Sherlock Holmes:

A Study In Regret

by

Claire Daines

Paperback ISBN 9781780924397
ePub ISBN 9781780924403
PDF ISBN 9781780924410

Published in the UK by MX Publishing
335 Princess Park Manor, Royal Drive,
London, N11 3GX
www.mxpublishing.co.uk

Cover design by www.staunch.com

To Madeline – best friend, muse and equally obsessed Sherlockian

Acknowledgements

My amazing family, for all of their support – especially my husband, Damon, who willingly puts up with me crying buckets and walking around with my head in the clouds for days at a time.

My hardworking translators, who freely gave their time and energy: Shirley Bain, Jana Mittelstädt, Dorothea Russell and Gerit Schwenzer. Your multilingual talents made this journey a lot less frustrating!

Sir Arthur Conan Doyle, for giving Holmes and Watson to the world.

Contents

Prologue

He was never entirely certain which pain was worse: the cruelties delivered by those guarding him, or that which was inflicted by his own mind and heart, fuelled by soul-searing memory. Not that he had to choose between them – there was an abundance of both as days and nights merged into a single constant blur of agony. But there were times when he was almost grateful to his captors for subjecting him to yet another round of their sadistic entertainment. At least then he could focus on the here and now, a distraction from the nightmares which plagued his every moment, waking and sleeping.

John Watson... *my beloved friend, dear God, I cannot bear it...* was dead, shot through the heart... *that noble heart, it held enough compassion for even such an undeserving wretch as I...* by Colonel Moran, Moriarty's aide-de-camp, at Reichenbach Falls. Holmes had no need of his brother's eidetic talents – every detail of that horrific moment was crystal clear, unclouded by any amount of time or drugs. How long had it been? A week, a year, an eternity... it made no matter, time was meaningless to a man who had lost all hope. Had Mycroft or anyone else miraculously come to his rescue, he would not even have made a move to follow. The prison of his own guilt was far stronger than his shackles, more torturous than anything his gaolers could have devised.

It should have been me... the sound of water thundering in his ears... *no, not again...* the kiss of mist on his brow, scrapes from the climb stinging his palms and knees... *let me be...* Watson's frantic calls to his friend as he gazed into the abyss in growing despair, the clatter of stone on the cliff face when Holmes' foot dislodged a loose rock... *please, God, make it stop...* Watson's head jerking upwards in surprise, the joy of seeing Holmes alive and well blossoming in his face... *for the love of Heaven, show me no more...* the red stain blossoming on the Doctor's breast as Moran's bullet struck true, the fear and understanding growing in his friend's eyes even as their light slowly

1

dimmed... Watson! It should have been me, Watson, I am so sorry! My cursed arrogance... I should never have allowed you to follow me! I failed you one time too many, my dearest friend, a thousand times too many!

He buried his face in his tattered hands, broken frame wracked with sobs. Burning eyes betrayed him yet again, as all tears had long since run dry. He had shed enough of them for a waterfall of his own, but one that was powerless to plunge him into the oblivion he craved. He would never have thought that he could envy James Moriarty, but the man had at least received a death of his own choosing, at the hands of his most respected enemy. For that poor mercy Holmes would have given his very soul, if he could only have reached down and reclaimed it from that seething cauldron where it lay, torn and bloodied, in the heart of the best and wisest man he had ever known.

Forgive me, John... forgive me...

Chapter 1

Downfall

Holmes lay crumpled where they'd thrown him, exhausted and shaking from their latest amusement, struggling against the waves of pain and nausea that washed over him. The small amount of food and water he had managed to choke down earlier now adorned the floor of the cellar and – his cracked lips curled weakly – one of his tormentors' boots. A small satisfaction, one that Holmes had paid for dearly with several vicious kicks to the gut. He would be passing blood for days, assuming he could actually crawl to the bucket.

The stone floor was cold and damp, the chill seeping into his aching body. He knew he would grow sicker if he stayed where he was, but he simply couldn't move; the little strength he had left was not enough for him to reach the sacks in the corner without passing out. Tired, he was so tired... If only sleep did not come at such a high price. His nightmares had changed, grown to include still more details of that accursed day, he couldn't face that again... He couldn't...let...

* * *

...His legs give way just as his feet touch the ground. He doesn't remember how he climbed back down – the last thing he recalls is Watson collapsing onto the path, shirt and coat soaked in blood. Panic-stricken, he forces himself to rise and stagger the last few feet to where his friend lies unmoving. Watson can't be dead, he cannot die, please, God, don't let him die! The Doctor is sprawled face down, one arm hanging over the edge, blood spreading slowly out from under him.

He falls to his knees at Watson's side and tries desperately to roll him, to pull him away from the edge. There has to be something he can do, he just can't be too late, not for Watson, God, not for him... but even as he turns the doctor over it is clear, horribly clear, that he can

3

do nothing. Watson's face is white as a sheet, torso glistening darkly crimson. His eyes are wide open, staring, chest still, he isn't breathing!

"Watson! Watson, *no*! Stay with me, please, you can't leave me!" He clutches his friend's hands, shakes him by the shoulders, cradles his head, but there is no answering spark in Watson's vacant eyes, no response to his frantic pleas. "Please don't die, Watson, come back, you can't die! Oh God, no..."

His voice cracks, the full realisation of what has happened, of what he has done, sweeping over him in a crushing avalanche of sorrow and shame. "This is all my fault! I'm sorry, Watson, I'm so sorry, *please*, Watson, come back! Come back...!" His vision blurs and he lets the bitter, scalding tears fall freely. Blindly, he pulls his friend's still-warm body into his lap and clutches him tight, heedless of the blood that soaks into his own clothes, his violent grief tearing from his throat, echoing above the roar of the falls.

Time passes, he does not know how much, he does not care. His only friend, his anchor in the storm, lies in his arms, cooling, lifeless. He cannot think, he cannot move, he can hardly breathe. His whole body is numb, but for the gnawing ache in his chest. Watson is dead... nothing else matters, not now, not ever...

* * *

Hands, so many hands... they filled Holmes' world, cruel and cunning and always, always bringing him fresh agony. Hands which caressed one moment and cudgelled the next, hands that slashed, hands that shattered, that could burn or freeze without warning – he never knew, couldn't predict what extreme would come to him next, or when it would come, only that it would. His body was an almanac of pain: each new hurt inflicted, every barely healed wound re-opened a brutal record of how much he had undergone and a sinister portent of things to come.

How much longer could he endure? A dark lesson he had no desire to learn, but there was no way to play truant from this. Sooner or later those hands would finish teaching him, in minute detail, exactly what was required to break him beyond repair. Perhaps by then he would no longer care, there might not be enough of him left to care. The thought was strangely comforting. Footsteps on the cellar stairs, they were returning already, no, not again, not so soon...

* * *

...Footsteps on the path, muffled by the water. Holmes does not even bother to turn as a shadow passes over the two of them, but suddenly, the glint of sunlight on metal catches his eye. He looks up in alarm, far too late. A blow to his head and he falls, darkness looming up to claim him...

When he comes to, he is face down on the path, hands tightly bound. Someone is crouched over him, a knee planted in the small of his back, pinning him to the ground. Struggling upwards out of the clinging shadows, he forces his eyes open. He groans as the late afternoon sun glares off the falling water, adding to his pounding headache. "He's awake, sir," a voice grates above his head. "You want I should knock him out again?"

"No, Briggs, I think he has rested long enough. We wouldn't want Mr. Holmes to miss his friend's funeral," comes a second voice, one that is all too familiar. The malicious words fill Holmes with dread, and he manages to turn his head, stiffly. Colonel Sebastian Moran stands at the end of the path in front of him, at the very spot where he fought Moriarty only a few hours since, although it feels like a lifetime ago now. Watson's body lies at the Colonel's feet... No, much worse – one of Moran's boots is actually resting on the Doctor's chest, for all the world as if Watson were one of his damned hunting trophies!

A mist swirls before Holmes' eyes, and a deadly fury wells up inside of him, lending him a desperate strength. Pushing with his legs,

5

he rolls suddenly to the right, throwing Briggs off-balance towards the edge of the path. Bound hands notwithstanding, he staggers upright with the help of the cliff face and rushes the Colonel, deaf and blind to everything but his own murderous rage.

Not five yards from his quarry, a shot rings out above the water's thunder, and a red-hot wire seems to pierce his left thigh. His leg folds under him and he crashes to the ground, wrenching his shoulder and striking his head hard on the path. Stunned and gasping with pain, he makes a valiant attempt to get back up, but is pinned by his bad shoulder under the Colonel's blood-stained boot. "Commendable effort, Mr. Holmes. Such a pity you forgot with whom you were dealing."

"A cold-blooded, murdering villain!" he snarls, glaring his venomous hate at the man, wishing with all his heart that looks could truly kill.

"It does take one to recognise one, doesn't it, Mr. Holmes?" Moran's voice is dangerously calm, but his eyes hold a savage gleam. "Excellent shooting, Briggs. Your marksmanship is improving, although your timing could use some work."

"Had to make sure I weren't goin' to hit no vital spot, sir," Briggs justifies smoothly, reloading a sleek black revolver. "Dint reckon yer wanted him bleedin' to death after all that trouble. Nice little flesh wound that was too, though I say it meself."

"As you can see, Mr. Holmes, I too have my trusted associates – although mine do seem to have better survival instincts." Those taunting words are a knife to Holmes' insides. He clenches his teeth, helpless to do anything save fantasise about breaking every bone in Moran's body. Briggs kneels, produces a knife and holds it to the detective's jugular, forcing him to lie still. The Colonel grinds his heel deeper into Holmes' shoulder, smiling evilly as he flinches, before stepping over to where the Doctor's body rests.

"It broke my heart to shoot him, Mr. Holmes, truly. I'm a military man myself, after all, and he seemed a decent sort of fellow, despite the company he kept. But orders are orders, and the Professor was very clear on that point. We couldn't have all these loose threads flapping about, much too untidy. On the other hand, if you had just laid low and played dead, perhaps we needn't have bothered about him. A shame there's no time to dig him a decent grave, but we are on a tight schedule. He can keep the Professor company."

With a slight grunt of effort, Moran shoves Watson's lifeless corpse over the edge with his foot, then strolls back along the path to look down at Holmes, pale and trembling in speechless outrage at the callous treatment of his friend's remains.

"My apologies, Mr. Holmes, although I can't imagine why you're so upset, really. What's that Scripture verse again: 'An eye for an eye, a tooth for a tooth'? In this case, I'd say you got the better end of the deal. You bagged the lion, I merely put down one of your hounds. Carry on, Briggs."

Holmes stiffens as a needle jabs into his upper arm without warning, only kept from jerking away by the razor-sharp blade at his throat. As the plunger presses down, the world begins to shimmer and buckle before his eyes, like looking through a soap bubble, until at last it melts away altogether...

* * *

Fire... searing, scorching heat, he is burning, what are they doing to him this time? He can hear someone moaning, is it him? He thought they tore his voice from him a long time ago, maybe they're torturing someone else, is that why they left him? Why have they left him, isn't he any fun anymore? Maybe they'll come back if he can find the voice to keep screaming, he doesn't want to be alone, it's so lonely down here, down here in the damp, silent dark...

Cold, so cold... the flames have suddenly vanished, he is grasped by long, icy fingers that nip and pinch and freeze him to the core. Shuddering, he tries in vain to curl himself up. Little wonder the Doctor detests winter... all except for the snow, he always greets the first snowfall with the delight of a child. He remembers saving a snowball in Mrs. Hudson's icebox for two months, greeting Watson with it on the first day of April at six o'clock in the morning... That was a good day, the look on his friend's face was worth the wait...

The snow is falling now, he can feel the crisp flakes kissing his face, melting on his lips, he should run and tell Watson... No, wait, it isn't snow, it's rain, a cool April shower. They can't go out to play now, the snow will turn to slush. Better to stay inside, let the Doctor ease his leg by the snug fire, although Mrs. Hudson does seem to have put on a large amount of coal. The room is growing far too warm, he is panting in the stifling heat, his lungs burning from the smoke, he can't breathe...

Another volley of hacking coughs ripped from Holmes' lungs, pain stabbing in his chest for the thousandth time. Strange, that pain now seemed to be at the head of the queue. The rest of his wounds that usually screamed at him with every laboured breath were merely shouting from a distance. So it had begun, they'd almost finished breaking him. The collective agony that wracked his body had lost its razor edge, he felt wrapped around with a strange softness, he wasn't even as thirsty anymore. He was still so tired, though; he wished they would simply get it over with...

"Mr. Holmes? Mr. Holmes, can you hear me?" A voice intruded on his drifting thoughts, far away at first but getting closer, oddly urgent. "Mr. Holmes..." What did they want? Why didn't whoever-it-was just kill him, how much more entertainment could be derived from a vegetable? If he pretended not to hear, maybe they'd leave him alone to die, surely it wouldn't be long now.

"Mr. Holmes! Come on, sir, wake up, now..." The voice was dogged, persistent, irritating beyond measure, and he was suddenly, impossibly glad to hear it: "I swear, Mr. Holmes, if you don't give me some kind of sign that you're still in there, I'll... I'll have your arrogant *bloody* hide for a new dartboard!"

The ridiculous threat cut into the fog in Holmes' mind like an ocean breeze, an old threat from a very worried, very familiar voice, one he had never expected to hear again. Relief flooded through him and he tried to move, to open his eyes, but his spent body would not obey. The most he could do was twitch his lips in a faint smile in answer to the Inspector's gruff bluster.

Lestrade obviously saw the weak response, if his delighted oath was any indication: "Lord's sakes, Mr. Holmes, that's a beautiful sight! Doctor! Doctor, get in here, he's awake!"

Doctor? Was it possible? The detective's heart leapt in his chest and he struggled to lift his leaden eyelids, strengthened by a sudden, painful hope... to see Lestrade hurrying back into the small, white room Holmes was occupying, followed by a tall, older man in a white coat who looked nothing whatsoever like *his* doctor. For a brief moment, all too brief, he was simply puzzled, wondering where Watson was, why this stranger was standing in his place. Then the Inspector's eyes widened in horror at Holmes' confusion, face pale as he realised what he'd just said, and at the worst possible moment.

That unguarded expression filled Holmes with terror. It told him beyond all doubt that there was no mistake, he had not merely dreamt his ordeal. Watson was dead, he was never coming back, *and Lestrade knew it, too* – that was the most terrifying thing of all. Lestrade sharing that knowledge, being a part of his sorrow, made it far more real than his nightmares had ever done.

Holmes set his teeth while the strange doctor looked him over, checking the detective's numerous bandages and dressings – so many,

9

God, he couldn't even remember what was beneath half of them. The man spoke to him, but he couldn't seem to understand the words, there was a ringing in his ears. His body shook, he could hardly breathe, colours dancing before his eyes. The tension mounted inside him – pain, fear, grief, rage and black despair all knotting and twisting together, burning like acid.

His eyes squeezed shut, he fought to keep himself in one piece, but he couldn't contain the tears that seeped treacherously from beneath the lids – where were they earlier? No, please, he couldn't *do* this right now! He didn't want to be alone, but he *would not* weep for his friend or himself, not like this, not in front of the Inspector and this complete stranger who knew nothing of Watson and never would...

He felt the mattress dip, then a touch to his shoulder. He couldn't help flinching at the contact, eyes snapping open in panic to find the doctor gone and Lestrade sitting on the bed beside Holmes, calloused hand coming back to rest lightly on the detective's shoulder again. The Inspector's face was affectionate, not accusing, eyes full of compassion and, merciful God, tears of his own! The sight of them proved Holmes' undoing, the last of his defences breached by this unexpected kindness. It had been so long, far too long since he'd last known such a thing, and a whimper escaped his throat, an involuntary plea for help that Lestrade instantly understood.

Holmes' blankets were drawn back, and a pair of wiry arms slid under his shoulders and knees to ease him a little closer to the wall, before covering him again. The movement made him moan in renewed pain, but even if he could have protested, he wouldn't, and Lestrade clearly knew it, although Heaven help them both when the doctor came back... The stray thought caused a fresh whimper to burst forth, and his tears began to flow in earnest.

He tried to turn his face away, but then the Inspector was beside him on the bed, arms wrapping carefully around the detective's shoulders and pulling him into a gentle embrace, not speaking, just holding him in silent sympathy. Holmes buried his face in Lestrade's shirt, tears soaking the coarse fabric as he let the flood carry him where it would, grateful beyond words that his colleague was able to do this, to offer him the gift of weakness when he most needed it. For now, just for now, that was enough to keep the terror at bay, and he followed the growing darkness down into an exhausted sleep.

Chapter 2

Scales of Justice

Holmes slept deeply and dreamlessly most of the night, unconsciously reassured by the solid presence of the Inspector beside him. Towards dawn, however, the ghosts of past torments began to reappear, slipping past his lowered defences. He remembered...

* * *

...Compared to some of the punishments they've inflicted on him, this is strangely soothing, although probably not for much longer. He has hung from the manacles on his wrists for hours, his hands, arms and shoulders now mostly numb. The real discomfort will come when they finally let him down again – no doubt they're looking forward to it. His lacerated back is currently towards the cellar's entrance, but he has learnt to distinguish between the different approaching treads on the stairs, each set of footsteps bringing its own particular brand of pain. A macabre kind of mercy, to have that slight forewarning of what could be in store, but it's one he is grateful for. Mercies are rare in his current world.

He drifts, half conscious in spite of his best efforts, but jerks awake at the sound of the trapdoor opening. He doesn't recognise these footsteps, although the soft tread puts him in mind of McAllister, whose favourite pastime is tattooing his name across Holmes' torso with a red-hot railway spike, one letter for every visit. He smirks grimly – no doubt the brainless ape needs the intervening time to memorise the next letter...

"Such a pleasant smile, Mr. Holmes, I'm flattered." His skin begins to crawl, hatred exuding from every pore at the sound of the Colonel's leering voice. "Did you really miss me that much?"

Holmes forces his swollen eyelids to open, wishing his mouth wasn't so dry. He would gladly endure a week's worth of beatings to be able to spit in the blackguard's face just once. He hasn't seen Moran since he first awoke down here, two days after his capture at the falls, dazed and sick from all the drugs they gave him to ensure a trouble-free journey. He wrenches his mind away from the memory of what came after, and focuses as best he can on the gloating face that looms into view.

"Moran," he rasps, glaring. "Dreadful to see you, it hasn't been nearly long enough. How's the butchering business?"

"Come now, Mr. Holmes, you know I never combine business with pleasure." The words fill Holmes with dismay; he well knows how creative this twisted old veteran can be when it comes to 'pleasure'. He has to fight to keep his expression neutral, although he knows the effort is futile, Moran is not fooled for a second. The man is loving every moment of this, cruel eyes glittering as he watches his prisoner's fear grow. The worst part is the uncertainty – at least with his other captors he has some idea of what to expect. Not so with this sadistic monster...

"Of course, my dear sir," he manages to rejoin, his casual words belying the panic quivering in his chest. "Shall we proceed, or would you prefer to converse further?"

"You're too kind, Mr. Holmes, but truth be known, I have never been a great raconteur." The Colonel puts his hand into his jacket and draws out a fist-sized wooden box, ornately carved. Holmes notes with rising dread that the box has several tiny holes in the sides, and a faint hissing is issuing from them. "However, my young companion here, I'm told she speaks most eloquently... I shall let you be the judge in this case."

No... oh God, no, please, not this! He has had a profound aversion to snakes all of his life, rooted in his subconscious decades before that awful night at Stoke Moran, where he was forced to confront his deepest phobia head-on. He doesn't believe he could even have done so without Watson at his back. The Colonel would not have chosen this at random, he *knows*, how does he know? It hardly matters – the real concern is directly before him, as Moran undoes the catch, lifts the lid and gives a low whistle.

The next moment, a tiny diamond-shaped head appears, emerald green, yellow devil's eyes fixed on Holmes, unblinking. The forked tongue flickers out of its mouth, quick as thought, and it is all he can do to keep himself from flinching.

Moran's face is a study in sinister delight, rivalling that of the snake. "Now, now, Mr. Holmes, no need to be so shy. Naja is a charming little lady – aren't you, my dear?" beaming at the serpent, which Holmes now recognises as an Indian pit viper. Moran advances on him, lifting the coiling snake out of the box with all the reverence of a butler bearing a porcelain vase.

He is petrified, shivering uncontrollably, heart pounding, he has to clench his teeth to keep them from chattering. The only thing that stops him from begging for mercy is the certain knowledge that Moran is waiting for that very reaction. Pleading with the man will only add to his enjoyment and prolong the session.

Delicately, the Colonel untangles Naja's coils from his fingers and grasps the serpent behind the head, squeezing gently to make her needle-fanged jaws open wide. "A curious thing about snakes, Mr. Holmes: the young are even more deadly than the adults. Do you know why?"

He shouldn't do it, he knows he'll pay for this, but in spite of his fear he just can't resist the urge to wipe the smile off the oily bastard's face, if only for a second. "Because... the adult snake can determine the amount of venom... it injects into its victims. The hatchling has... no such control, it must expend all its venom in one strike." He grins shakily at the sight of Moran's darkening countenance, steeling himself for the approaching retribution.

"Very good, Mr. Holmes," the Colonel grates, scowling. "But did you also know that it only takes a few hours at most for the hatchling to replace its store of poison? Naja now, she was last milked two hours ago, and I've yet to discover exactly how long she needs to replenish. I imagine she has not fully returned to her normal, deadly self, but the effects should be interesting, nonetheless."

Before Holmes can respond, Moran places his pet on the detective's right shoulder and releases her, stepping back to get a better view of the entertainment. Hissing furiously, the angry reptile coils for a moment, then lunges for the nearest thing within reach, burying her fangs in Holmes' upper arm.

His choked cry of pain and terror echoes around the cellar... echoed in turn a moment later by an enraged bellow from the Colonel at his victim's next reaction, completely unexpected by either of them. Holmes has no idea how he manages it, or where his sudden inspiration springs from, but with the desperate strength and speed of a man who truly believes he is about to die, he whips his head around and seizes the snake's body in his teeth. Viciously, he bites down through scale and flesh and bone, crushing the serpent's spine.

He rips the bloody, still-writhing corpse from his arm, the fangs inflicting more damage as they tear free, then spits the loathsome thing in Moran's direction with a savage joy, completely taken aback himself by his own audacity. He doesn't get to savour his victory for long. The next instant, the fresh wounds begin to burn, and the Colonel's hands close around Holmes' throat, the villain's normally ruddy face now purple with fury.

Ironically, it is one of Moran's own men who intervenes: Parker, their sentinel, clattering hastily down the steps and thrusting a folded piece of paper at the Colonel. "Message just received, sir, begging your pardon. Looks like you were right, but we're pressed for time. You need to come now, sir... Sir?"

Moran's hands linger on Holmes' neck for a moment longer, fingers twitching, torn between duty and vengeance. Finally, he steps back, recovering his composure, although his eyes still burn with undisguised malice. "Well played, Mr. Holmes. I must confess I wasn't expecting such an audacious move. Even at this late stage of the game, you prove a worthy opponent. However, you will have to excuse me, as I do have other pressing issues to attend to. I look forward to resuming our conversation when next we meet." To Parker, "Tell Briggs to keep him strung up until the venom runs its course. Remind him that we have more in stock. Good day, Mr. Holmes..."

Anything else the man might be saying is lost in the sound of his own full-throated screams, as the blood turns to fire in his veins, a thousand fangs piercing his flesh...

* * *

Holmes woke in a blind panic, gasping, soaked in sweat, the last tendrils of the hellish memory still gripping his mind. Distantly, he heard Lestrade's voice beside him, heavy with sleep: "Mr. Holmes? Oh, bloody Christ... Hey, Mr. Holmes, look at me!" Strong hands grasped his shoulders. "Come on, man, snap out of it! Breathe..." He obeyed instinctively, responding to the authority in the Inspector's voice, and his vision began to clear.

"That's it, now... calm down... easy..." Lestrade relaxed his grip on Holmes' shoulders, brow still furrowed in concern. "You're safe, Mr. Holmes, it was just a dream. Are you all right?"

"Uhh… yes, I… think so..." Thank God, he finally had the strength to speak again. His throat felt completely raw, he couldn't manage more than a whisper.

16

"Good Lord, sir, you're white as a sheet. That must have been one hell of a nightmare!"

"Not... a nightmare..."

"It was a *memory*? God in Heaven... Do I even want to know?" Holmes shuddered, and Lestrade took the hint. "Right, never mind – how are you feeling now? Anything you need?"

Holmes shoved the obvious answer to the back of his mind, and tried to respond normally. "I could... use a stiff drink." He smiled weakly at the Inspector's relieved grin.

"Sorry, Mr. Holmes, but we're a long way from the Thames. You'll have to make do with the fancy foreign muck."

Lestrade carefully raised him higher against the pillows and fetched a glass of water from the nightstand. Unthinking, Holmes tried to reach for it, but his hands were stiff with bandages and his arms refusing all orders until further notice. He coloured, but the Inspector took his helplessness in stride, sitting on the bed without comment to hold the glass to his lips.

Holmes' mouth felt as dry as a desert, an uncomfortable reminder of the dream he'd just left, and the cool, sweet water was a blessed relief. He had to force himself to go slowly, he didn't want it returning. He hoped fervently that he would never need to be reacquainted with his stomach contents ever again, he'd had enough of that for several lifetimes. Lestrade made him rest after a few sips, clearly having similar ideas.

An awkward silence descended. He had so many questions, and no doubt Lestrade had even more, none of which Holmes was anxious to answer. At least there was one thing he didn't need to divulge, but how on earth did the Inspector know what had happened?

"You told me, Mr. Holmes." Lestrade's voice broke in on his thoughts, apparently reading them. There was no anger in the man's voice, only understanding, and Holmes dared to look up, letting his expression ask what his mouth could not. "We're in Zurich, in case you didn't know. You've been in hospital for three days, most of which you spent with a fever. You didn't say much, but what you did say... it confirmed what we already suspected."

'We'? Ah, of course. Mycroft must have sent Lestrade with one of his agents – he certainly would not have allowed the Inspector to travel alone.

"I trust I... did not put you to... too much trouble, Lestrade. How long...?" How long had Watson lain beneath the falls in the arms of Moriarty? How long had he stayed in that hellhole at the mercy of his enemies? How long before anyone had even noticed they'd disappeared?

"How long have you been gone? Well, today's June 5th, and you two left England on April 24th, so you've been away from London for about six weeks. Your brother gave me all the details he could, but it wasn't very much to go on. You and the Doctor seemed to have vanished off the face of the earth, and we had a hard time determining whether it was a deliberate ploy on your part, or foul play by Moriarty's gang."

"Then how...?" Six weeks... and he and Watson had only travelled together for ten days.

"You sent your brother that coded telegram from Geneva, so we had a place to start from, although the police force there had already decided it was a lost cause by the time Mycroft sent me over." Lestrade shook his head. "Not that I can blame them, really. Most of the evidence seemed to point to one conclusion..."

"What evidence?"

18

"Just wait, Mr. Holmes, I'm getting to that. Your brother pulled some strings for me so that I could go where I needed to and bypass the chain of command when necessary. 'Bureaucratic immunity', I believe he called it. I'd wager it cost him more than a few favours in some very high places, too. When we got to Geneva, I went straight to the authorities and showed them my credentials – they practically fell over themselves in their hurry to roll out the red carpet." Lestrade chuckled lightly. "Things went fairly smoothly after that, for a time. Do you remember the last village you stayed at, before... well, before you went missing?"

"Meiringen." Yes, Holmes remembered that village very well, the more was the pity.

"That's right. Seems you caused quite a stir in that area when you disappeared. Don't look so surprised, Mr. Holmes, it's a close-knit community; folks keep an eye on each other in those parts. A good thing, too, given the terrain and all. It was the landlord at the hotel who raised the alarm."

"Steiler, of course... We left our carpet bags... at the hotel when we started... for Rosenlaui. He saw us off."

"When you didn't come back the next day, he sent a messenger to the hamlet and learned you'd never arrived. A search party went out to scour all the different paths you might have taken..."

"...including the falls..."

"Exactly, and what they found... You need to understand, Mr. Holmes, the police report wasn't pleasant." Lestrade's face was a picture of concern and embarrassment. "Are you certain you're all right with hearing all of this? I mean, it can wait until another time, when you're stronger."

"Quite all right, Inspector. Please... continue, you are assisting... more than you know." Lestrade's calm, steady voice was surprisingly soothing, and it kept Holmes from having to face his own thoughts alone.

"Only if you're sure. If Dr. Joubert catches me keeping you awake at this hour..."

"He will probably... banish you from the room... and then sedate me... so please... do not get caught."

"All right, as you like. If anyone comes in, pretend to be asleep."

Chapter 3

Missing Pieces

Lestrade had not exaggerated about the police report being unpleasant: full-length impressions of at least one body in the soft earth, a spent casing from Briggs' revolver... and blood, *Watson's* blood... staining the earth and the torn plants at the edge of the path... It would have been too easy for the Swiss police to take one look at all the obvious clues and draw entirely the wrong conclusion.

"So everyone thought... that one of us had... murdered... the other?" On second thought, perhaps the police had not been so far from the truth.

"The police certainly did, and most of the villagers as well. Fortunately for you, Steiler didn't." Lestrade stopped expounding long enough to give Holmes some more water, then continued. "He was one of the first on the scene, if you can believe it. For an old gaffer approaching seventy, he's as spry as a mountain goat, with a good head on his shoulders besides. He told the police what he knew when they first started investigating, but by then a lot of other people had visited the scene, trampling over the evidence. The police thought he was daft when he told them that he'd been up there before all that. It's a two-hour climb up that track, as I'm sure you know – I wouldn't have believed him either without seeing it firsthand. Left me in the dust, he did." Lestrade grinned ruefully. "My knees may never be the same again, or my pride."

"What did... Steiler tell you?"

"That there were a lot more footprints on the trail than there should have been. He counted at least five different sets, possibly more, all made around the same time as each other. You're looking very sceptical, Mr. Holmes. Didn't you know Steiler used to be a guide in those mountains? He can read more from a rocky path than most people can from a newspaper. You two should get together and trade stories."

Holmes raised an eyebrow, impressed. "So he deduced that... we were not alone... up at the falls?"

"Which was suspicious enough in itself, but he also remembered what happened after you left the hotel. I've no idea how much of this you know already." Lestrade took a notebook from his pocket and skimmed the pages.

"I have to confess, Inspector... most of what you are saying is... new to me." He hated having to admit that he knew less than Lestrade did about anything, especially when it came to a case. "I... greatly appreciate your... filling in the gaps." At least the man wasn't going to hold it over his head, this time around.

"All right then, I'll start at the beginning. Steiler saw you both off on the path to Rosenlaui, then went back to the hotel. He and Roland Brenner, the hired boy, were splitting logs not half an hour later when they were approached by another Englishman, one whom Steiler had never seen before. He didn't give his name, but from the description the landlord gave me, Mr. Holmes, there's no doubt in my mind as to who it was."

"Moriarty..."

Lestrade nodded grimly. "Tall and thin, Steiler said, with a face like a lizard. He spoke pleasantly enough, however, and asked after you. He said you were old acquaintances and had heard that you were staying in the village, but couldn't wait for your return. He asked for paper to write you a note, so Steiler gave him one of the stationery tablets from the writing desk, before going back to work. When Moriarty had finished the note, he requested that the boy be sent to find you with the message. Steiler did think it was a little unusual that he didn't simply leave the note at the hotel, but at the time..."

"I understand, Inspector. Steiler is... a good man, he had no reason... to be suspicious. Please continue."

"Steiler told Roland to try at the falls, and to come straight back again if he didn't find you there. Moriarty thanked him, gave him a generous tip in Swiss francs, then left. Steiler didn't see him again after that. In fact, nobody else in the village seemed to know anything about him while the investigation was going on. It was as if the man had never been there in the first place, which didn't make Steiler's tale any more believable to the police."

"Brenner... did the police question him?"

"I'm sure they would have, Mr. Holmes, if they could have found him. Roland never came back to the village. I'm guessing from your expression that this doesn't surprise you."

"No... The boy did find us with the message... at the falls... but it was a forgery. He had to have been... in Moriarty's employ."

"Yes, I know. When the Doctor came back to the hotel, he showed Steiler the note that the landlord was supposed to have written, begging Watson to help the sick Englishwoman. Poor old Steiler was completely at a loss, he had no idea what was going on. When he told the Doctor about the man who had actually written the note, Watson must have realised it was Moriarty. Steiler said he turned white, then rushed back down the village street to the path as if his feet had wings. That was the last he ever saw of him." Lestrade sighed and put the notebook away.

The thump of the pages closing was like the slamming of a door in Holmes' face. He blinked hard, trying to collect himself. "It would seem... it is my turn to fill in... some of the gaps, Inspector."

"Not until you have some more water and take a rest." Lestrade supported Holmes' head as he drank. "You're exhausted, sir; I really shouldn't be letting you do this."

"And yet your curiosity… will not allow you to rest... any more than mine."

"Hm, sad but true. Couple of blasted cats, the pair of us. Is that enough?"

"Thank you, no more." Holmes lay back and closed his eyes, summoning up his courage to face the challenge ahead, while Lestrade took the opportunity to turn down the gas and open the curtains, letting in the grey morning light.

It suddenly occurred to the detective that this was the first real sunlight he would see since his capture. The only light in the cellar had consisted of candles, lanterns, branding irons... and what little had come through the cracks in the floor above. Yet he was here now, alive, and soon to view his first sunrise after a month of living in the dark. He took a deep breath. "Well, Inspector... what do you wish to know?"

"What happened at the falls after the Doctor left you? Please, just tell me what you can, Mr. Holmes. I know this can't be easy for you to talk about."

Trust Lestrade to state the most obvious fact, yet it was also the most accurate. Holmes would far rather simply bury his head beneath the pillows and pretend none of this had ever happened, but he did not have that option. Lestrade deserved an explanation, Holmes owed the Inspector this and infinitely more for all that the man had done on his and Watson's behalf. As for what he owed Watson... the complete and unvarnished truth seemed an immeasurably poor beginning for such an unpayable debt; however, it was the best he could do for the moment.

Once Holmes actually began the account, it became slightly easier – there was a strange relief to it, like drawing poison out of a wound. He told Lestrade the whole story: Moriarty's arrival, their wrestling match, the fall... he had to pause for a minute to breathe at that point, the Professor's scream as he teetered on the brink ringing in his ears. He braced himself and continued, the worst was still to come: his sudden decision to disappear, the climb to the ledge, Watson's return... and the moment when everything had gone so tragically wrong. He faltered, the rising emotions in his chest choking him, eyes stinging. How was he meant to describe *this* to the Inspector?

He felt Lestrade gently grip his shoulder. "It's all right, sir. You already told me this part, while you were battling the fever."

"How much... detail?"

"Enough to know what happened with Moran. I'm so sorry, Mr. Holmes..." Tears slid down Holmes' cheeks, he couldn't hold them back, but at least with Lestrade he did not have to. "If only I'd known where... where the Doctor was when I was up there with Steiler." Why did Lestrade sound so remorseful? There was no need for the Inspector to feel ashamed, none of this was his fault.

"What could you... have done... even if you had?"

"I don't know. Could have paid my respects, at least. He was... a damn good man, Mr. Holmes. They don't come any finer than the Doctor. We're all going to miss him."

"...thank you..." A memory stirred at the back of the detective's mind, one that seemed vaguely significant... He shied away from it, burying it with all the rest, he didn't want to see any more.

Lestrade pulled out a handkerchief and blew his nose vigorously. "Well, I suppose... it must be my turn again – that is, if you feel up to listening."

Holmes nodded gratefully, a lump in his throat – anything to distract himself from his own thoughts. Lestrade retrieved his notebook and continued.

"We almost lost the scent after Meiringen. There wasn't enough real evidence to tell us exactly what had happened at the falls, and even Steiler's account of the crime scene didn't shed much more light. All we knew for certain was that there had been some kind of a struggle, a gun had been fired and at least one person had been badly wounded, although not necessarily the same person that went over the edge. There were just too many questions, and too many directions the survivors of the incident could have gone. I didn't dare form any theories without more solid evidence – it looks as if you've been rubbing off on me, Mr. Holmes."

Holmes' lips twitched at the back-handed compliment. "Quite right. Yet something occurred... to narrow the search?"

"I should say so. We had one slim lead, young Roland Brenner. According to Steiler, his parents had lived in Rosenlaui, but his mother died of pneumonia five years ago, and his father was killed in a house fire last winter. He didn't think the boy had any other relatives, but we went along to Rosenlaui all the same, and made inquiries. No-one in the hamlet knew anything more about Roland or his family that could help – or if they did, they weren't willing to tell us. We visited the place where his parent's chalet had been, on the off chance, and that was when we got our next lead. Steiler suddenly realised where we might find a record of Roland's next of kin – the family Bible."

"Of course... all of their family records... births, deaths, marriages... would be written inside."

"Precisely. The house had burnt to the ground, but Steiler was certain a treasure like that would be protected, most likely inside a metal box of some kind. It could have survived the blaze, depending on where it was hidden when the fire started."

"You found the box, then." Lestrade's grin was all the answer Holmes needed.

"That we did, Mr. Holmes, behind a loose brick in the chimney, above the mantelpiece. Not that there were many places to look, the chimney was almost the only thing left standing. Fortunately, the box hadn't been damaged, and we discovered some very interesting things when we opened it back at the hotel."

"I gather that there was... a good deal more in the box... than just a Bible."

"You're right, the box contained a number of different papers. Letters, family photographs, the marriage certificate for Roland's parents... but it was the Bible that gave us the best lead. Steiler was right, the Brenner line was recorded inside the front cover, going back at least six generations on either side of the family. The most interesting thing, however, was what had been crossed out, or rather who."

Holmes was going to enjoy this... "Young Brenner's... elder brother, Erik, no doubt..."

Lestrade's mouth dropped open in astonishment, eyes popping. "Good God, Mr. Holmes, how in the world did you know that?"

"I encountered young Brenner at the hotel... and he was also at the falls with me... for some little time before Moriarty arrived. It was more than enough to gain... an insight into the boy's circumstances. Up until now, however... I had not had a chance to make the connection."

"So how did you know about Erik Brenner?"

"As you said, Inspector... the brothers are orphans. Roland was wearing Erik's outgrown clothes... which were too big for him, with several crude patches. Steiler is also a widower... there was no maternal figure in Brenner's life... to sew him new clothing or decently

27

repair the old. His face bore fresh signs of grief... therefore he had lost another loved one recently... there was also his attitude... towards Steiler as an alternate father figure. I knew his brother's name... because it was inside the band of his cap, another hand-down."

He paused for a moment to catch his breath. "The family is of the Catholic faith, deeply religious. The boy's fingers twitched nervously while we were awaiting Moriarty... in the unconscious movement of saying a rosary. That degree of guilt meant that he was not in Moriarty's employ by choice... therefore his involvement was through coercion. Keeping his brother's cap, which was also a size too large... spoke of the great affection he had for Erik... he would do anything for him. In a family of such devout faith... with an eldest son who had sunk so low... as to be ensnared by Moriarty... it was only logical that it would be Erik's name... that was struck from the family record... indicating his disownment by his disapproving father."

Holmes had to smile as Lestrade shook his head in admiration. "Confess, Inspector: I have restored your faith... in my abilities."

"Well, begging your pardon, Mr. Holmes, but you'd be wrong there." Lestrade gave the detective a warm smile in return for his raised eyebrow. "I never doubted them in the first place, sir – not for a moment."

That simple, forthright assertion left Holmes speechless. He stared at Lestrade, thoughts in a whirl, utterly bewildered. He could hardly believe the man was sincere, and yet... he knew that in all the time they had worked together, Lestrade had never once told him a lie. He did his best to regain his composure, no easy task when his face was scarlet with embarrassment.

"Inspector, I... am truly honoured... by what you have said..." Confound it, why could he not stop stammering? "Although how you can still retain... such confidence in me... after the utter mess I have made of this whole business... I confess, I am completely at a loss."

"That's because you're being far too hard on yourself, as usual." Lestrade sighed. "Seriously, Mr. Holmes, do I really have to give you the same talk I give the new recruits? Nobody's perfect... You can't save everyone, or guard against every possibility, not even you. The Doctor knew that, and he went along all the same, because you were his friend and that was worth the risk. Are you trying to tell me that he was wrong? Save your breath, because I believe the same thing he did."

The Inspector ignored Holmes' dumbfounded expression and carried on. "Besides, you didn't make an 'utter mess' – far from it. Thanks to you, we managed to convict most of Moriarty's gang, and as for the man himself..." Lestrade smiled with grim satisfaction. "I can't say that I'd have preferred to arrest him, Mr. Holmes – there's no justice on earth that could have given that monster what he deserved. You did a good job, sir, whether you believe it or not. I'm only sorry that events turned out the way they did afterwards, for both your sakes."

For both... Holmes stiffened in horror as the evaded thought, one that he should have acknowledged long before, rushed to the front of his mind. "Oh, dear God... Mary!" Of all the egotistical, self-absorbed fools... How could he have forgotten her? Groaning, he turned his head and buried his face in the pillow, dread and remorse knotting together in his chest. How on earth was he going to tell Watson's wife the truth? How could he possibly face her?

He didn't realise that he had been speaking aloud until Lestrade answered him, sounding decidedly awkward. "Well, about that, Mr. Holmes... I have some good news and some bad news..."

Holmes turned his head back and looked at the Inspector warily. After a few moments of silence, Lestrade took a deep breath. "All right... The first thing is that Mary already knows about her husband, you don't need to break that to her."

"How much… did you tell her?" Lestrade must have cabled Mary while Holmes was still feverish, although how the Inspector had worked up the nerve to send that kind of news in a telegram...

"Only that the Doctor was shot by Colonel Moran, and that... his body lies under the falls. We thought it'd be best if she heard the rest of the story from you, which leads me to the second thing: you may be able to get that explanation over with sooner than you think."

Holmes certainly would not be able to travel for some time, which most likely meant: "Mary is... coming to Zurich?" How long did he have before she arrived, before he had to attempt to explain the unexplainable?

"No... Mary is *in* Zurich, here at the hospital. She's been travelling with me almost every step of the way."

Chapter 4

Paper Trail

"Mary is... here? *She* is the other person... you have been referring to?" This time, Holmes really couldn't believe his ears; either Lestrade was hoaxing him or he was still dreaming, and he was not certain which idea he liked less.

"Indeed she is. This hospital is quite large, we're both staying in the guest quarters – although I haven't seen much of my room, for obvious reasons." The Inspector's face was completely serious, no trace of humour anywhere, and even the detective's worst nightmares had never lasted this long. When one had eliminated the impossible...

"Lestrade, have you gone insane?! How could you bring Mary into this? If Watson had had the least notion... that you, or anyone, would involve his *wife*..." If only Holmes had thought of this while attempting to persuade his friend to return home.

"You talk as if I had some kind of choice in the matter, Mr. Holmes. The first I even knew that Mary was following me was on the boat from Newhaven. Came up beside me while I was hanging over the rail and offered me a ginger pill, as calm and unruffled as you please." Lestrade looked ill at the mere memory. "I was hardly in a fit state to lecture her. Even if I had been, it was much too late to turn around. Took care of me for the whole crossing, bless her. I did try to convince her to go back on the next ship when we reached Dieppe, but she wasn't having any of it."

No wonder Lestrade had regretted not knowing about Watson's resting place at the falls. "Watson told me... Mary was away visiting friends."

"She was, but only for three weeks. The Doctor had left a note for her at home, saying that he'd gone on a case with you, but should be

31

back in a fortnight at most. So when she arrived home on May 14th and learned how long he'd actually been gone... she didn't even wait to unpack, just went straight to Pall Mall and barged into Mycroft's rooms while he was having breakfast." Lestrade chuckled. "I wish I'd been there for that, your brother's face must have been priceless."

"I gather that Mycroft had already... been in touch with you by then."

"Two days earlier; I've never seen the man looking so anxious before. When Mary went to see him, he did his best to calm her fears, even going so far as to tell her he was putting his best people on the task. He probably shouldn't have said that, in hindsight. Mycroft would never have gone to such lengths if there was nothing to worry about, and Mary knew it." Lestrade gave a rueful grin. "It took a little time to make all the necessary arrangements for my departure, and by then Mary had made an educated guess and some 'arrangements' of her own. I thought Wiggins was hanging around the Yard a bit more than usual."

"She sent the Irregulars... to spy on you?" Holmes was still wrestling with the mental image of an indignant Mary Watson bearing down on an unsuspecting Mycroft in his dressing gown and slippers.

"Not only me: Gregson, Patterson and Morton, too, as well as Mycroft. Honestly, what those young urchins wouldn't do for the three of you doesn't bear thinking about, by God." The Inspector's disapproving tone was completely belied by the affectionate twinkle in his eye. "It didn't take the boys long to find out that I was the one going, and all Mary had to do next was head to the train station. She didn't even have to pack her bag..."

Holmes had to admit he was impressed by the woman's resourcefulness. Even so... "There is still no excuse, Lestrade! You could simply have... handed her over to the gendarmes in Dieppe – you had all the necessary jurisdiction from Mycroft, if you recall!"

Lestrade snorted, folding his arms. "I'm a police inspector, Mr. Holmes, not a magistrate! Since when do I have the right to tell a woman she can't go looking for her husband? Besides, Mary made it very clear that I could either have her alongside, helping in the search, or constantly be looking for her over my shoulder. I have to say, that was rather a persuasive argument, and it's one I've been glad to concede ever since we left England. The lady has some very useful talents – without her, I might never have found you. I don't know exactly what she learned at that Scottish boarding school, but it certainly wasn't all stitching samplers and playing the haggis."

Holmes disdained the man's feeble joke, obviously meant to distract him from the matter at hand. "So, you abandoned your principles... for a winning smile and a stomach remedy – for shame, Inspector."

"Mary's 'winning smile', as *you* so interestingly put it, helped to open a lot of doors, Mr. Holmes. That, and she speaks both French and German like a blessed native. I've never been much good at that sort of thing, and the few phrases I remembered from my school days would scarcely have been helpful where we were going. I've no idea why your brother thought I was the best person to send off to foreign parts, but who am I to argue?"

"Indeed; very little arguing seems to have occurred in your case, Inspector," Holmes sniffed, but without much conviction. It was not as if he had succeeded in that endeavour, either. "Go on, Lestrade," he sighed, trying to convey his apology without actually having to say it aloud. "You were saying?"

Lestrade nodded and picked up the thread again. "As I said, Mary's assistance was invaluable. She's done a good deal of travelling in her earlier days, which meant we could keep a lower profile along the way, in case anyone was looking for us. She even took off her wedding ring and assumed the role of my sister when necessary – her idea, sir, you don't need to scowl like that! She charmed the epaulettes off the Commissionaire in Geneva; combined with Mycroft's letter of introduction, we probably could have borrowed the Swiss Army for a short stroll up the Matterhorn, if the situation had called for it. Either way, we had no trouble acquiring the relevant files and evidence from the investigation – what little there was."

"Please tell me you did not let Mary read... the police report from the crime scene!"

"You tell me how I was supposed to stop her, Mr. Holmes! I know you don't have a high opinion of females in general, but you can at least credit Mary – who was brave enough to marry the best friend of Sherlock Holmes, mark you – with a little more fortitude than most. I warned her it wasn't going to be pretty, but she took the file out of my hands and read it from start to finish without stopping. She dashed for the water closet to be sick a minute later, but that was understandable. She came straight back again afterwards, too." Lestrade smiled with quiet pride. "I'll tell you what, Mr. Holmes, that woman has the heart of a lioness."

"Lestrade... you..." Words failed the detective, he couldn't think of any that were at all worthy of a gentleman.

"And there was something else as well, which wasn't mentioned in the police report. You can thank Mary for noticing it – I never would have known." Lestrade reached into his jacket and pulled out a slim silver object, one Holmes recognised instantly: his cigarette case. "This *is* yours, isn't it, sir? If not, then I've begun a promising new career in petty larceny, which probably won't sit too well with my current profession."

"It is undoubtedly mine." Holmes would have known it anywhere, Watson had given it to him for Christmas last year. "Where did you... acquire it from?"

Lestrade's face was grim. "Commissionaire Beaumont's pocket."

Holmes' cigarette case, which had been left resting atop the letter he'd written to Watson; he was appalled to think that he could have failed to recollect something so vital. Considering that Watson had never found that note before he... before he died, how had its paperweight come to be owned by one of Switzerland's most prominent authorities?

"A damn good question, Mr. Holmes, but what letter are you talking about?" Lestrade's brows knitted themselves together. "There was nothing like that in the police report, either."

"And Steiler did not notice any such thing when he first arrived on the scene? I left both items and my alpenstock... in plain view for Watson to find, when Moriarty and I... had our last encounter. Moran, or one of his associates, must have... disposed of them before we departed."

"What was in the letter? I'm sorry, sir, but it's important you remember as much as you can. If you wrote anything that might have been useful to Moriarty's gang, which Scotland Yard doesn't know about, or your brother..."

"Then we could be in grave trouble. You have a pencil, Inspector? I will attempt to relate its contents *verbatim*." This was not going to be easy. Holmes closed his eyes and cast his mind back to when he'd written it, the first and only time he tried to tell his friend what was in his heart, which Watson had never even gotten to read. He recited slowly, the words fresh and clear in his memory as if he had only just written them:

"*My dear Watson, I write these few lines through the courtesy of Mr. Moriarty, who awaits my convenience for the final discussion of those questions which lie between us. He has been giving me a sketch of the methods by which he avoided the English police and kept himself informed of our movements. They certainly confirm the very high opinion which I had formed of his abilities. I am pleased to think that I shall be able to free society from any further effects of his presence, though I fear it is at a cost which will give pain to my friends, and especially, my dear Watson, to you.*

I have already explained to you, however, that my career had in any case reached its crisis, and that no possible conclusion to it could be more congenial to me than this. Indeed, if I may make a full confession to you, I was quite convinced that the letter from Meiringen was a hoax, and I allowed you to depart on that errand under the persuasion that some development of this sort would follow. Tell Inspector Patterson that the papers which he needs to convict the gang are in pigeon-hole M., done up in a blue envelope and inscribed "Moriarty." I made every disposition of my property before leaving England, and handed it to my brother Mycroft.

Pray give my greeting to Mrs. Watson, and believe me to be, my dear fellow, very sincerely yours... Sherlock Holmes...'"

Holmes was supremely thankful that he managed to dictate the whole thing to Lestrade without faltering, for he found himself shaking once he had concluded. When he'd written the letter, he was at peace, convinced he was about to die, leaving a bereaved Watson free to return home to his wife. Now, their positions were utterly reversed, and he still had no idea how he was going to tell Mary... but that was not the most pressing issue at present. "Well, Lestrade?"

"Bravo, Mr. Holmes." The Inspector's voice sounded a little awkward, but mostly impressed. "We found that envelope before the trials, although I did have to leave before the proceedings began. Even if Moran was able to get his hands on those papers now, I seriously doubt they'd do him much good."

Holmes stiffened, Lestrade's words and his own dictation stirring yet another memory, this one far more alarming. "He may yet, Inspector. Moriarty... he told me...

"That there was an informant inside Scotland Yard?" Lestrade shook his head in grim amusement at the detective's look of surprise. "Lord love you, sir – that was obvious from the moment Moriarty gave us the slip. There's been a silent investigation of internal affairs going on since then; although now that the man's dead, we'll probably never discover just how far in the rot really goes. Why d'you think I still haven't made contact with Mycroft or the Yard since I left London, even after you were found? Your brother made it very clear that I was only to message him as a last resort, or..." Lestrade broke off abruptly.

"Or if you discovered... that a continued effort... was unnecessary," Holmes finished, taking pity on his red-faced colleague.

Lestrade nodded gratefully, looking marginally less embarrassed. "As far as he's concerned, no news means good news." The Inspector shook his head, respect written clearly on his face. "Mycroft might be even more cold-blooded than you at times, Mr. Holmes, but I'll say this for him: the man has nerves of steel. Can you think of anything else in the letter that could be important?"

"Nothing that Moran... did not already know."

"Which leaves the question of how Commissionaire Beaumont managed to end up with your cigarette case – I'm assuming you don't want me to return it to him." Lestrade placed the case reverently on the nightstand. "The Doctor gave this to you, didn't he? Mary said she was with him on the day he chose it, she recognised the engravings. When she came back after recomposing herself, Beaumont was all sympathy and patronising smiles, and invited her to sit down in his office. I went to fetch her some water, and when I came back, the pompous fathead was lighting a cigarette and offering Mary one – as if that was going to make her feel any better. She went even paler when she saw the case,

37

but pretended the smell of tobacco was the reason for it. Beaumont begged her pardon and left the room to finish his cigarette, which gave Mary the chance to tell me what she'd seen. In hindsight, it might have been better to leave the case with its new owner, especially since we had no proof that the man knew who it had belonged to. But if he did know..."

"Then he would be one of Moran's contacts... and alerting him to your suspicions... incredibly dangerous. It was most unwise, Inspector... You should not have taken such a risk."

"I know. Believe me, sir, the case would still be sitting in Beaumont's coat pocket, if the perfect opportunity hadn't presented itself."

Holmes groaned. "Lestrade, what did you do?"

"It was none of my doing, Mr. Holmes. Since there was no more information to be had from the police, we left soon after; the Commissionaire escorted us out. We were saying our farewells, when we heard a rumbling crash and shouts of alarm from further up the steep street. We looked up in time to see several large barrels rolling straight towards us. Mary was alert and jumped to safety, I didn't have to worry about her, but Beaumont was standing frozen to the spot, mouth open. I grabbed him by his coat front and dived out of the way with him, just in time. He hit his head on the cobbles and lay stunned for a minute..." Lestrade spread his hands like a conjurer, grinning. "I simply couldn't resist, I knew I'd never have a better chance than that."

The blood had drained from Holmes' face during Lestrade's tale, concern giving his voice a sardonic twist. "A masterful heist, Inspector – but did it not occur to you that... the opportunity was a little too convenient? You and Mary blundered straight off in search of us, causing a considerable stir in high places... then the minute you stepped back outside the gendarmerie... both of you nearly came to grief."

Lestrade looked decidedly offended. "What kind of an idiot do you take me for, Mr. Holmes? I knew right away that it wasn't just an accident, and Mary's no fool – she knew it, too. We took advantage of all the mess and confusion, and disappeared into the growing crowd as fast as we could. All the same, looking back, it did seem rather a crude effort, more like a warning than an actual attempt on our lives."

"No need to ask... whether you heeded the warning..."

"Only so far as acknowledging that we needed to drop out of sight, and quickly. Fortunately, we were travelling light, with just two carpet bags between us. We found a guest house in a quiet side street where we could catch our breath and make new plans. The more we discussed it, the more obvious it seemed that, however it got there, the cigarette case being in Beaumont's possession was no coincidence. It was a subtle message that we were being watched, right before the more emphatic message out on the street. Somebody knew that Mary and I were coming, in spite of all precautions. There was definitely a leak in communications somewhere, which meant we couldn't rely on the authorities any longer – we were on our own."

Chapter 5

Switch Track

"I trust your subsequent voyage was a pleasant one, Lestrade?"

"Actually, it wasn't as bad as... wait, what?" The Inspector stared at Holmes. "God help me – should I even bother telling this story, or are you simply going to deduce the rest of the journey from my shirt cuffs?"

"Elementary, Inspector. Geneva is at the western end... of the region's largest lake. You could not initially use the roads or railways... without running a grave risk of being detected... therefore your wisest course would be to travel by boat. If those watching you had observed your crossing the Channel... they would hardly expect you to take to the water again. Where did you put ashore?"

"La Bretagne. We found an unexpected ally in the landlady of the guest house, a Madame Fauvel. Mary can tell you more about her, she hardly spoke any English, but the two of them were thick as thieves in five minutes. She could see we were in trouble just by looking at us, and insisted on hearing the whole story. Fortunately for us, Madame was no stranger to trouble herself. Her son Henri is a smuggler, it was his sloop that took us across the lake the next night."

Lestrade shook his head at Holmes' sceptical look. "Luxuries, Mr. Holmes, no firearms; we might have been hard pressed for options at that stage, but even my abandoned principles can only take so much. I won't say I wasn't glad to set foot on shore again – however, it was still another eighty miles from La Bretagne to Meiringen, as the crow flies."

"Since you were not blessed with wings... north or south?"

"South first, then northeast. We were able to follow the Rhône river up the valley, all the way to Oberwald."

Holmes couldn't quite hide a smile. "I am impressed, Inspector... I was not aware you could ride a horse. The way you are shifting in your seat at the recollection, my dear Lestrade... tells me everything I need to know. Saddle sores can be extremely painful, can they not?"

"Wonderful, I'm glad I amuse you. You're having far too much fun at my expense here, I hope you realise."

"My sympathies, Lestrade. Please, continue... this is a most compelling account." The detective tried his hardest to look contrite.

"You want to watch the blatant flattery, Mr. Holmes. The horses were spent by the time we reached Oberwald. We rested them for a day, then set off again up the mountain pass. That was an exercise in patience – those hill roads are rough, it took us two days to get only halfway."

"How did Mary fare in all of this?"

"As well as could be expected, I suppose. She's a much better rider than me; I think the hardest part for her was the crawl up the pass. That, and we were both on edge, not knowing what to make of the few details we had, and doing our best not to assume the worst or upset each other with useless speculation. Meiringen was a sight for sore eyes when we finally reached it, late on the afternoon of the 28th. We found the hotel, and the landlord welcomed us with open arms, even before he knew why we'd come, to his credit. We'd been travelling almost non-stop for over a week – we weren't exactly respectable-looking when we arrived on his veranda, or very fragrant, either. I've never been so glad for a bath in my life... and if you dare to voice that thought, Mr. Holmes, I'll cut the story short right here! As I was saying, Steiler took us in without hesitating, and Mary didn't even need to translate, for once. When we told him the reason for our being there, the poor fellow almost wept, he was that relieved to have someone who'd listen to what he had to tell. The next part you already know."

"Indeed, I believe you left off... after finding Erik Brenner's name... struck from the family records."

"That might not have been very helpful in itself, if events hadn't taken an unexpected turn. It seemed our activities in Rosenlaui had attracted a bit more attention than we thought, which became apparent when we received a late-night visitor. Care to speculate, sir?"

Holmes did not have to, the answer was obvious. "Roland Brenner."

"The very same. He'd been hiding up in the hills in an abandoned cabin, ever since he left you with Moriarty. He was meant to sit tight and wait for further orders, but when he received the message from the hamlet that we'd been poking around up there... One of the locals must have been spying on us when we found the box in the chimney."

"No doubt he could not leave his... family's treasured possessions in enemy hands... regardless of instructions."

"Steiler had locked the box away in the hotel safe, but Roland knew where the key was kept. Too bad for him I'm a light sleeper these days." Lestrade grinned like a wolf. "I'll admit, I'd been itching for an actual fight for ages, so I might have been a little overenthusiastic while apprehending him... not that Mary complained. She and Steiler were both woken by the noise and came rushing to the study where I had Roland pinned. Thank God we were the only guests. Up until that point, we'd had few leads and no contact with anyone who knew anything definite about the two of you, so when Mary learned who he was..."

Lestrade gave a low whistle. "I've seen some chilling sights in my time, Mr. Holmes, but never anything like Mary Watson's face at that moment. All I'll say is that the pleasant smile she was wearing didn't match her eyes... It made the hair on my neck stand straight up, and I wasn't even the one she was looking at!"

42

"You had no trouble... extracting what you needed... from Brenner, I gather." The Inspector's description of Mary was not making Holmes feel any better about their approaching interview – quite the opposite.

"No, *she* didn't."

"You allowed Mary... to question him alone?" Perfect, it was now official: Lestrade had gone stark, staring mad.

"'Allowed' is hardly the word for it, Mr. Holmes... and if you'd ever seen Mary when she has a bee in her bonnet, you wouldn't need to ask. We'd secured Roland to a chair, so he couldn't do anything to harm her. She insisted on Steiler and I leaving the room – neither of us had the nerve to cross her right then, I'm not ashamed to say it – and the look in her eyes told me plainly that eavesdropping was not an option."

Lestrade shivered. "I don't know what she said to that young man in our absence and, by Heaven, I hope I never do. Mary didn't even raise her voice... but in quarter of an hour, she summoned us back in to find Roland slumped in the chair, sobbing like a child into his freed hands. Unfortunately, it seemed that he was sent away immediately after Moriarty arrived, so he didn't know what had happened to either of you, or the Doctor. However, Roland did tell Mary one useful piece of information – a mailing address in Zurich that his brother gave him. We had our next lead and, most importantly, a strand of our own in Moriarty's web."

"You decided to trust Brenner... or was that Mary's idea?"

"I'll never understand how the woman inspired such devotion in someone she'd just reduced to tears." Lestrade shook his head in wonder. "Still, I can't deny that her confidence in the lad was well-founded. He more than proved himself during the next stage of the journey. At this time, we decided that speed was slightly more important than stealth, so the obvious choice was to take the train.

Meiringen having its own station, it wasn't hard to stow away on one of the boxcars in the next train bound for Lucerne. Not the most comfortable way to travel, I'll grant you, but at least it was low-profile. Well... that was the idea..."

Lestrade shifted uncomfortably in his seat. "It only took an hour to get to Lucerne by train – except that we almost didn't reach it at all. Looking back, it's clear we should have stayed away from the railroads completely, tracks give precious little room for manoeuvring. I suppose all the successes we'd had in getting so far had made us careless; we'd... *I'd* forgotten that there were still unfriendly eyes and ears in a lot of walls." The Inspector's face was mortified, eyes downcast. "I should have known better, I walked us headlong into danger like a blasted raw recruit. If it hadn't been for Roland's quick thinking and a decent-sized miracle..."

"Yet you clearly emerged... relatively unscathed, Inspector." At least Lestrade's mistake hadn't cost anyone their life, as far as Holmes could tell from the man's expression. "Please, go on... if you feel able."

"Well, it won't hurt anything except my pride. I'm just glad to be sitting here to tell it. Bear in mind that I couldn't understand half of what was being said at the time, Mary had to fill in the gaps afterwards. The boxcar we were in was stacked full of wooden crates..."

* * *

...There was barely enough room for the three of them to stand together in the remaining floor space. Lestrade and Roland clambered to the top of the stacks and shifted some cases around to hollow out a space big enough for three. It wasn't much of a hiding place, but they might escape a casual glance, if it came to that. They were still working when the train jolted into life and threw Mary off-balance.

Roland moved quickly to steady her as she staggered, face etched with concern. *"All right, little mother?"* Lestrade remembered enough German from his school days to understand that, at least.

"Yes, Roland, thank you." Mary smiled at Roland affectionately; she'd clearly already adopted him, and Lestrade wondered anew what had passed between them in the study.

Roland made a bed in the nook with their coats and bags and offered his hand to help her climb. *"You should rest, Maria. It's an hour's journey to Lucerne – we'll keep watch, the Inspektor and I."*

Lestrade wasn't surprised when Mary followed the lad's suggestion gratefully, no doubt she was exhausted. The pace they'd set over the last fortnight would have knocked anyone off their feet – he was amazed she'd made it this far without collapsing. Then again, considering what drove her... His brow furrowed, lips tightening. They hadn't talked about what they'd do if... if they learnt that the worst had happened. Now was not the time for thoughts like that, there was too much at stake, they had to keep hoping for the best. He climbed down to sit on the floor and leant back against the cases, trying to make his mind go blank. Too few clues, random pieces of a puzzle, and not even a picture for a guide...

He snapped awake as Roland shook his shoulder frantically. *"Inspektor, wake up! Please..."* The lad's eyes were wide with alarm, this couldn't be good.

"Roland? What's happening?" Mary's voice was tense but controlled as she rolled up their coats and stuffed them into the carpet bags.

"Something's wrong, we're stopping too soon!" Something about 'too soon'...

Mary peered through a gap in the door. "He's right; we're only on the outskirts, why are we stopping? Shh, listen!" They could all hear: raised voices outside the train, coming closer. No mistaking the tone, if not the words – the voice of the policeman was universal.

Roland paled. "*The police, they're searching the train! Hide, quick!*" Lestrade didn't need telling twice, scrambling up the crates. He joined Mary in their crude cover and they huddled down as low as they could.

"*Roland, hide!*" Mary's frantic whisper mirrored Lestrade's own bewilderment. Why wasn't the boy hiding, there was enough room in here!

A dreadful suspicion suddenly tingled down the Yarder's spine, but there wasn't a damn thing he could do about it now. The voices were rapidly closing in, he could hear orders being barked in German: "*Open them! Look everywhere!*" He cursed himself for several dozen kinds of fool, why hadn't they used the horses? It was only a matter of seconds before their car was ransacked as well.

Lestrade heard Roland breathe, "*Do you trust me, Maria?*"

"*Of course, but...*" Mary's voice trembled as she lifted her head from their hiding place. She'd been so brave, she shouldn't be here, Lestrade should never have let her come with him.

"*Goodbye, little mother... I'll see you in Zurich.*" Roland winked, curled up in the small floor space and started to snore.

"*No, Roland!*" Mary tried to scramble up, but Lestrade knew now what the lad was up to. Mercilessly, he held her down, hating himself for it, but there was no sense in all of them getting caught.

"No, Mary, stay down!"

"But Roland..."

"...knows what he's doing, it's our only chance..."

Mary's eyes widened in horrified understanding as the sliding door crashed open, and a shout went up: *"Here!"*

"Eh?" Roland's sleepy, panicked voice would have done credit to any amateur theatre company. *"No, no, please..."*

"Keep searching, this one's mine!" The voice was a young man's, strident and cruel. Lestrade's fists clenched at the bully's evident delight at having found such a prize. Footsteps pounded away over the stones, continuing the search of the other cars, as the young man leapt into their car and the sounds of a scuffle ensued.

"No, let go!" Mary's hand found his and he held it tight, bracing her as they listened helplessly.

"Stand up, little rat!" Then... *"Roland?!"* No, it couldn't be...

"Erik? Erik, thank God!" Hope squeezed Lestrade's heart painfully, echoed by Mary's grip on his hand. Could they just possibly all get out of this in one piece?

"Roland! Little brother, what are you doing here?" Erik's voice was thunderstruck, and not a little angry.

"I... I had to find you. Papa..." Roland's voice was tearful, lost. Their father had died only last winter, perhaps his disowned eldest son hadn't known.

"Anyone with you?" Erik's demand had a slight panicked edge.

"No, no one. Please, Erik..."

Roland was cut off by his brother's frantic hiss, as the footsteps approached their car again. *"Shut up, you little fool! I don't believe this..."* Erik harshly called out to the other searchers. *"He's alone, the train can leave. Move, little rat... Take him!"* as if the boy were nothing more to him than a random stowaway.

Erik must have had his reasons for not wanting his associates to know who Roland was, but would he really allow his younger brother to be taken – and yet how could the man avoid it without giving himself away? Those questions were answered the next moment by a sudden yelp of pain and a curse from an unknown voice, followed immediately by angry shouts from many voices: *"Hey, stop! Grab him!"* Roland had clearly seen his chance and made a break for freedom. Lestrade could only pray that they wouldn't think the boy worth pursuing for long...

* * *

Chapter 6

Stage of Resistance

The Inspector sat back, suddenly realising that he was perched on the very edge of his seat. Holmes had to admit, the feeling was mutual. "The police came back empty-handed, with Erik cursing a blue streak at them, although it was clear to Mary and I that he'd wanted Roland to escape. The cars were closed up again, and the train moved on a minute later. We were safe, for the moment, although the police search did indicate that getting back out of Lucerne was likely going to be much harder than we first believed. However, we had no choice – Roland's last words to Mary were that he would meet us in Zurich, so that's where we had to go. We waited another minute, then jumped from the train before we got to the edge of the town, it was going slowly enough. With the police looking for us, and no idea where Roland had run to, we were forced to keep moving and hope he'd catch up..."

* * *

...But Roland could move faster than the two of them, and would have a much easier task avoiding the authorities. They couldn't just blunder their way through this time, they needed a plan. Both of them had bathed before they left Meiringen this morning, but they still stood out in their travel-stained clothes. Thankfully, Mary had wisely kept one dress in reserve, and did her best to smarten Lestrade up as well. The summer season was just beginning, and they hoped that Lucerne would have enough tourists for them to fade into the background.

It was midday by the time they reached the river in the town centre with its covered wooden bridge, which Mary told Lestrade was called the Chapel Bridge. It was the first time she'd spoken to him conversationally since they'd left the train. He knew she was still upset about Roland, one more worry on top of everything else.

They strolled casually out over the water, pretending to admire the religious paintings that gave the bridge its name, but staying alert for anything that seemed out of place, not that they'd know it even if they saw it without Roland... God help them, what were they *doing* here? A sudden combined rush of panic and homesickness almost knocked the Yarder off his feet. He stopped and gripped the rail, breathing deeply, head bowed.

"George?" Mary's low, urgent use of Lestrade's assumed name brought him back to himself. "George, are you all right? You need to compose yourself, we're attracting attention." She took his arm and pressed it, speaking aloud for the benefit of the curious onlookers. "Come, brother dear, we'll find a coffeehouse. It must be at least half an hour since you breakfasted, no wonder you grow faint!" Her teasing smile and the concern in her eyes helped to brace him up again. He couldn't let her down, not like this... and she wasn't the only one relying on him, either.

Emerging from the other end of the bridge, they wandered into a small plaza with a brightly painted fountain. Mary made him sit down at an outdoor café and they ordered coffee and sweet rolls. As they finished eating, their attention was caught by the fuss a little way across the square. An extremely fat Englishwoman, with her mouse of a husband in tow, was attempting to make herself understood to the driver of an open carriage. They were having little success, as the lady's French was even worse than Lestrade's, and the driver's patience was plainly wearing thin.

Mary winced at the woman's merciless butchering of the elegant syllables, then leant forward, looking thoughtful. "George... The police aren't looking for a large party, are they – only an English couple?"

"I suppose so, but... Martha, where are you going?" as she stood quickly, expression resolute.

"To find transport, wait here a minute." Mary approached the frustrated woman, radiating calm and assurance. "Excuse me, madam, I am so sorry to intrude... Might I be of some assistance to you?"

"Oh, my dear, could you? This simpleton of a peasant cannot understand a word I say, I thought they could speak French in this country!"

"If you will allow me, madam? Perhaps he is merely accustomed to a different dialect, there can be a wide variation between regions." With a winsome smile, Mary turned to the driver and addressed him in German. The man's irritation rapidly faded and he touched the brim of his hat respectfully, responding in kind. Mary turned back to the lady. "Where do you wish to travel, madam?"

"Oh, thank heavens! My husband and I simply must reach Zurich by this evening, how much to hire the carriage? I confess, I am all at sea with this confounded currency; why can they not replace these silly francs with honest English pounds?" Mary negotiated with the driver and, amazingly, both parties seemed to be satisfied with their end of the bargain. The lady seized Mary's hand and wrung it. "My dear, we are indebted to you, you have been so helpful! Might I ask your name?"

"Martha Lethbridge, madam. It is a pleasure to make your acquaintance."

"The pleasure is ours, my dear, I assure you! I am Mrs. Rachel Peabody, and this is my husband, Alistair."

"Delighted, Miss Leth..." The man was clearly one of those unfortunate husbands destined never to finish a sentence.

"And what of you, my dear, are you bound on the same journey? Might we offer you a place with us?"

"Oh, no – it is most kind of you, madam, but we wouldn't dream of imposing. My brother and I will be quite all right. No doubt they will have repaired our carriage by tomorrow."

"Tomorrow! My dear Miss Lethbridge, I simply won't hear of it; you both must come with us. We English have to band together in times of crisis!" If the woman only knew...

"You are too kind, madam, bless you! Please excuse me, I must go and tell George the good news."

She escaped and rejoined Lestrade at the table. "That was charming," he remarked dryly. "Are you sun-touched?"

"No, although the driver thought Mrs. Peabody was," Mary chuckled.

"Ha! Seriously, Martha, we still have to get past the police. Do you really think this is going to work?"

"Safety in numbers, dear brother, I do believe it will. Mrs. Peabody's personality should provide sufficient cover." Or, if need be, a battering ram. "Shall we?"

"Absolutely, my dear Martha. By all means, introduce me to our charming new friends!"

Lestrade rose and offered her his arm, grinning as Mary murmured, "Bite your tongue, George..."

"And why is the driver now beaming at our good benefactress? I thought he was going to hit her with his whip a little while ago!"

Mary gave him an innocent smile. "Well, I may have slightly exaggerated to her the fee that the driver told me. I think it could be the largest fare Franz has ever collected. Why do you think the two of us are riding free of charge?"

"I didn't know we were – does she?"

"Least said is soonest mended, dear brother…" Moriarty might have to concede his title of criminal mastermind.

* * *

"The subterfuge worked perfectly. The police didn't even stop the carriage when we reached the road block, just waved us on through. According to Mrs. Peabody, they were looking for two dangerous spies on the run from Geneva. She and her husband had already been through several checks on the passenger train from Berne. Mary carefully steered the conversation towards less dangerous topics, playing up to the lady's vanity shamelessly. The journey to Zurich was as uneventful as we could have hoped for."

Lestrade shook his head ruefully. "I couldn't shake the feeling that things were going just a little too smoothly, however, which only lasted until we arrived at the rendezvous. None of us had considered the possibility that the mailing address Erik had told Roland wasn't for a house. All he knew was the street name and number, Falkenstrasse 1. When we finally found it…"

* * *

…Lestrade had to bite back an oath, remembering the company he was in. They were looking at the large and extremely ornate new Stadttheater, still under construction. Exactly how long ago had Erik left home? What had been here before this?

"According to the sign, this is where the old theatre was. It must have burnt down since Erik gave Roland the address." Mary peered at the posters on the billboards. "The grand opening is set for October: Wagner's 'Lohengrin.'"

"Well, we can't just camp outside for four months, I'm not that much of an opera lover. It's a building site – there must be an easy way in..."

"Wonderful. Are we about to add breaking and entering to our accomplishments?"

"What would you suggest? Wait out on the street, maybe? This is where Roland will come to find us, and we don't have anywhere else to stay."

"In that case, lead on, Inspector."

They found a window around the back that had only been loosely boarded; it was the work of a minute to pry them free.

"Do you think perhaps we're not the first ones to do this?" Mary joked, half-serious. Lestrade wouldn't be surprised, which made him wonder if they might not be the last tonight either, even if Roland didn't make it... They'd better take turns to get some sleep. It was still too early for that, though, only half past three. Thankfully, the building seemed completely deserted at the moment. It was a Saturday, after all – the workers must have gone home early.

The sheer size and opulence of the place put Lestrade in mind of St. Paul's combined with the Clarendon Hotel. He and Mary took the grand tour, walking out onto the stage and surveying the mostly complete auditorium, craning their necks to admire the jewel-bright paintings on the ceiling. Lestrade whistled softly, the sound carrying right around the vast room. "Impressive, isn't it? Imagine what it'll be like when it's finished!"

"The dressing rooms are, at least – we can camp in one of them tonight."

"Speaking of which... Mary, we need to think about what we'll do in case we get uninvited guests. Roland may not be the only one to arrive after dark."

"I gather from your expression, Lestrade... that your suspicions were correct."

"You have a genius for understatement, Mr. Holmes." Lestrade's *expression was grave. "I'll give you fair warning, this part of the story isn't going to be easy to hear, but I'll be hanged if I leave it for Mary to tell..."*

It was nearing the end of Lestrade's second watch when he learnt that they had company. The damn building had been echoing and creaking since their arrival, but even an empty theatre couldn't produce the sound of footsteps. He woke Mary with a hand over her mouth and signed to her to hide. She swiftly concealed herself behind some scenery flats with what he thought was a reassuring smile, it was hard to be sure in this light. Hopefully, their night vision would give them a slight advantage.

Breathing a silent prayer, the Yarder slipped out of the room and down the corridor. He trod softly on the bare boards, edging towards the weak light that spilled out from under a door standing slightly ajar. If he remembered correctly, that was one of the practice rooms, a large empty space with full-length mirrors and handrails on all four walls. With any luck, he might hear something interesting...

A slight breeze on the back of his neck had him ducking instinctively, the blackjack missing him by a hair as it whistled over his head. The misjudged blow made his assailant lose his balance, and Lestrade's arm was around the man's throat the next instant, cutting off his air in a choke hold as the thug opened his mouth to yell. As his would-be attacker clawed frantically at his arm, a newly-familiar voice rang out from inside the practice room. "Good evening, Inspector

Lestrade. Would you do me the honour of your company? There is someone here who is anxious to be reunited with you."

His heart lifted at those words. Erik might have Roland, but he wouldn't want his brother to come to any harm – time to call his bluff. Lestrade loosened his grip on his prisoner's neck slightly, revolver jabbing into the small of his back."Let's not keep your friend waiting, sunshine, move your arse."

As they edged slowly into the room, the situation appeared to be a stalemate at first glance. A dark, well-built man in his late twenties leant against the wall, a single lantern at his feet, pistol casually trained on the figure huddled in the middle of the floor. The resemblance between the brothers was surprisingly faint, made more so by the fresh cuts and bruises on Roland's face. Lestrade squashed his rising anger at the boy's appearance, hoping for Erik's sake that the man had had one hell of a good reason for allowing such treatment of his own kin. Or was any of that *his* handiwork?

"Evening, Brenner. This belong to you? It was lying around in the passage."

"Thank you, Inspector, you are too kind." Erik inclined his head graciously. "And where is the radiant Mrs. Watson? You should invite her to join us – it is time we had a little talk."

"Enough of the dramatics, Brenner," Lestrade responded bluntly. "Roland's your brother, you're hardly going to kill him after letting him go from the train. Drop the gun."

"You make a grave error, Inspector, confusing lack of desire with lack of ability. Release my colleague and put your weapon down, or yes, I will shoot my own brother, if only to force you to take me seriously. It might or might not be fatal."

Erik's eyes glittered, and Lestrade felt a chill crawling down his spine... He'd just made a huge mistake, the man was most certainly not bluffing. The Yarder let go of his hostage and stepped back, placing the gun on the floor. The other man darted forward and scooped it up, rubbing his neck, malice-filled eyes fixed on Lestrade.

"Harrison, make our guest comfortable. Please do not try anything foolish, Inspector, this is a hair trigger." Erik kept his gun pointed at Roland, while Harrison shoved Lestrade over to the rail on the other side of the room then, without warning, viciously clubbed him over the back of the head with the revolver. Lestrade's knees buckled and he slumped to the floor. Dazed, he felt his wrists seized and tightly tied above his head to the wooden bar.

Erik switched guard duty with Harrison and crouched in front of Lestrade. "Just so you know, Inspector: Roland did not betray you, not directly. I will confess I was surprised to find him on the train, but he forgot something important. Whatever else I despise about my family, our sainted father and I share one exceptionally useful talent: I always know when someone is lying to me. It was no great leap of logic to realise who else was on the train and where you would go next. Roland never was very good at hiding when we were younger. Nothing has changed, it seems."

"So you were a smug, boot-licking reptile... back then, too? That doesn't surprise me." Lestrade's head was throbbing, and he could feel the blood trickling down through his hair.

"Language, Inspector," Erik replied calmly. Footsteps sounded in the passage and, to Lestrade's dismay, Mary entered the room with a second thug holding a knife to her throat. "Ah, Mrs. Watson, I am so glad you could join us. Good work, Klaus."

"My apologies, Inspector." He winced at the self-reproach in Mary's voice as Klaus moved her to stand against the opposite wall to him. "*Roland, your face!*"

"I'm sorry, Maria... I couldn't stop them..." The poor lad sounded utterly wretched.

"We did warn you in Geneva, Inspector," Erik sighed. "The Colonel is a tolerant man, but you are both rapidly becoming a nuisance."

"Well, that *is* what I do for a living..." Lestrade dropped his voice to a murmur, not wanting Mary to hear. "Which reminds me... where are Mr. Holmes and Dr. Watson? I get the distinct impression that if anyone knows what happened to them, you do. Indulge my curiosity, won't you?"

Erik matched his quiet tone, smiling faintly. "Persistent to the last, Inspector, I admire that. Yes, I do know – but sadly, it is more than my life is worth to tell. My sympathies to you both, but you have come as far as you can..."

Harrison's leering rasp cut in. "Don't suppose we got any spare time while you're jawing with the flatfoot, Brenner? The lady seems like the spirited type... I reckon we're owed a little fun."

The look in the thug's eye made Lestrade feel sick. "Don't lay a finger on her!" Please, God, *no* – not this, not Mary!

"Why not? *Roland, your hands are free.*" Erik drew a pair of handcuffs from his pocket and turned to toss them at Roland. "*Cuff the lady to the rail.*"

"*Erik, no, please...*" Roland was pale, eyes wide with horror and disbelief, and Mary was in much the same state.

"*You or them, little brother? Choose...*" Erik's voice was cold and hard as steel. Mary shuddered, lips pressed together tight, clutching the rail behind her in a death grip. She looked like she was about to faint – if anything, that would probably have been a mercy.

Roland hesitated for a long moment, then set his teeth and picked up the restraints, bowing his head. *"Forgive me, Maria..."*

"Roland, no, don't you bloody *dare!"* When Lestrade got his hands on the coward, death would be a very distant mercy. "Mary...!"

"Inspector, please... don't worry about me... I'll be all right..." Mary's voice was trembling, but she managed to lift her head, her expression one of scathing contempt. Her sheer courage staggered Lestrade, he prayed it wasn't just an act. His hands clenched convulsively, wrists wrenching against the ropes – futile or not, he couldn't just *sit* here...

Roland slowly approached Mary and closed the first cuff around her left wrist, circling the bar with the chain... then, before anyone could react, clasped the second cuff around his own right wrist, securing them both to the rail. The boy stuck out his chin defiantly, eyes blazing. *"If you hurt the lady, sirs, you have to hurt me, too!"*

"You little fool..." Erik's voice was a mixture of disbelief, anger and amusement.

"Aw, look... the little worm's grown a backbone!" Harrison sniggered, digging an elbow into Klaus' ribs.

"Well, Brenner?" Klaus grinned, sounding sickeningly pleased about the new development.

The brothers locked gazes for several tense seconds; then, to Lestrade's immense relief, Erik was the first to look away. "No... Leave them, we do not have the time for this," turning back to the chained pair and driving his fist into Roland's gut, *"But* never *defy me again, little brother!"* Roland dropped to his knees with a gasp, and Mary sank down beside him, clinging to the lad as best she could with only one arm, whispering what Lestrade could well believe was fervent gratitude. He'd have given a lot to be voicing his own right now; he could only imagine what it had cost Roland to stand up to his brother that way.

"You two, go and scout ahead." Both thugs muttered darkly, scowling, but did as they were told. Once they'd left the room, Erik's voice changed from steel to stone. "As for you and the lady, Inspector... be wise, return home. You cannot help your friend, but you can save your own lives. Take Roland with you, I would rather not have to kill him, either. Be out of Zurich by tomorrow, Inspector. Should we meet again..." Erik picked up the lantern and walked out, leaving the three of them stunned and stranded in the dark.

"Mary, are you all right? Mary! Roland...?"

"*I don't know, Inspektor, she's had a terrible fright. Maria...? Shh, it's all right, I'm here... You're safe, little mother, calm down...*" Lestrade could only listen helplessly as Roland gently soothed her, weak from relief and pain, his head hammering. Even if there'd been any light in here, he still wasn't sure he could have seen anything. His eyes felt unfocused... "*Inspektor? Inspektor!*"

"What, Roland...?" Why was the wall moving? He was so tired, if he could just lie down...

"*Damn... I'm worried, Maria, the Inspektor was hit on the head.*"

"*He might have... a concussion. Talk to him, don't let him fall asleep.*" Oh, good, she was sounding much better... "Inspector? Geoffrey! You may have concussion, you mustn't go to sleep. Stay with me." How was Lestrade meant to do that, it was too far to reach... "Talk to us, Geoffrey, you need to stay awake."

"I'll do my best..."

"*I'm so sorry, Inspektor, this is all my fault.*"

"He says..."

"Don't worry, Mary... I think I got that one. Tell him I don't blame him... I shouldn't have underestimated his brother like that. Cold-blooded bugger... No wonder his father disowned him... he should have been drowned as a child! Oh, hell, don't translate that..."

"Well, obviously!" A few moments later, "Geoffrey... what did Erik say to you before? I know you were asking about... about John and Mr. Holmes. And then... when he left, he said..."

"I know." 'You cannot help your *friend*.' Had Erik been mistaken, or was there really only one of them still alive? If so, it was almost certainly Mr. Holmes, he would have been the most valuable to Moriarty. But that was the odd thing: Erik had said 'The Colonel is a tolerant man,' not 'The Professor.' What the hell was going on? Lestrade had been lost in thought for too long – he suddenly realised Mary was frantically calling his name. "I'm still awake, Mary... it's all right."

"Is it?" Her whisper was anguished. "If Erik was telling the truth…"

"Are you telling me you believe anything that crawled out of that bastard's mouth? Mary, I... I know I can't promise you we'll find either of them alive, but... whatever's happened, wherever they are... we *will* find them – I swear it." Lestrade wasn't about to let the blessed woman return home without some kind of solution to this whole bloody mess; whether it was her husband at her side... or worst case, the knowledge of where and how he'd died. Before any of that, though, they had to get out of here. Erik had said to leave town by tomorrow, but it would take a lot longer than that for the builders to come back and find them – tomorrow was Sunday.

* * *

Chapter 7

Dawning Hope

"Mr. Holmes?" Lestrade's hand on his shoulder brought Holmes back to the present with a start. "Take a deep breath, sir, you look like you're going to be sick."

"It would seem that I am not... the only one with a genius... for understatement, Inspector." Lestrade's account had been the verbal equivalent of a kick to the stomach. The thought of what could have happened to Mary, without Roland's intervention, made Holmes feel physically ill.

Lestrade brought him some more water. "I'm sorry you had to hear that, Mr. Holmes. I know you're not looking forward to speaking with Mary, and I don't blame you – but I thought if you knew what she's gone through to get here, it might make things... I suppose 'easier' is the wrong word..."

"I understand." Holmes was surprised to find that he meant it. Hearing about Mary's journey had not made his task any easier, but it had helped to strengthen his resolve. The woman had run towards the unknown without hesitating, undeterred by overwhelming odds. She might not have done it for him, but he could do no less for her. "When will I be able... to see her?"

"That's for Mary to decide. I don't know when she'll be ready to talk, but I can at least tell her that you are. Do you want me to?"

"No... but please do so."

"That's the spirit, sir. In the meantime... there's something you have been wanting to see, I think. The rest of the story can wait." Lestrade drew Holmes' covers back and draped one blanket around his shoulders, then began carefully gathering the detective into his arms.

"Don't worry, Mr. Holmes, I'm not going to drop you. You're far too scrawny at the moment."

"Thank *you*, Inspector. Where are we going?"

"To the window, you can't see the sunrise from where you are." In the space of a few hours, the Inspector had been continually surprising his colleague, and now was no exception. "A child could have deduced that, Mr. Holmes. You've been constantly glancing at the sky since I opened the curtains. Is this going to hurt you too much?"

"No, it is all right." Holmes tried not to wince. In fact, his body was protesting vehemently, but he needed this more than he needed the bed rest at the moment. Lestrade raised a sceptical eyebrow, but lifted the detective regardless and carried him across the room. Holmes' pain was forgotten as they approached the window. It was... There were no words that could adequately describe what lay in front of him.

The second floor room faced south, looking out over the park-like grounds of the hospital and the rustic town centre, and beyond that... Blue, everywhere: the lake, the mountains, the airy, cloudless arch of the sky... Dear God, Holmes had forgotten how large it was... The sun was just beginning to peer over the thickly-wooded hills, although the snow caps of the distant mountains had already been turned to gold.

After being locked away underground for so long, this first view of the outside world was breathtaking... and *terrifying*. He suddenly couldn't look anymore, squeezing his eyes shut to block out everything crowding in on him, it was too much, too soon... but when he closed them, his sense of touch was heightened, and he could feel the sun on his face. The warmth was soothing, gentle... Holmes turned towards it and savoured the feeling, staring at the glow from behind his closed eyelids.

His eyes were watering from the brightness, he had been in the dark so long... How had he even survived, *why* had he? He'd never begged his captors to kill him, but he'd silently prayed for it every moment – perhaps death had been too much to ask for, too great a mercy. He shouldn't be here, he didn't deserve this, it should have been Watson here, not him, Watson watching the sunrise with his wife... He couldn't blame the light for his tears now, there were too many of them... and the name echoing in his mind as he wept into Lestrade's shoulder was joined by another...

When the door opened and the other doctor entered, the detective was surprised to find himself back in his bed and Lestrade sprawled in the bedside chair, snoring. Holmes must have cried himself to sleep again. How long had the Inspector stood at the window holding him? Come to think of it, how long had Lestrade been in this room, when was the last time he'd seen his own bed? The man looked exhausted, face haggard, dark circles under his eyes.

"Good morning, Monsieur Holmes. I am Dr. Joubert." The doctor stood at Holmes' bedside, shaking his head ruefully at the noise. "I trust Inspector Lestrade has not kept you awake with his thundering? The man has barely left your side – I hope not to have the stubborn idiot as my next patient. You have come a long way from when you first arrived here, monsieur, you will do well. How are you feeling? Is there any improvement since last night?"

"A little, perhaps. Last night... monsieur..." Holmes couldn't bring himself to use the man's medical title, the word was still too painful. "I hope I did not..."

"That is all right, Monsieur Holmes; the Inspector has told me of your friend. I am truly sorry for your loss, although perhaps that does not mean much, coming from a stranger." Joubert smiled gravely. "I can only imagine how difficult this must be for you, to submit to the care of someone you do not know or trust. I will do my utmost to spare you more pain, and I assure you I shall not be offended by your merely tolerating me."

"Thank you..."

"My apologies, but you will have to endure my presence for some time this morning. Your dressings need changing, monsieur; that cannot be put off any longer, although the worst of the infection has healed. First, however, you must eat – and so should the Inspector, when he wakes."

Holmes shuddered; the thought of eating anything was hideous. What little had been thrown to him in the cellar was usually spoiled, he had often lost the food almost as soon as he'd eaten it. The look in Joubert's eye told him he would be wise not to argue the point right now, however. Besides, this *was* Switzerland – the hospital fare here couldn't possibly be as bad as Charing Cross, could it?

Apparently, it could. Lestrade was awake by the time a nurse brought in Holmes' breakfast and excused himself with a sympathetic grin, no doubt off in search of something actually edible. Holmes almost envied the man; he could only manage two bites of porridge before his throat closed, in spite of the nurse's coaxing. Eventually, she gave up and removed the tray, threatening to send the doctor after him if he did not eat more at dinner – he thought that was what she'd said, his German was not exactly fluent. At least he'd kept down the food he had managed to swallow, a genuine surprise.

True to his word, Joubert returned soon after breakfast with Lestrade, his colleague looking marginally improved in a clean set of clothes, although he still hadn't washed or shaved. "Later, Mr. Holmes. Joubert says he needs to change your bandages, I thought you might want me here for this. You haven't really had the chance to take stock of your injuries yet, have you?"

"No..." Holmes had been trying hard not to think about that. His wounds were of a piece with his memories – he was not certain he could deal with either at the moment. "How badly...?" Perhaps hearing before seeing would help somewhat.

"Well, your face isn't too bad – for some reason, they left that mainly untouched. What bruises and cuts you do have are fading nicely, although your eyes are a bit bloodshot, and you could definitely do with a shave. I can find a mirror for you, if you'd like."

"No! No, I... I would rather not... just yet."

"Fair enough. As for the rest, I think the doctor had better tell you."

"No... Inspector, please... I would much rather... hear it from you."

Lestrade glanced uncertainly at Joubert, who nodded in understanding, and left the room with the nurse in his wake. "Call when you are ready, messieurs."

"So... Lestrade..." Holmes took a deep breath. "Exactly how much of a mess am I in?"

Lestrade knit his brows awkwardly. "Depends on what you mean, Mr. Holmes. Individually, you don't have any life-threatening injuries; the worst damage at the moment is a couple of cracked ribs and your right knee. The doctor thinks it was dislocated, then forced back again. Do you... remember anything about that?" Holmes swallowed hard, he remembered that excruciating episode only too well... "The joint is still swollen, you're going to be on crutches for a while. Joubert is hopeful that you'll get back most of your mobility, though, especially if you do the exercises he has in mind. As for how it'll affect your work, it's far too soon to tell, but I don't imagine you'll be able to race around London at quite the same speed anymore."

"I see... What else? If that is the worst injury... why can I not move my limbs?"

"You're just weak, with proper food and rest you'll be able to strengthen them again. Your shoulder muscles are badly strained, though – they'll take a little longer. They strung you up, didn't they?" Holmes nodded, shuddering. Lestrade consulted the file the doctor had

66

left behind, peering at the scratchy handwriting. "I know you're worried about your hands, sir; it says here you have two broken fingers and a fractured meta...carpal, whatever that is. Anyhow, they've been splinted and the doctor thinks you'll be able to play the violin again in a few weeks, as long you go carefully in the meantime."

"Is there... more?" Holmes was still trying desperately not to think about what had happened while he'd hung from the ceiling.

"Nothing serious, but... Mr. Holmes, you have to understand, you weren't a pretty sight when we found you. You had a lot of cuts and burns, most of them badly infected. Joubert says that if you had spent one more night in that cellar, we would have been too late. As it is, you're going to be carrying a large number of scars from now on, and there's one in particular..." Lestrade looked distinctly uncomfortable.

"Just tell me, Inspector."

"Do I want to know who or what 'MCALLIST' is?"

Having his wounds redressed felt very much like opening Pandora's box, although that unfortunate incident probably only lasted a few moments. Holmes had to lie still for what seemed like hours, trying to relax and breathe deeply as each revelation delivered a fresh onslaught of nausea-filled memory. He knew he did not have to watch, but he seemed to be in a contrary frame of mind at present – looking away felt too much like giving yet more satisfaction to the ones who had done this to him. At least most of his scars could be concealed when he was able to dress in normal clothes again.

His hands were the worst – he nearly lost his meagre breakfast when Joubert and the nurse unwrapped them, the splints doing nothing to conceal the fact that they both resembled badly-prepared portions of steak tartare. What skin remained intact was covered in bruises, several fingernails were cracked and two were missing altogether.

The detective had to forcibly remind himself that his hands would not always look like this, he *would* use them again. They did not hurt overmuch at present, kept immobile by the new splints and bandages, but he would have to come to terms with them a second time once the bones had knit. His front torso took second prize, McAllister's unfinished signature only one of many permanent mementos of his ordeal. He was not remotely ready to even think about his back yet...

He was shivering violently by the time they'd finished, although he did manage to hold back the tears on this occasion. Joubert tactfully refrained from saying more than "Bravo, monsieur," before quitting the room. The man was doing an admirable job of minimising the necessary contact between them. Holmes wished he didn't feel so relieved about that; it was not Joubert's fault the detective could hardly bear to even look at him.

Holmes' thoughts were interrupted by Lestrade, who had been sitting on the bed beside him the whole time, much to the disapproval of the nurse. Her pointed sniffs had provided a welcome distraction from the matter at hand, especially when the Inspector courteously offered her a handkerchief, eyes twinkling. Lestrade put an arm around Holmes' shoulders and braced him until the shaking subsided. "Well done, sir, it's all over..."

"...until the next time. Perhaps I ought to... ask for a blindfold." The feeble joke was a poor disguise for the embarrassment Holmes felt at being so easily overwrought.

"Not a bad idea, I wish I'd thought of that."

Now that Holmes looked at Lestrade properly, the man did seem a trifle pale as well. It was perversely comforting to know that he had not been the only one affected. "You should rest, Lestrade. How long since you last slept... on an actual bed that was not already occupied, I mean?"

"Honestly, I think it was back in Meiringen; but if you'll pardon me, Mr. Holmes, you don't seem like you want to be left alone at the moment. Should I let you rest, or would you rather hear the rest of the story?"

"As long as you promise immediately afterwards... to sleep, shave and take a bath. I do not think Fräulein Bessner... was merely sniffing in disapproval."

Lestrade chuckled ruefully, seating himself back in the bedside chair. "All right, it's a bargain. Where was I up to?"

"Sunday, I believe."

"Oh, yes. We couldn't do anything to free ourselves until the morning. We just had to sit and wait until there was enough light coming through the door from the passage..."

* * *

...Even then, their efforts seemed useless. The ropes were cutting into Lestrade's wrists – he was able to slide his hands together, leaving his skin behind on the wooden rail, but he still couldn't reach the knots. Even if he could have, his fingers were numb. The other two had been trying all night to slip their hands free of the cuffs. Roland borrowed a hairpin from Mary to try and pick the locks, but neither of them had the skills. If only Harrison hadn't taken Lestrade's knife as well... The Yarder thumped his head back against the mirror behind him in frustration, wincing. He'd forgotten about the friendly tap the thug had given him earlier. Wait a moment... His eyes widened. A friendly tap...

"Mary, I've got it!"

"What is it?"

"The mirror behind you, use the handcuffs to break the glass!"

69

Mary's eyes glowed. "Of course, we can use a shard as a knife – Geoffrey, you're a genius!"

"Wrap some cloth around it to make a handle, then find a way to get it over here. I'll try to grab it with my teeth and cut these ropes."

Mary turned to her fellow captive. *"Give me your hand, Roland, we need to break the mirror!"*

Roland stiffened in excitement. *"Maria, that's brilliant! Oh – sorry, Inspektor..."* The boy cast an apologetic look at Lestrade as he helped Mary to her feet.

"All right, Roland, it doesn't matter. Be careful, you two."

It took the cuffed pair several blows to even crack the glass, but then Roland delivered a few well-placed kicks, and they were able to collect the shards. Mary selected the thinnest, longest piece and wrapped her handkerchief around one end. "I won't throw this over to you, Inspector, I have a better idea." She used the blade to cut the end off one of the ribbons on her dress and unravelled it, giving herself a goodly length of thin, strong thread, then tied one end to the knife handle. "Don't move, I don't want to hit you."

"No offence, Mary, but shouldn't Roland be doing that?"

"No, Roland is right-handed, the same as me. Keep still, please." There was an odd glint in her eye; questioning the woman's aim while she was holding a sharp object might not have been a wise idea. Mary moved as far forward as she could and carefully swung the knife by the thread like a pendulum, aiming at the wall to Lestrade's left. After a few tries, it fell behind the rail to the floor, leaving the thread draped over the bar. It was easy for Mary to position the knife so that he could grasp the handle in his teeth. Once he had a secure hold, she let the thread go slack, but kept hold of the other end. "It's up to you now, Inspector. We'll make another in case you break that one."

Now who was being insulting? Unable to reply at the moment, Lestrade managed to crouch under the bar and started gingerly sawing at the left-hand ropes. The fibres parted slowly, this was painstaking work. The last thing he needed was to give himself a wider mouth or slit his own wrist. The cord finally broke, and his hand slipped free, the blood rushing painfully back into his fingers. He let the pins and needles fade before cutting his right hand loose, then pulled himself upright with the railing... and nearly fell over again – he kept forgetting about his head wound.

"Damn... Remind me to 'thank' Harrison the next time I see him. Let me try with that hairpin, Mary."

Lestrade turned back to the other two, but just then a burly figure suddenly appeared in the doorway. "*My God!*" Whoever it was took one look at the scene and charged straight at Lestrade before he had time to react, grabbing him by the throat and slamming him back up against the wall. As fresh pain shot through the Yarder's head, he dimly heard questions being barked at him in rapid German: "*Who are you? What are you doing with them?*"

"*Inspektor!*"

"*No, mein Herr,* stop, *please! He's our friend!*"

"*Excuse me?!*" Thank God, Mary's desperate plea had penetrated the unknown attacker's fury, none too soon. The vice-like grip around Lestrade's neck loosened, and he gasped for breath.

"*It's true, mein Herr!*" Roland added his earnest voice to Mary's. "*Look at his wrists.*" The stranger looked down to where Lestrade's hands were locked on his... The next instant, the dazed Yarder was gathered up in the man's arms and carried across the room to sit against the wall next to Mary.

"*Forgive me, mein Herr, I didn't realise.*" The man sounded extremely sheepish, and more than a little bewildered. "*Your friends are hurt, Fräulein – what's happened here?*"

"*It's a long story, mein Herr... We're in great trouble.*" Lestrade knew that tone of voice: he'd last heard Mary using it on Madame Fauvel in Geneva. She'd decided the man could be trusted, and her instincts were excellent.

"*Clearly... Allow me, lad.*" The man took the hairpin from Roland and released both handcuffs in a few seconds. "*My name is Werner Schultz, I'm the foreman for this site.*"

"*Thank you, Herr Schultz.*" Mary made Lestrade lean forward so she could examine the gash on the back of his head, hissing in sympathy. "If you ever do meet that brute Harrison again, Inspector, send him my regards as well. I don't think you need stitches, but I will need to clean it soon."

Roland offered his hand to help Mary rise, while Schultz lent Lestrade his support as he struggled to his feet, swaying. "*Does your friend need a doctor...? Fräulein, what's the matter?*" Lestrade looked up sharply at the concern in the foreman's voice.

Mary was leaning heavily on Roland, her face drawn and pale. "*Maria, sit down.*" The lad helped her sit down on the floor again. "*Breathe, little mother, it's all right. Her husband is a doctor, Herr Schultz; he and his friend are missing. She has come far to find him...*"

"*God in Heaven... I'm so sorry, mein Frau! How can I help you?*"

* * *

"We were lucky that the foreman found us when he did – he'd left his pipe at the theatre on Saturday, but didn't realise it was missing until dusk. When he came back to search the next morning, he found the boards we'd pried off the window, although he didn't think too much about it – until he let himself in the normal way and heard strange voices." Lestrade massaged his neck, wincing at the memory. "The man's as strong as an ox. It's too bad we didn't have his help the night before, the odds would definitely have been in our favour."

"I can well believe it. What assistance did he give you?"

"He took us back to his house, to start with. His wife made us welcome and saw to Roland and me, she wouldn't allow Mary to do a thing. She's a fierce hawk of a woman, gave 'ruling the roost' a whole new meaning. She didn't even let us explain ourselves until we'd finished breakfast..."

* * *

...Roland had barely eaten since yesterday morning – the lad fell to and stuffed himself. Frau Schultz scolded him roundly for his lack of table manners, but kept filling his plate. Mary caught Lestrade's eye with a faint smile and he could guess what she was thinking: their hostess reminded him of Mrs. Hudson, too.

Herr Schultz had been looking strangely at them ever since they'd introduced themselves to him – their real names, Mary had been insistent about that. He suddenly left the room and returned with a small, linen-wrapped bundle, placing it on the table with a reverent expression.

His wife stopped what she was doing abruptly and pressed a hand to her mouth. *"Werner, you told me... You promised!"* She sounded almost in tears. Schultz moved to her side and held her close, murmuring in her ear. Their guests sat in awkward silence, trying not to draw attention to themselves or stare at the mysterious object.

"Get ready for church, dear." Schultz escorted his wife gently out of the kitchen towards the stairwell. *"I'll stay home with our guests.*

73

They need to understand, Klara." She looked unconvinced but didn't argue, climbing the stairs.

"What were they talking about?" Lestrade murmured to Mary, who frowned at him, shaking her head. All right, he could take a hint... although from the look on Schultz' face as he sat back down at the table, the Yarder was about to learn far more than he wanted to, anyhow. The foreman carefully unwrapped the linen and revealed a book.

Mary gasped, fingers trembling as she reached out her hand to trace the bold words on the cover: '*A Study in Scarlet, by Dr. John H. Watson, M.D.*'

* * *

Chapter 8

Walking the Edge

"The book had belonged to the Schultz' young son, Tobias. They'd given it to him for his twelfth birthday eighteen months ago, his father read him a chapter every night. Sadly, they never got to finish it – a few days after, there was an accident on the lake ice..."

Lestrade sighed and shook his head. "Frau Schultz came back downstairs several minutes later, dressed to go to Mass. Roland tried to hide the book under the table, but she smiled bravely and told him not to bother, I think... then asked him if he'd like to have it for his own. Whatever her reasons were for giving the book away, Roland was completely overwhelmed. I don't think he'd ever been given a gift like that before. Mary then told our hosts the whole story, although Schultz didn't need much telling – he'd already put two and two together from our names, and what Roland said to him in the theatre. You're a lot more famous than you might think, Mr. Holmes."

"So it would seem..." It was incredibly ironic that the thing Holmes had deplored most about his friend had been a vital factor in his rescue. If Watson had known, he'd never have allowed the detective to hear the end of it... If only...

"Herr Schultz ordered all three of us off to bed, promising to wake us in the evening. His wife wasn't merely going to church. She was inviting some friends over for supper who Schultz knew could be trusted not to turn us in, to Moriarty's men or the police – although how much difference there was between them now was anyone's guess."

"A war council, of sorts?"

"That's a very good term for it, especially considering what happened that night..."

* * *

...With the doors bolted and the shutters closed, the three companions came downstairs and were introduced to their new allies. The people assembled here tonight were an odd collection. Three workers from the building site: Heinrich Luft, a joiner, and Peter Kaufmann, a bricklayer, with his grown son Wilhelm. Also present were Lukas Dresner, a sharp-looking young clerk from the council chambers; Fräulein Schmidt, a middle-aged spinster, who was cursed with a permanent haughty expression; and Monsieur and Madame Girod, whom Lestrade didn't need telling were the local baker and his wife – he and Mary had bought bread from the elderly couple before locating the theatre.

Schultz brought everyone up to the mark during supper. Once the meal was over, Monsieur and Madame Girod opened the bags they'd brought and produced a fiddle and concertina. The music was a distraction, and would hopefully make what they had in mind much easier. Lestrade was certain that they were still being watched. Their enemies weren't about to make the mistake of simply believing they'd actually retreat, despite the grim warning. Tonight could very well be their last chance to even the odds, and get some much-needed answers.

There, the signal they'd been waiting for: the long, piercing yowls of a pair of stray cats. Two spies, then, one watching each entrance. It was time...

"We had divided our forces into four. The outside signal was from the first group, a handful of street urchins that Frau Schultz had half-adopted after Tobias died. I never would have expected to have a Swiss version of the Irregulars helping us, but they played their part with no trouble, and got the hell out afterwards like they'd been ordered. Willing or not, we weren't going to risk those youngsters in the next stage, there were too many things that could go wrong. Now that we knew both doors were being watched..."

76

... the next two groups were ready to move. Lestrade, Fräulein Schmidt, Lukas and Heinrich were set to go out the front; Herr Schultz, Mary, Peter and Wilhelm were waiting by the back door. Two men, a youth and a woman in each party... Hopefully that was a good enough decoy, the next part of the plan depended on it. The Girod couple struck up the music in the kitchen, with Frau Schultz and Roland remaining behind as well. Five minutes later, both parties slipped out their chosen doors and into the night, heading in opposite directions: the front party to the lake shore, the back party to the forest. The snare was set, but would either watcher take the bait? This was an old trick, but there was a reason tricks got old – sometimes they worked.

At least they didn't have to worry too much about being quiet, not at the moment. The loud music should have helped to muffle their synchronised exits, preventing the two watchers from hearing what was happening on the other side of the house. Now they just needed to get far enough away to spring their individual halves of the trap, and hope for the best elsewhere. They were getting very close to the lake now, one more corner...

Lestrade stepped away into the shadows and the other three bunched up a little tighter, continuing down to the dock where several small craft were moored for the night, a plausible escape route. Half a minute later, stealthy footsteps approached the Yarder's hiding place and moved on past without slowing. Lestrade smiled grimly at the familiar silhouette, he would be settling scores with Harrison much sooner than he'd thought.

The sound of the hammer cocking on the revolver Schultz had loaned to Lestrade stopped the thug in his tracks. Harrison raised his hands carefully, putting them behind his head without needing to be told. "Evening, Inspector, I was wondering where you'd wandered off to! Go ahead, shoot! Let's see how many people you can get out of bed."

"Don't tempt me, Harrison, I'm in the perfect mood to humour you just now!" Lestrade growled, giving the low signal whistle to bring the other three decoys back from the dock.

"Oh, dearie me – and here I was, thinking you wanted me alive! Shows how much I know, doesn't it?" Harrison slowly turned, grinning. Something wasn't right, Lestrade's quarry was far too relaxed for someone with a gun pointed at him.

"Funny you should mention that." Lestrade had never been a particularly violent man, but Harrison's satisfied smirk made the Yarder itch to remove it – with Frau Schultz' bluntest kitchen knife.

"No, what's *really* funny, Inspector, is your thinking that any one of us is going to tell you where to find your snivelling little friend – not when it's so much more fun watching you dance..."

A chill swept through Lestrade – once again, 'friend'... Thank God Mary wasn't here. By now, the other three had returned, looking greatly relieved at the successful capture. Lukas and Heinrich kicked Harrison's legs out from under him and knelt on his back, tying his hands and relieving him of any weapons before hauling him up again. One down, one to go. Time to return and find out what results the other two groups had gotten. "You want to talk about 'dancing', Harrison? Happy to oblige."

"Aw, what are you going to do, flatfoot? Hand me over to the police and let them hang me? After you!"

Fräulein Schmidt handed Lestrade her head scarf and he stuffed it into the man's mouth, silencing him, although hopefully not for long. "No, Harrison – after you. Move..."

There was no sign of the other decoy party as they headed back to the house. Harrison laughed silently to himself all the way, grating fiercely on Lestrade's nerves. Now that they'd actually snared their prey, it did seem just a little too easy... What had they missed? Lestrade got his answer a second later as Harrison stiffened with a muffled scream, then staggered sideways. The thug's sudden movement caused the silent sniper to miss with the second shot, gouging a hole in the wall beside Lestrade as he flung himself at Harrison. Why couldn't he hear any gunshots? Hauling desperately, the Yarder dragged Harrison towards the nearest shelter behind a rain barrel as a third bullet clipped the cobbles at his feet.

Lestrade couldn't see what had happened to his companions. He prayed they'd found their own cover – he had bigger problems at the moment. Blood was pouring from the hole in Harrison's upper torso. The man had only minutes left to live at most, and that was being generous. Lestrade snatched the scarf from his prisoner's mouth and clamped it down on the wound. Harrison was sinking fast, but the Yarder would be damned if he let him go without a fight.

"Come on, Harrison, stay with me, curse you! You don't get to die, you smug bastard – that's too bloody easy!" Harrison gave a glistening, scarlet smile, matching the mist that clouded Lestrade's sight as he snarled into the man's face. "Your friend shot you because he thought you'd talk, so *do it! Where's Holmes?!*"

"Blimey, flatfoot... Brenner... pegged you good... didn't he?" The man used the last of his strength to raise his head and whisper, "Bless you, Inspector..." The light faded from Harrison's eyes and his head fell back.

"*No!* God damn it, Harrison...!" Lestrade grabbed the man's shoulders and shook him like a terrier with a rat, heedless of the fact that he was clutching a corpse, there were no answers left here. Firm but kind hands pried Lestrade's free, and lifted him to his feet. It was Fräulein Schmidt and Lukas, the young man looking extremely dishevelled. "What's happened, where's Heinrich?"

Lukas beamed at him, revealing that one of his front teeth was missing. *"Come and see, Inspektor. It's a beautiful sight."*

Lestrade left the thug's body leaning against the barrel for the moment and followed the pair to where Heinrich was waiting for them in a dead-end alley, looking almost as battered as Lukas... but with a bound and unconscious Klaus on the ground, a large gash on the thug's forehead trickling blood into his eyes. *"A present for you, Inspektor,"* the joiner said with a weary smile, clapping Lestrade on the back. *"Although I wouldn't open it here."*

Lestrade had no idea how the three of them had done it – he didn't even want to know, especially not Fräulein Schmidt. The gleam in the woman's eye reminded him too much of Mary's face at Meiringen two nights ago. "Right," he nodded, feeling a grin spread across his face that had nothing to do with humour. "Good work, gentlemen, Fräulein. Let's cart this filth off the streets." Finding the second party would have to wait, but he suspected they wouldn't be too far away.

They made it back to the house without difficulty, Roland flinging the door open before anyone could knock. The others swarmed out and helped them carry the two bodies inside and down to the cellar under the scullery. Klaus was starting to wake up, but Lestrade was in no hurry to speak with him yet. It'd do the man good to sweat next to his dead colleague for a while, all the more time to imagine what he had coming...

A triple knock sounded on the back door, then two, then one – the other group had returned. Lestrade dragged the heavy bolt back and opened the door, just managing to catch Mary as she flung herself at him. "Geoffrey, you're back, thank God! Where are you hurt? You're covered in blood!"

The others piled in through the door behind her, exclaiming at the state of Lestrade and bearing them both off to the kitchen. The Yarder waved Herr Schultz towards Heinrich and Lukas, who were getting fussed over by the three other women.

"It's all right, Mary, I'm fine. None of it's mine, I promise. How did things turn out at your end?"

"Our decoy didn't work, Geoffrey, we never saw anyone! *Roland, are you all right?*"

"*It's all right, Maria! The Inspektor caught both spies...!*"

"All right, Roland, calm down! Let the lady sit and catch her breath." Lestrade wasn't keen for Mary to hear about what had happened with his group, not until he'd had a chance to come to terms with it himself. The part that upset him the most was his own question to Harrison: 'Where's *Holmes*?' He could try telling himself that he was just keeping things simple all he wanted... but deep down, he knew. Only one of the pair remained now, and it wasn't the Doctor, although he'd rather have taken Harrison's fatal bullet himself than break the news to Mary one moment before he needed to. Wait a second...

"Mary, ask Heinrich: what did he do with Klaus' gun?"Mary looked at Lestrade strangely, but translated all the same. Heinrich passed over a German Reichsrevolver, which didn't answer the Yarder's question at all. This gun would definitely make a noise when fired – so what kind of weapon had Klaus been using to shoot Harrison, and where was it now?

Fortunately, all the information Lestrade needed was within reach. He nodded to Schultz. "Mein Herr, I could use your help downstairs." Both of them rose. "Mary, I want you to stay up here with Roland; Fräulein Schmidt and Heinrich can fill you in on what happened out there." Her lips tightened, making his heart sink. He knew what she wanted, all too well, but this was one battle she wouldn't be winning.

81

Whatever else they'd been through together, Lestrade had to walk this road alone."No, Mary, I'm sorry... You're not coming with me!"

"But Geoffrey, you need me..." Her pleading voice stabbed at him like a knife, strengthening his resolve further, and he cut across her protest sharply.

"*No*, Mary! I don't care how good your German is, you aren't setting one foot on those steps! This isn't going to be like it was with Roland, and Klaus can speak English well enough. This is an order, not an argument. Don't force me to tie you up as well – because you know I will!" Mary stared at Lestrade, speechless, eyes filling with tears. The sight filled the Yarder with a mixture of pain and relief. She hadn't cried since their first night on the run, even while at the Meiringen hotel; he'd been seriously worried about that.

Lestrade crouched in front of Mary and took her hands, looking up into her anguished face... then drew a deep breath, hating himself for what he had to say next – he was going to pay for it later. "Mary... How do you think John would feel if he knew what you were prepared to do, even for his sake? And what would he say to me if I simply stood back and watched you become the kind of person who could do this?"

"Then how can *you*...?" Mary's voice trembled, Lestrade couldn't tell with what emotion. Her eyes would not meet his, she did not want to admit that he was right. He didn't despise or blame her, not in the least. She'd come so far... All she could see now was the journey's end, heedless of the path she took to get there, or its cost. For her sake, until she learned the truth, Lestrade had to count the cost for them both.

"I'm a copper, Mary – walking the edge is what I do. This badge of mine already has its fair share of tarnish, I think it can stand a little more. Ask the Girods to start playing again, and Mary... don't wait up for us. We could be down there for some time." Before she could protest further, Lestrade stood and strode into the scullery with Schultz and Peter following...

"And that, Mr. Holmes, is all I'm ever going to say on that subject." The Inspector's expression was grim. Holmes opened his mouth, but Lestrade raised a hand abruptly, cutting him off before he could say a word. "Save your breath, sir. I don't regret anything I did down in that cellar, but I'll be damned if I'll describe it, to you or anyone. And truth be told, I don't like the look in your eyes right now, any more than I did Mary's at the time. All you need to know is what happened when we came back..."

Frau Schultz brought clean clothes and stood over the three men with a rolling pin until they were in a fit state to leave the scullery. To Lestrade's vague relief, there was no sign of Mary or Roland. Hopefully they were both asleep, it was four in the morning. His hands felt raw from all the scrubbing, but the rest of him was completely numb. In a daze, he drifted through the kitchen, ignoring his new friends' sympathetic looks as they came together and talked in low, anxious tones.

The Yarder's legs carried him unbidden down the passage and out the back door to stand in the middle of the small courtyard, firewood stacked along the wall under the eaves in neat piles. The night was completely still, peaceful in the last few hours before dawn – if only that peace wasn't a total lie... Lestrade's eyes stung, but he couldn't let himself cry, not now, that was too much like giving up... *Damn* it, who was he trying to fool here? A wave of exhaustion and despair crashed over him, just like on the bridge, only much worse this time, because at least then... He stumbled over to the stacks of firewood and sank down on one of them, burying his face in his hands, breath ragged, throat tight, eyes burning...

"Inspektor? Are you all right?" Oh God, no – the last thing Roland needed was to see him like this, and the last thing Lestrade wanted right now was company.

The Yarder made a valiant effort to pull himself together, rubbing his eyes to try and remind them who was in charge. "Roland... this isn't a good time, lad. Go on back inside, please."

"Forgive me, Inspektor." Roland's voice was hesitant, full of concern. *"You seem troubled, and I know that Maria..."*

That grabbed Lestrade's attention. "Mary? What about her? Is she all right?"

"Yes, yes, the little mother's fine – she's sleeping." Roland nodded upwards to the dark windows of the second floor, sitting down next to Lestrade. *"But you, Inspektor? You're exhausted. Your eyes..."* Shaking his head, the boy put his fingers under his own eyes and pulled the skin downwards.

"All right, very funny, I get the point." And exactly how was Lestrade meant to sleep at a time like this? The lad's concern was touching, but hardly helpful at the moment.

"Really? We need you, Inspektor – especially your two friends!" The lad was plainly upset, although how Lestrade was supposed to understand why... *"If you don't take care of yourself..."*

"Roland, please – I don't know what you're saying! Just... leave me alone, will you?" The instant the words were out of the Yarder's mouth, he wished he could take them back – the lad had understood his irritated tone perfectly, flinching as if stung. Lord's sakes, Lestrade couldn't do anything right tonight, could he? He sighed deeply and put a hand on the boy's hunched shoulder. "Roland... I'm sorry."

Roland turned his head to look at him, eyes wide in what seemed to be amazement, then beamed. *"That's all right, Inspektor! It's nothing."*

His reaction took Lestrade aback. Was this the first apology the lad had ever heard from anyone? Given what little Lestrade knew of Roland's past, especially his father and brother, perhaps it was. All too soon, however, the smile faded as Roland kept looking at the Yarder's face. *"Inspektor, what is it? Talk to me, please."*

The young man looked genuinely confused, he didn't know. How could Lestrade explain this without Mary? On second thought, no... It was better that she was still asleep. "The others... didn't... tell... you?" He did his best to make the meaning clear with gestures. Roland shook his head, waiting for more. "Roland, Klaus is... dead. I... killed him."

Lestrade wasn't expecting the lad's calm reaction to the news: Roland looked thoughtful, and more than a little pleased. *"So? What did he say?"* The boy used Lestrade's own gesture to sign talking.

"Nothing, Roland! Klaus... didn't... say... *one word!*" Lestrade's chest tightened again, along with his fists. He abandoned his efforts at signing, surging to his feet and pacing the courtyard like a caged bear, words pouring out of him in a torrent. "Harrison was right, curse him! We're all the way back to square bloody one. Every time, just when I think we're getting somewhere, those murdering villains turn out to be two steps ahead! What am I supposed to do, Roland? I'm not Mr. Holmes, I can't pull miracles out of thin air! God... this is madness! What was Mycroft thinking, sending me? All I've done is make a total mess of things since we started, I'm going to get us all killed – just like the Doctor..." He faltered and leaned against the nearest wall, head bowed.

"The Doctor? What about him?" Roland's voice was full of apprehension. No doubt Mary had told him what Erik said in the theatre, right before he left. *"Inspektor... what do you know about Dr. Watson?"*

Lestrade couldn't bear to say it out loud, the words escaped his throat in a whisper. "He's dead, Roland, he must be... The Doctor...

dead... Understand?" Roland paled, hand flying to his mouth. "Only Mr. Holmes is still alive, *maybe*, Heaven only knows for how much longer, and we can't find him! He could be a hundred miles away, or right under our noses, for all I know... And what the hell am I going to tell Mary? I can't keep this from her, she's going to find out about her husband sooner or later, and it's going to break her heart! I don't even know where his body is... and I promised her...!"

Lestrade's misery rose in his throat, choking him, and the sobs he'd held back for so long began to wrench free. He sank to his knees, letting them take over. Roland hunkered down beside him and wrapped both arms around Lestrade's shaking shoulders, riding out the storm with him.

Gradually, the Yarder became aware that Roland was murmuring something, although he couldn't make it out in his current state. It did sound vaguely soothing, though, and strangely familiar the more Lestrade listened, as his tears began to subside. *"...Pray for us sinners, now, and at the hour of our death. Amen. Hail, Maria, full of grace..."* Of course, Roland's family was Catholic, it made sense that he would fall back on old habits at a time like this. Lestrade had never been too sure about that sort of thing – his own upbringing had been rather threadbare of such trappings, apart from what his grandmother had tried to drill into him. Besides, a policeman's work didn't leave much room for belief in anything apart from himself, his colleagues and, if he was fortunate, the law. All the same, he appreciated the gesture; at this stage, he was desperate enough to try anything.

Lestrade waited for Roland to finish his latest 'Hail Mary', before pulling out his handkerchief and wiping his face, feeling only slightly less wretched. "Bless you, lad." He patted the boy wearily on the shoulder and glanced at the sky, it was close to dawn. "Shall we go back in? I think we could both do with some breakfast, it's going to be a long day." He climbed stiffly to his feet, knees protesting, and offered Roland a hand up. "Roland?"

86

There was a far-off look in Roland's eyes, his brow furrowed with intense concentration. "Bless you..." What was the matter with the lad – the phrase wasn't that unusual, was it? What would it be in German? 'Gesundheit', or something like that; Frau Schultz had said the same to her husband when he sneezed while shaking pepper on his soup. No sooner did Lestrade say the word out loud, however, than Roland leapt to his feet, eyes shining. "Bless you... Gesundheit!" The boy smacked himself on the forehead in disgust. *"I'm an idiot! Aaspitz... Now I remember!"*

"Roland, what is it? What do you know?" The boy's reaction was starting to stir Lestrade's own memory; Harrison's very last words before he'd died in the street were: 'Bless you, Inspector.' Had the man been taunting him... or trying to give him a clue? Either way, the Yarder wasn't about to look a gift horse in the mouth – although this horse's mouth was going full speed, he couldn't make out a word. "Roland, slow down! Go and wake Mary, all right? We'll need her for this."

Roland nodded vigorously, dashing back inside, and Lestrade wasted no time in following him. They found Mary already awake, helping Frau Schultz in the kitchen. She looked better than she had last night, although that wasn't saying much. Her face was pale and worn, with dark circles under her eyes. She also seemed slightly more composed, which only lasted until the two of them entered the room. One look at Roland's face, and her own face began to glow with a faint hope that hadn't been there a moment ago.

"Roland...? Geoffrey, has something happened? Frau Schultz said..."

"I know, Mary – it's true, Klaus didn't talk... but we may have a new lead, anyway. Go on, Roland."

Roland broke into rapid German, punctuated once more by the word 'Aaspitz', which caused Frau Schultz to run to a small chest in the sitting room and bring out a roll of parchment, a map of the lake region. She left the room for a minute and returned with her husband, who scrubbed the sleep from his eyes furiously as he listened in growing excitement to the boy's frantic spiel. Schultz stabbed his finger down on the map to the east of Lake Zurich, at the southern end of a much smaller lake called Greifen. There... at the southernmost edge, a name: Aaspitz.

"I've heard that name before! I didn't understand..."

"For God's sake, Mary, what's Roland saying?" Lestrade demanded.

"He says he's heard the name 'Aaspitz' before, but he didn't understand at the time, he was only half-conscious... oh, Geoffrey, they'd been beating him! Harrison and Klaus were guarding him afterwards... Erik wasn't there... they were speaking in English... *Roland, please, speak slowly!* He heard Klaus say 'Aaspitz'... and Harrison laughed and said 'Bless you!' Roland thought it was a real sneeze, he didn't realise they were talking about a place!" Mary clasped her hands before her tightly, eyes wide. "Geoffrey, do you think...?"

"I don't know, Mary, but we're damn well going to find out! Roland, you're a wonder!" Lestrade seized the boy's hand in both of his and wrung it. Roland flushed scarlet and stared down at the floor, muttering under his breath. The Yarder sighed. "Mary, tell the young idiot this isn't his fault – Harrison said exactly the same thing to me, and I was wide awake!" He turned to their hosts, who also had been conferring together urgently. "Herr Schultz, I hope one of your friends is from that area – we're going to need someone who knows Lake Greifen like the back of their hand..."

Chapter 9

Left to Live

"Aaspitz isn't far from Zurich – roughly ten miles, as the crow flies. The chalet we found you in, if a shack like that even deserves the name, wasn't marked on the map. Fortunately, our bricklayer friend, Peter, had grown up in the lakeside village of Greifensee, and knew the area very well. We had no idea what kind of resistance we'd meet with, so we just had to prepare for the worst, and hope for the best..."

...Peter and Wilhelm volunteered to scout ahead and insisted that Lestrade went with them, the Yarder's eyes and ears supposedly useful in detecting any surprises that might be in store. Lestrade hoped like hell that they were right – he'd never be a country man, despite the adventures of the last fortnight. Give him a foggy London street any day of the year. Privately, he vowed never to set foot outside his beloved city again without a damn good reason, if... *when* they got back.

"Inspektor?" Lestrade shook himself from his reverie to see Wilhelm nodding eastwards at the rapidly lightening sky. *"We need to leave, the sun will rise in an hour."* The young man was right, they needed all the advantage they could get, including what little was left of the night. Time was running out, they didn't dare wait one more day – but if they sacrificed stealth for speed, they might lose this opportunity altogether... Heaven help them. Please, God, let Aaspitz be the right place, let them find Mr. Holmes, alive, it didn't matter in what condition, just as long as they weren't too late...

Lestrade turned to Mary, who was helping to load the handcart in the courtyard. Ever since he'd started coming to terms with the Doctor's almost certain fate, he'd been searching for the right words to broach the subject, without the least success. Now was probably the worst possible time, but he couldn't leave without saying something. Mary and their other companions would be right behind the advance party, although taking a more direct route on the main road through the forest. This was Lestrade's last chance to prepare her for what they might find – or not...

Mary looked up at him, eyes searching his, and shook her head. "It's all right, Inspector. You don't have to say it." Lestrade really wished she couldn't read him that well. She put her hand on his arm, smiling sadly. "Geoffrey, I've known since we left England that we... that we could be too late to save John or Mr. Holmes... but it still hasn't kept me from hoping, even now. Does that seem incredibly foolish?"

He was appalled at her needing to ask such a question. "No, Mary. You... you must be the least foolish person I've ever known, that hope is what's kept us all going! Without you, I never would have gotten this far, I'd probably be rotting in a Swiss prison; and Roland... The boy's becoming a man, because of your faith in him... and his love for you." Lestrade smiled at Mary's blush. "Yes, I have seen the way he looks at you. Don't worry, Roland's no fool, either – he knows your heart belongs to John."

Lestrade took her hand in his. "That promise I made you still stands. Whoever or whatever's waiting for us over there, we *will* eventually find out the truth – all of it. That's something I know you can handle, Mary. You're far stronger than you think. I'll see you soon." The Yarder put his arm around Mary's shoulders and hugged her for a moment, before turning away to where his two guides were waiting with the horses. "Let's go, gentlemen."

"The three of us rode south along the shore of Lake Zurich as far as Küsnacht, then turned due east. Thanks to Peter, we made excellent time through the forest, and managed to get down the other side of the ridge before the sun rose. It wasn't trees all the way, unfortunately, and we had to tie the horses close by the road at Letzi for the others to find, covering the last half mile on foot..."

...which was mostly fields, with only a few sparse stands of trees for cover. There was no way the second party was going further than the horses until they were sure of what they were up against. Lestrade shouldered his pack and checked his weapons, Peter and Wilhelm doing the same, then followed father and son out through the thinning treeline. This had to be the worst possible terrain for reconnaissance, let alone a rescue mission; he'd never felt so vulnerable. He had to hand it to Moriarty, the mysterious Colonel, or whoever was behind the scenes these days: they certainly knew how to choose a hideaway.

"We're coming, Mr. Holmes, don't give up. Just hold on, just a little longer..." It was only when Wilhelm turned and gave Lestrade a fierce scowl that the Yarder realised he'd been saying it out loud. Bloody hell, he was getting seriously distracted – mind on the job, damn it!

By now the sun was up, painting the landscape with long stripes of light and shadow, a blessing and a curse as the three men edged nearer to their goal. Eventually, they reached the last copse before the final stretch of open ground, less than a hundred yards from a small patch of woods. A cabin-sized building could barely be seen lurking amongst the shadows, close to the water.

Peter reached into Wilhelm's pack and pulled out a pair of field glasses, careful to keep them out of the sunlight. After a minute or two of intense scrutiny, he handed them over to Lestrade, voice a low murmur. "*Inspektor, do you see anyone?*"

"Thanks..." Lestrade peered through the glasses, frowning as the hulking structure came into clearer focus. "It could just be too early for anyone to be up and about yet, but... no, they should at least have a sentinel posted. Oh, hell... there's no smoke!" Surely someone would have lit a fire, if the house was occupied by any of Moriarty's men... and if it wasn't... An icy fear started growing in his gut. "We have to get in there, Peter, I've got an awful feeling about this. Another two minutes and we move!"

"Five, Inspektor, five minutes," Peter showed the Yarder five fingers, his expression stern, *"and Wilhelm will stay hidden."* Lestrade didn't need that translated as Wilhelm started to protest, but was silenced the next instant by his father's glare. *"You will obey me, boy! Your mother would use my bones for soup..."* The young man nodded ruefully, grinning. Peter gave Lestrade a painful jab in the ribs with his elbow, which was probably meant to be encouraging. *"Be patient, Inspektor!"* Easy for him to say, if that meant what Lestrade thought it did...

Five minutes later saw the two elder men creeping forward through the long grass and weeds on either side of the open ground, with Lestrade slightly ahead, every sense tingling, mind shouting at him that this was the very worst idea he'd ever had in his life. He wasn't about to argue, but what choice did they have? At this point, stealth was their only ally, albeit a poor one. The closer they got to the house, though, the more it appeared that the place was completely deserted – he prayed he was wrong about that, prayed fervently every second.

They made it to the shelter of the woods without mishap, readying firearms, then Peter led the way through the trees, both crouching low, until they fetched up against the south wall. The bricklayer signed to Lestrade to circle to the left, slipping around to the right as silent as a shadow. He followed the man's example as best he could, stepping quietly, ears straining for any sound that seemed out of place. He and Peter reached the front at the same time, so much for the outside...

The veranda roof was sagging and looked as if it was going to collapse any minute, much like the rest of the building. As they neared the warped front door, all was quiet from inside, but Lestrade's copper sense was screaming. The door wasn't locked; it creaked open onto a single large room, damp and musty, but above the smell of mildew... A horribly familiar mix of scents intruded on Lestrade's nose: the rusty reek of old blood, the acrid stench of vomit, and a lot of other things he'd rather not think about, but which made his stomach tie itself in knots. There were no obvious traces of any of that in this room, in spite of all the rubbish, which left only one real possibility: "Check the floor, there has to be a space below – hurry!"

Peter joined Lestrade in kicking aside the debris, hauling up a large piece of mouldy carpet to reveal a trapdoor, bolted shut. *"Here, help me!"*

The smell was ten times stronger when they heaved the hatch open, making them both gag. "Bloody Christ..." Lestrade choked. "Mr. Holmes? Can you hear me, sir? Mr. Holmes!" There was no sound and it was too dark to make anything out. Lestrade was about to plunge on down the steps, when Peter stopped him.

"You'll need light, Inspektor, and this air could snuff out a candle." The bricklayer struck a match and held it over the hole, which went out before it had burnt halfway. *"We need to break the floor,"* stamping his heel on the creaking floorboards.

"Get Wilhelm in here, I'll make a start!" Lestrade took out the knife he'd reclaimed from Harrison and began levering at the nearest gap between the planks. His stomach was churning – he wished he hadn't eaten breakfast, because he was certain he'd be parting with it shortly. Peter and Wilhelm soon lent their hands and tools to the job, Peter having the wise idea of taking single planks from different places so that the whole floor wouldn't give way. Wilhelm handed Lestrade a wet cloth and indicated he should tie it over his nose and mouth, he and his father doing the same. The masks helped to filter out the worst of the foul air, and the holes in the floor should give them enough light so that they wouldn't break their necks.

Lestrade squared his shoulders and took a deep breath. "Let's get down there..."

"And if it's all the same to you, Mr. Holmes, I'd really rather not go into fine detail for this part." The Inspector shook his head, looking decidedly ill at the memory. "We couldn't get the shackles off your ankles right then, but Peter and Wilhelm managed to pry the ring loose from the wall. Once we'd decided your injuries weren't too serious for you to be moved, we turned our coats into a makeshift stretcher..."

...which was frighteningly easy to lift, the chains seemed heavier than the wraith-like figure wearing them. With infinite care, the three men eased their fragile cargo up through the hatch and outside, Lestrade's heart aching with every rattling breath. Mr. Holmes' skin was burning hot, eyes twitching beneath his swollen lids – Lestrade really didn't want to know what the man was seeing right now, but he could guess.

As they emerged from the house, the detective started to whimper, face creasing. Peter swore and whipped the still-damp cloth off his own face, draping it over the man's eyes, using Lestrade's and Wilhelm's masks to cool his brow and cheeks. Of course, the sunlight, Lestrade was an idiot for not thinking of that. How long had Mr. Holmes been down there in the dark? What had those monsters done to him? Whatever it was, it was nothing compared to what was in store when Lestrade caught up to them – Klaus and Harrison had both gotten off far too lightly.

They set the coat stretcher down softly in the shade at the edge of the trees. *"Wilhelm has signalled the others."* Peter nodded in the direction they'd originally come from, pulling supplies out of his pack. *"They'll be here soon."* He placed his hand on Lestrade's shoulder, shaking him gently. *"Your friend is alive, Inspektor. Don't worry, we'll do everything we can for him."*

With that mysterious reassurance, they set to work. Since they had no idea what kind of internal injuries Mr. Holmes had, all they could do was deal with what was right in front of them, namely trying to cool him down with the water they'd brought – even Lestrade knew better than to use the lake. The detective was already covered in angry, livid wounds, there was no need to make them worse. In the end, the easiest solution was to soak their own shirts in canteen water and wrap them around him. They didn't need to remove Mr. Holmes' shirt – the only clothing he had left was a pair of trousers, little more than filthy rags, to match the rest of him.

As might have been expected, Mr. Holmes didn't take kindly to their clumsy efforts, but he was far too weak and confused to even try and prevent it. Lestrade could only imagine what the poor man thought was happening to him, and did his best to calm him, smoothing the detective's greasy, tangled hair, the only part of him left relatively untouched, although he was missing a few patches. "Shh, it's all right, Holmes, easy now... No-one's going to hurt you, Holmes, never again, you're safe... I've got you, I won't let go, it's all right, Holmes..."

It took Lestrade a few seconds to realise that he was using the Doctor's name for the man, the only one allowed to use it, and that every time he did, Mr. Holmes relaxed a little more. The Yarder kept murmuring soothingly in the detective's ear, trying to recall all the things he'd ever heard the Doctor say to his friend while patching him up after he'd rushed headlong into danger, so many times... things that Watson would never say again. God forgive him for this, but right now the lie was far kinder than the truth...

* * *

"...leave..."

"Mr. Holmes…"

"I said '*leave*', Lestrade, *get out!*" Curse the man, could he not even understand a simple instruction?

"I'm sorry, Mr. Holmes, I didn't know what else to do!" Understatement of the century – Holmes had always known the Inspector was a blind, blundering fool, but the man had completely surpassed himself this time.

"You had no right, Lestrade – none!" The Inspector was fortunate that the detective was unable to move, although if looks could kill, Lestrade would now have been a pile of ashes. "Do you have any idea... How *dared* you?!"

"Because you needed a reason to stay alive!" Lestrade shot back furiously, eyes flashing. "Do you have any idea what it's been like for *me* these last three days, seeing what those bastards had done to you, and having to just sit here, praying that we hadn't been too late, that you still had something left to fight with? I'm not the religious type, Mr. Holmes, but I've never prayed so hard in my entire life, and it wasn't just me, either! I'm sorry, all right? I admit, I crossed the line, but if you let me explain..."

Holmes turned his face away, he did not want to hear another word, but he couldn't shut out the Inspector's treacherous voice, determined to the last...

...all the comments Lestrade and his colleagues had ever made about this essential, life-saving partnership were coming back to haunt the Yarder – but he'd be damned if he let it happen. The death of one would not be the death of the other, not if Lestrade had anything to say about it. Mr. Holmes had survived this long, he never would have if he didn't possess the will to live, in spite of everything he'd been through. Now, it was up to the friends the detective had left to make sure he remembered that, whatever it took...

"Admit it, sir, what really gets up your nose is that we didn't just leave you to die! That's what you wanted, wasn't it? I'm sorry if you feel that what I did was a betrayal, but I'd do it again in a heartbeat, if that's what it took to keep you from giving up! The Doctor wasn't the only one who cared about you, Mr. Holmes, not by a long way..." Lestrade's eyes narrowed. "But I can see that doesn't mean anything to you at the moment. Forgive me, forgive all of us, for having the nerve to actually give a damn!" The Inspector stood up and strode towards the door, his expression thunderous.

"Lestrade..." Perhaps Holmes had been a trifle hasty.

"Save it, Mr. Holmes. Besides, I thought you wanted me to take a bath after I'd finished." The Inspector stalked out of the room and closed the door none too gently after himself. It only occurred to Holmes once Lestrade had gone: he hadn't said when he would be coming back.

Chapter 10

Bitter Truths

To Holmes' acute dismay, Lestrade did not return at all that day. The detective was painfully aware that the Inspector had been pushing himself to breaking point. Hopefully, the man was merely following Holmes' earlier injunction and finally getting some uninterrupted sleep. He wished he could do the same... Although Lestrade had essentially concluded the story of his and Mary's journey, there were many aspects of the account that continued to haunt Holmes, particularly his rescue from the cellar.

Despite the Inspector's view of Holmes' admittedly excessive reaction, the detective was by no means certain himself how he felt about living to fight another day. His moods seemed to alter from one minute to the next, whirling freely as a gyroscope, with as much rhyme or reason. His appetite did not improve – the mere thought of food sickened him to the point where he could barely swallow – nor did his dreams. He only mildly protested that evening when Joubert insisted on sedating him so that he could get at least one night of unbroken rest. Unfortunately, that only made it harder to escape from the next onslaught, his memories no less terrifying with his mind wrapped in fog.

Holmes was profoundly thankful when he struggled awake the next morning to find Lestrade asleep once more in his customary chair, head and arms resting on the bed within reach – which Holmes took advantage of a few moments later when he noticed that the Inspector was also dreaming, by no means pleasantly. Lestrade's face was turned towards the detective, the Inspector's eyes darting beneath his closed lids, brow furrowed, right hand curling around the handle of an imaginary revolver. This was not going to end well.

Without thinking, Holmes weakly reached out and touched the Inspector on the shoulder, arm trembling with the effort. He was rewarded for his exertion a moment later by Lestrade starting awake, eyes wide before they focused on Holmes' concerned face, his own face slowly relaxing into a grateful smile. Holmes returned it briefly, raising an eyebrow as if to say: "Well, how was I supposed to sleep with that going on?" before closing his own eyes again. They seemed to have reached a truce, God only knew for how long. A mere two hours, as it turned out...

The next several days passed at a snail's pace. There was very little for Holmes to do, except rest, eat, and let himself heal – and none of these options were in the least attractive. All this forced inaction was by turns intolerable and overwhelming. There were times when he felt he couldn't stand another minute of lying in bed, his wounds burning and itching beneath the dressings, trying desperately to turn his thoughts elsewhere, anything to keep from spiralling down into madness or, even worse, stagnation; and other times when he barely had the will to keep breathing, let alone speak coherently to Lestrade, drained by the sheer weight of his accumulated misery.

It took Holmes until his third re-dressing to work up the courage to look at his back, with the assistance of a pair of mirrors. The sight put him morbidly in mind of a railway disaster, all those scarlet criss-crossing lines, old and recent... Even with Lestrade holding him, it took half an hour for him to stop shaking afterwards. The detective was slowly growing stronger, able to move a little more easily every day. His injuries still pained him greatly, however, and his movements cost him in more than just discomfort – he was always tired, quite often falling asleep mid-conversation with Lestrade.

It was his colleague who was keeping him sane – Holmes could freely admit that, if only to himself. Coaxing, nagging, almost bullying at times, the Inspector constantly pushed him to talk, to move, even to eat. Although his nightmares were beginning to plague him a shade less, the man was always there when they occurred to shake Holmes awake and calm him down, thanks to the extra cot Joubert had moved into the room for convenience's sake. The awkwardness both of them felt at becoming official bunkmates only lasted until the next time the detective woke in a cold sweat.

Lestrade hadn't said anything more about Mary after the story's end. Holmes knew the Inspector was deliberately not volunteering information, but he couldn't bring himself to ask after her, either... not yet. They would come face to face soon enough at any rate, he hoped – the suspense was becoming intolerable. The afternoon of Holmes' tenth day in hospital, he finally got his wish. Waking slowly from a troubled sleep, he thought he was still dreaming at first when he heard her, talking quietly to someone else.

The second voice was vaguely familiar: young, male, speaking in German: "...back to Meiringen when the theatre's finished; Herr Steiler will need my help over the winter. Besides you and the Inspektor, he... he's the closest I have to family, now."

"I'm so sorry, Roland – I know how much you wanted to believe the best of Erik. Your brother hurt you terribly..."

"I was a fool, Maria! I should have seen him for what he really was, like Papa did, instead of blindly following him into the dark. It was me who lured the Doctor away from Herr Holmes in the first place. If I'd never given him that message..."

"Then Moriarty would have found some other way. You meant no harm, Roland, you couldn't have known what was going to happen. And with all that you've done since then... Geoffrey and I are both very proud to call you a friend. You've been so brave."

"Not nearly as brave as you, little mother... I should leave, I don't think Herr Holmes will want to see me when he wakes. I'll come back when I can – Herr Schultz has everyone working double shifts at the moment, the building inspector's coming in two days."

100

"It was kind of you to visit, Roland; I'm so glad you've found a place here. Give my love to Klara and Werner, won't you?"

"Of course. Goodbye, Maria."

"Goodbye, Roland – be careful."

Footsteps across the floor, quick and light, then the door closed and Holmes and Mary were left alone together. A rustle of pages told Holmes that she had found a better way to pass the time than simply staring at him. As far as he could tell, Mary believed him still asleep, but getting this over with was strangely preferable to continuing the charade. He sighed, turned his head and opened his eyes to see Mary sitting in Lestrade's customary place, eyes lifted from the book on her knee to his face, smiling anxiously. "Mr. Holmes? How are you feeling?" The woman's own face was drawn and weary, etched with sorrow, eyes red-rimmed – the sight twisted Holmes' insides.

"Mary... I mean, Mrs. Watson... My apologies, I... did not hear you enter. Have you been sitting here long?"

"An hour or so. This is a very comfortable chair, I can understand why the Inspector has been sleeping in it."

"I confess I had... expected to see Lestrade." Except... oh, yes, he'd thrown the Inspector out of the room this morning for shaving him during his last sedated sleep, without his permission. The detective was still seething over that, despite Lestrade's abject apology. The man should have known how Holmes would feel about having a blade anywhere near his face, unconscious or not. To make matters worse, the doctor's furious expression when he came to investigate was agonisingly familiar – although, for the first time after that, Holmes had been able to call him 'Doctor', thanks largely to Joubert lapsing into his native language, threatening to sedate Lestrade and shave his entire head if he ever dared to do anything so stupidly presumptuous to one of *his* patients again...

"Dr. Joubert ordered him to take a walk in the grounds. Even the Inspector cannot do without fresh air and exercise indefinitely, and I..." Mary set the book aside and looked down at her hands, blushing. "I would much prefer not to remain idle, as I have been. Is there anything that I might do for you?"

"You are most kind, madam..." Which had to be the greatest understatement of all time. "But rather, I believe... there is something that I... might do for you."

Mary raised her head at that, tensing. "The Inspector said... that you had more to tell me... about John." She was trying hard not to appear overly affected, but her eyes gave her away, filled with equal measures of apprehension and longing.

"Yes... I... " Merciful God, Holmes was already starting to shake. How were either of them going to get through this without losing all composure?

Suddenly, Mary leant forward and laid her hand on his arm. "If I may speak plainly, Mr. Holmes? I know the Inspector thinks that this will, to use his words, 'be good for both of us' – but you need not tell me, if it will cause you more pain. You have borne enough already. I know now where John... where his body lies, at least – it will suffice. The rest may remain unsaid, sir, if you wish."

Yet again, the woman's courage put Holmes to shame. The lie was a kindness he had not expected, but it was also one he couldn't accept. He drew a shuddering breath – it was time. "Madam, please... permit me to do what little I can. Your husband died bravely, through no fault of his own... whilst trying to protect me. If hearing what happened... might help you to understand, or find some measure of peace... I owe it to you both to make the attempt. Will you... allow me?"

Mary hesitated for a long moment, eyes searching his face, then nodded. "Very well... If it will help you to help me, Mr. Holmes, then... please do so. I would be... truly grateful."

As dispassionately as Holmes could manage, he forced himself to tell Mary the relevant details, nothing more, every last damning fact of Watson's death that was branded onto his memory. Of all the things the detective loathed about his chosen profession, this was the worst, and the knowledge that it was *Watson's* widow to whom he must recount his catastrophic failure made the task infinitely more difficult. Unable to even look up at her, sitting so still and quiet at his bedside, he stared at his bandaged hands. He could feel Mary's fixed gaze on him all the while, it was almost unbearable.

"The fault is entirely mine, madam... I failed him... and you. If... if I had not given myself away, if I had remained hidden... then your husband would still be alive. He would be at home with you this very moment, convincing the world that Moriarty and I were both dead... and the villain that... took his life would instead be hunting me."

Finally, he gathered enough courage to look the woman in the face, only to find it ghostly pale, eyes wide with growing disbelief. "But... Mr. Holmes, no, you cannot mean... you would have allowed John to... You meant to let John believe that you had died, that he was too late? Mr. Holmes, *why*?" Mary's voice was pleading, begging him to give her reasons that she could comprehend. "Why would you make my husband, your friend, suffer so?"

The question caught Holmes completely by surprise, he had never expected her to ask him this! "Because at least then he would have been safe! None of Moriarty's gang would have thought him a threat, they would have let him alone. I meant to return and tell him the truth once all of them were locked away. It would have been better for everyone if he had believed me dead until then..." He shook his head in confusion, why was Mary so distraught about what had never happened? Did she not care more about her husband's actual fate?

"And how would that have been better for John, Mr. Holmes? To make his way back to England alone, grieving over the death of his dearest friend... only to find that he had been lied to, that you did not trust him to keep your secrets?"

"It was the only way I could think of to save him, I could not allow..."

Mary cut Holmes off, eyes flashing indignantly. "It was a most shameful deception, sir! How dared you presume to decide for John what dangers he could not face? I am... I was his wife, Mr. Holmes, and I know that he would have counted it a privilege to lay down his life for those he loved."

He stared at her, mouth agape. "My 'daring to presume' might have kept him alive, madam, brought him back home to you! Why would you not wish for that?" Now Holmes was the one pleading, all of his honourable intentions lost in the storm of Mary's wrath.

"It would have torn him apart, Mr. Holmes! My John... his heart was large enough to contain half the world. His memories of Afghanistan did not fade after he married me, sir. I lost count of the nights he awoke in my arms, screaming, believing himself drenched in the blood of his comrades-at-arms... friends he was powerless to save. Can you not understand the weight of the shame and sorrow you were prepared to inflict on him so thoughtlessly? No... Of course not, how... how naïve of me!" Holmes winced at the scorn in the woman's voice, if she only knew how well he understood... "However much I miss John, Mr. Holmes, I will thank God every day that he did not live to see this – to realise such a betrayal by one he trusted as a brother. Better a bullet to his heart than a knife to his back!"

The detective was no stranger to the lash, but the angry, bitter truth of Mary's words flayed him to the bone. He had nothing left to say, no defence, no apology that she would ever accept from him, but still he made one last attempt as she rose abruptly and turned to exit the room. He simply could not watch her leave in so much pain, pain of his own damned making.

"Mary..."

She blanched, and he fell silent. Mary's next words were cold as ice, as the blue depths of her eyes, glistening with tears that she would not shed before him. "My name, sir, is Mrs. John Watson. Save your feeble excuses for the Inspector, I imagine he is well accustomed to them. Good day to you."

Holmes did not know how long he sat desolate after Mary... Mrs. Watson swept out of the room, her last stinging rejoinder echoing in his mind. All too soon, however, he was brought rudely back to the present by the very last person he wanted to see at the moment. "Hmm, that went well, didn't it?" Lestrade leaned on the doorframe, arms folded, shaking his head. "You certainly have a way with women, sir; can you tell me what I'm doing wrong?"

"Be quiet, Lestrade, you are not amusing." The words emerged in a petulant growl. "Go away..."

"Sorry, Mr. Holmes, I can't do that. Doctor's orders. He asked me to have a word with you... several, in fact." The Inspector's voice was sickeningly cheerful – why wouldn't the man leave Holmes alone?

"So help me, Lestrade, if I could get out of this bed..." And who invited the annoying clod to sit down on it?

"Well, that's the problem, isn't it, sir? Dr. Joubert says you're still not eating enough. You're never going to get back on your feet if you don't make more of an effort. He'd much rather not have to use the feeding tube on you again, now that you're conscious... although on second thought, given your current state of mind, it's probably better that you can't go anywhere." Lestrade's attention was riveted on Holmes, and he suddenly had difficulty meeting the Inspector's penetrating gaze.

"And what is that supposed to mean?"

"Come on, Mr. Holmes, remember who you're talking to! I've seen that look in your eye many times, usually right before you go and do something incredibly stupid."

Lestrade's stare nailed Holmes to the bed, but he would rather have eaten his own mattress than acknowledge that his colleague could read him so well. "Really? Do tell, Inspector! What brilliant conclusion have you arrived at this time?"

Lestrade shrugged off the sarcastic barb with the ease of long practice. "Well, I'm no owl, but it wasn't hard to get the general idea of the pleasant little chat you two were having just now; especially that remark about the difference between a quick death and a slow one."

"Do not play games, Lestrade. Admit it, you were eavesdropping on the entire interview!" And Holmes had not even noticed the man at the time... What on earth was the matter with him?

"Guilty as charged. You think I got to where I am at the Yard without listening to things I shouldn't?" To add insult to injury, the Inspector sounded completely unrepentant. "I have to admit, that was the most impressive tongue-lashing I've ever heard, and I started out on the beat down at the fish market. The point I'm trying to make is that one angry tirade from your best friend's widow is no reason to top yourself."

Holmes flinched from the blunt delivery. "What would you know about it?"

"Clearly, more than the great Sherlock Holmes does! I'm not surprised she stormed out on you – that really was a pathetic excuse for an apology. You'll have to do a damn sight better than that if you want her to forgive you, and I'd say it's going to be one of the hardest things you'll ever do. You should probably consider how to go about it, starting with getting yourself out of bed." The Inspector's pragmatic tone softened. "For the record, Mr. Holmes, I don't blame you for what happened to the Doctor."

"You should..."

"Do you want me to?"

"No..." Strange to say, Lestrade's opinion mattered a great deal more to Holmes than he cared to admit – when had that happened? "But why not?"

"Because you didn't shoot him. That's reason enough."

"For you, perhaps." What Holmes wouldn't give for it to be that simple.

"And it should be for you too, although I know damn well it isn't! Knocking that stone off the ledge was an *accident*, Mr. Holmes, it wasn't your fault; and you didn't kill the Doctor, Moran did. Let me know when you finally decide to stop torturing yourself... Mr. Holmes...?" Lestrade's exasperated voice was fading swiftly... *glaring sunlight, thundering water, blood staining Holmes' clothes, his hands, Watson's lifeless eyes staring straight through him...* "Mr. Holmes, wake up!" ...the impact of Lestrade's hand against Holmes' face – thank God, he'd never been so glad to be struck in all his life. "Bloody hell, sir, please don't scare me like that; you looked like you'd seen a ruddy ghost!"

Lestrade grasped Holmes' shoulders carefully but firmly, anchoring him in the present once more. "You were back there again, weren't you? Has that happened before while you were awake?"

"No..." Holmes still couldn't look the man in the eye, but now the shame had a different cast.

"You're a terrible liar – you know that, Mr. Holmes?" Lestrade reached into his jacket with a furtive glance back at the open door, pulling out a small flask. "Here... I shouldn't do this, but you look like you need it." The liquor burned its way down Holmes' throat, dispelling the lingering chill in his bones. "Not too much, now. The doctor will kill me if you get soused."

"Lestrade..." Somewhere in the last few minutes, Lestrade had gone from insufferable jack-ass to... well, nothing had changed in that department, but Holmes was grateful nonetheless to have the man at his side. "Thank you."

"Don't mention it... No, really, I don't want Joubert coming after me with a loaded syringe." Lestrade flashed the detective a guilty grin as he returned the contraband to his pocket.

Holmes smiled back faintly in spite of himself. "You're a terrible nurse – you know that, Lestrade?"

"Yes, I know; that's what the lady said, too..." Lestrade suddenly cut himself off, looking chagrined.

"Mar... Mrs. Watson? Why, what happened?"

"That's right... She didn't tell you, did she? But... seriously, sir, you didn't notice? She was sitting right next to you!" Lestrade's voice was a mixture of concern and amusement. Was Holmes losing his mind? What crucial detail had he overlooked now?

"Lestrade, what the devil are you talking about? What happened to Mrs. Watson?"

"Relax, Mr. Holmes, Mary's fine. She's pregnant."

Chapter 11

Suffer the Parent

'Mary... pregnant...' The two words echoed in Holmes' head, they appeared to be the only ones in there at the moment. Of all the things he'd imagined Lestrade could be about to tell him, this was most certainly not included, although that suddenly seemed ludicrously naïve. Holmes had known that Watson and Mary wanted children, had been trying for months, and now... Mary had been given the joy that they'd both longed for so greatly, only to be plunged into deepest sorrow immediately after... Merciful God, what had he done?! "How...?" The words caught in his throat.

"The usual way, I'd imagine... Do I really need to draw you a picture?"

"Lestrade!" Holmes' cheeks were strangely warm. "I was *going* to ask, 'How long have you known?'" Come to that, how long had Mary known? Had Watson? No, surely not...

"Since the day after we brought you in; you could have knocked me down with a feather when Mary told me. Don't ask me how she hid it for so long, especially with all the sick turns she must have had! According to Joubert, she's seven weeks along, and doing very well, considering everything she's been through lately."

"And Watson..." So the Doctor hadn't known... would never know...

"...is the father, yes!" Naturally, Lestrade took Holmes' dazed whisper in the worst possible context. "Lord's sakes, sir, it's a good thing Mary *didn't* tell you; she'd certainly have slapped you for asking something like that, and I wouldn't blame her! Whose did you think it might have been: mine, perhaps, or possibly Roland's?"

Why did that name suddenly make Holmes uneasy? "Roland... No, Lestrade, that's not what I meant! Be silent for a moment, will you?" Now he remembered. "Roland calls her 'little mother'... He's known since Meiringen! That has to be what Mary said to him in the study... and if he knew before he left the train..." He froze, an icy dread churning in his gut, "Then *Moran* knows!"

"Oh, come now, Mr. Holmes, you can't honestly think that Roland told Erik!"

"Whether he meant to or not." Holmes cut off the Inspector's protest with a glare. "Do you know anything for certain about what happened between the brothers, Lestrade? All you have to go on is what Roland told Mary!"

"And Brenner said himself at the theatre that Roland told him nothing! Erik may be a cold-blooded killer, but a liar he isn't, and either way..." Lestrade shook his head emphatically. "The young man's been through too much for Mary's sake, sir – he'd never betray her, I'm sure of that."

"Forgive me for not having copious amounts of faith in your assurances, Inspector! Regardless of who told him, Moran certainly knows about Mary's condition. That's why he let me live!" *Why* hadn't Holmes seen this earlier?

"What! Mr. Holmes, you were nearly dead when we rescued you! If that's Moran's idea of mercy..."

"No... it's his idea of sport... I've been blind, Lestrade! You didn't rescue me, Moran let me go! It isn't me he wants dead now – it's Mary!" The detective had to force himself to speak calmly, no easy task with terror hammering in his chest. "He's going to kill her, and her child... *Watson's* child..." And yet... it was over a week since Holmes had regained consciousness. Why had the Colonel still not made a move; what on earth was the man waiting for?

111

The colour rapidly drained from Lestrade's face. "You really believe Moran would do that – just to get revenge on you?"

"You have no idea what Moran is capable of, Inspector, you've never met him. Pray God you never do without a gun! Mary is in grave danger; you have to get her away from here, now!"

"Right." Lestrade stood abruptly, expression grim, and strode swiftly towards the door. "I'll find her, then we'd better..."

"I think not, Inspector." Joubert suddenly appeared in the doorway, pointing a revolver straight at Lestrade's face, stopping the Inspector in his tracks. "Please, be so kind as to sit back down."

"Joubert!" Lestrade was forced to step back and reseat himself, fists clenching. "What have you done with Mrs. Watson?"

"Merely locked her in her room, Inspector. I would never wish to cause the lady harm, believe me." Joubert frowned, clearly deeply upset about the role he was having to assume. "I am sorry, messieurs... but none of you are going anywhere, not for some time." And with those last words, Holmes finally understood what sadistic game was being played here, at least in part.

"Until I can walk again, do you mean – or merely pull a trigger? Exactly how fit do I need to be, *Doctor*, before Moran decides I am enough of a challenge?" Holmes knew he could say nothing to deter Joubert, but there was satisfaction nonetheless in watching the man writhe under the detective's scornful gaze.

"Forgive me, monsieur – I... I have no choice...!" The doctor's face twisted in agony, and he swiftly backed out of the room, shutting the door and locking it.

"Joubert, no, wait! Joubert!" Lestrade raced up to the door and hammered on it, eventually giving up in disgust. "The crawling coward! Do you think he could be the one? No, forget that – he couldn't have known about Mary before Moran. Curse it, how did they get to him?"

"His wife, they must have threatened to kill her if he doesn't cooperate."

"His wife? But he doesn't even wear a wedding ring! I may not have your talents, Mr. Holmes, but I'm not completely unobservant."

"There's a very faint band of paler skin on his left ring finger, he doesn't wear it while on duty."

"So we can't convince him to help us escape. Any suggestions?"

"*You* have to escape, Inspector, alone. Joubert could be back any minute with reinforcements to separate us, but if we don't wait for him..." Holmes nodded at the chair Lestrade had just vacated. "Block the door, then knot these sheets together, you'll have to use the window."

"Think again, Mr. Holmes, I'll be hanged if I'll leave you and Mary here unprotected!" Lestrade jammed the back of the chair under the door handle, then began stripping the sheets off his own bed. "We go together, or not at all!"

"Then you're a greater fool than I ever thought possible, Lestrade!" Holmes snapped. "Mary is under lock and key as well, and there is no way both of us can get out of that window in time. Moran doesn't care about you nearly as much as he does about Mary and I – as long we two are here, his men won't pursue you. You're expendable, so make use of that! Head for the woods, get yourself back to Herr and Frau Schultz, then cable Mycroft. Trust *no-one* else, understand?"

"And what's Moran going to do to both of you while I'm gone?" Lestrade finished knotting the corners of the two sheets together and dragged Holmes' bed to the window, the heavy frame shuddering over

113

the waxed wood floor. Holmes hoped the noise wasn't going to bring their enemies down on them any sooner.

"Use your head, Lestrade! Moran *wants* me to get stronger; he'll not harm either of us, not yet. You have time to go for aid, and I will do what I can here to give you more."

The Inspector tied the improvised rope to the bedhead, before opening the window and throwing the rest out over the sill. "All right, but on one condition: you have to keep eating."

"That rather defeats the purpose, Inspector." Food would only speed the healing process, which Holmes was now even more anxious to avoid.

"The hell it does! I mean it, sir – you eat, or I don't leave!"

The detective sighed, the obstinate look in Lestrade's eye all too familiar. "Very well... Now, go!"

"Blimey, if I'd known all it took was climbing out a window..." Holmes wasn't as bad a liar as his colleague believed... "I'll see you again soon, Mr. Holmes – that's a promise." Lestrade slid carefully over the sill and dropped out of sight.

Holmes watched the twitching sheet like a hawk, his only way of knowing how the Inspector was faring. To the detective's great relief, the sheet suddenly slackened, then was tugged twice – his colleague had reached the ground safely. "Godspeed, Lestrade," Holmes murmured, then reached out and hooked his wrist over the sheet, slowly pulling it back in, arms and shoulders aching with the effort. No need to leave an obvious clue for any outside watchers, even though the alarm was most likely already being raised. Seconds later, footsteps sounded outside the door, and the key turned in the lock. Holmes grinned at the angry voices on the other side when the door failed to open, and continued to wind in the sheet, enjoying the modest entertainment, although he was not looking forward to when they finally broke it down...

The detective couldn't decide whether it was flattering or insulting that Joubert had him transferred to the ground floor asylum wing. It might have been the logical choice from the doctor's perspective, but it was most inconvenient from Holmes' position. His new room was empty of any furnishings but the bed, which was bolted to the floor. Eating was an unarguable point; he awoke later that evening after his first refusal to cooperate, held immobile by the restraints, with a head full of mist and a sore throat and nasal passage. Joubert had obviously been serious in his threat about the feeding tube – the man would do nothing to jeopardise Holmes' recovery, for fear of having to answer to Moran.

Holmes' own situation was the least of his worries, however. What effect would being confined to quarters have on Mary, or the baby? Her courage was undeniable, but to be forced to merely sit and wait for the worst... assuming she had any idea of what was coming... But in the early hours of the next morning, Holmes learned just how resourceful the woman could be, as he was woken suddenly by his shoulder being shaken, a hand over his mouth.

"Mr. Holmes! Mr. Holmes, wake up!"

"Mary!" Was he dreaming or was she actually wearing a nurse's uniform? "Thank God... Are you all right?"

Mary ignored the question and began unbuckling the straps on Holmes' wrists. "Have they hurt you?"

"No." There was a heavy bandage on Mary's left forearm beneath the sleeve, but she seemed to be otherwise unharmed... and now that Holmes knew what to look for, it was evident that she most certainly was pregnant. He had not quite dared to believe it before. "Where is Lestrade?"

"I've not seen him since I left you yesterday. Dr. Joubert said you helped him escape."

"Joubert? Where is he?" Mary did not answer, but there was an odd smile lurking at the corners of her mouth. "Mary... what did you do to him?"

"Nothing he will not recover from, mein Herr." Another figure in a nurse's uniform entered, pushing a wheelchair, with what appeared to be a strait-jacket draped over it.

"Fräulein?"

The nurse closed the door, and assisted Mary in undoing the last restraints. "My apologies, Herr Holmes. Had I known earlier what my father was being forced to do..."

"You are Joubert's daughter?" There was not the slightest resemblance between the two.

"Stepdaughter, mein Herr. Bessner was my late mother's name... but that is not important. Your lives are in danger here, you need to leave as soon as may be. Will you let me help you?"

"We do not appear to have much choice."

"Unfortunately. It would be wise for you to wear this, in case we are seen." Fräulein Bessner and Mary helped Holmes to sit up and put the strait-jacket on, buckling the straps behind him. "I am sorry, Herr Holmes; I will not fasten the sleeves, merely wrap them around you."

"Quite all right, Fräulein, this is not the worst disguise I have ever worn." It definitely placed in the top five, however. "But you did not answer my earlier question, Mary. What happened to your arm?"

"I'll explain later, Mr. Holmes; right now, we have to leave." The women settled Holmes carefully into the wheelchair. "If you don't want to act the part, I suggest you pretend you're still under sedation. Hannah?"

"No-one is about, follow me." The nurse led the way down several corridors, which gradually became more dingy and neglected, stopping at last in a large supply closet, empty except for a pair of battered carpet bags tucked away in the corner, Lestrade's and Mary's. Holmes wondered briefly whether Herr Steiler still had his and Watson's belongings; he would be needing some clothes soon, to replace this hospital gown. To wear real clothes again, and not feel a draught halfway down his back every time he leant forward...

"This wing is set to be torn down next spring to make room for the new laboratories. I shall not be sorry to see it demolished, but it does have one redeeming feature." Fräulein Bessner pulled at a shelf, swinging it and the rest of the shelves away from the wall in one piece, then placed her hands flat on the wall and easily slid the whole partition to one side. A shallow flight of steps was revealed, going down into the dark... Holmes' throat was closing...

"Mr. Holmes? Oh, dear God... Mr. Holmes, breathe!" Panic-stricken, the detective clawed weakly at the jacket with clumsy, cloth-covered hands. "Hannah, shut that panel and help me get this off him, quickly!" Hands fumbled at the straps on his back and peeled the smothering garment away. "Just breathe, Mr. Holmes... that's it... easy, now... breathe..." Bent almost double in his seat, Holmes focused on Mary's voice, on her hands bracing his shoulders, drawing in large gulps of air, trembling. She removed her cap and used it to wipe the sweat from his face. "I'm so sorry, Mr. Holmes, I never thought! He can't go down there like this, Hannah – is there any other way out?"

"Besides riding in an ambulance? Either one of you could be missed at any time. This is your best chance to get away unseen!"

"Then... that is the way... you should go, Mary. Fräulein Bessner... can show you."

"To quote the Inspector, Mr. Holmes: save your breath. I'm not leaving you here alone – we're getting out together."

"And how do you plan... to accomplish that?" Holmes' face was burning with the humiliation of his sudden breakdown, before *Mary*, of all people. Weeping in front of Lestrade for the first time had been nothing compared to this...

"Well, I do have an idea... but it means you will need to trust me, Mr. Holmes." Mary knelt in front of him, placing a hand tentatively on his arm. "Can you do that?"

"As I said... I do not have much choice..."

"There is always a choice, Mr. Holmes." She took Holmes' bandaged hands carefully in hers, smiling kindly up at him. "Will you trust me?"

"...yes..."

"Hannah, please hand me my bag."

Chapter 12

Run and Hide

"I mean to blindfold you, Mr. Holmes – will it upset you overmuch if you cannot see?" Mary drew a peasant-style headscarf from her bag and folded it into a bandage.

"On the contrary, I would prefer it..." Holmes was still shaking; the mere thought of the gaping dark behind that wall was ghastly.

"Then close your eyes." Soft cloth pressed down on the detective's eyelids and tightened around his head. "I'm sure you've already realised we're going to be carrying you, we can't take the wheelchair down into the tunnel."

"Do not worry, Herr Holmes, we can bear your weight easily enough." Holmes heard the wall panel slide back again, smelt the damp earth and stone, a sickeningly familiar scent... but it was mostly overwhelmed the next moment by the smell of antiseptic and lavender, as the two women wrapped a blanket around his shoulders and gathered him up.

"Are you certain about this, Mary? In your condition..." The detective clenched his jaw as they descended the steps and concentrated on breathing.

Mary gave an exasperated sigh. "You're as bad as the Inspector, Mr. Holmes. It's only been seven weeks! Do bear in mind that a fortnight ago I was riding a horse and climbing mountains."

"All the same, I do not think that Watson... would have approved." Holmes would have to devote mental energy later to constructing a more convincing argument.

"I beg to differ, sir... but is that really the pertinent issue at the moment? The most important thing is for us to get out of here and find the Inspector."

"Which reminds me, Mary, you promised to tell me what happened to your arm. Who did that to you?" For once, it was a relief to have something else to worry about.

"She did it to herself, Herr Holmes."

"What?" Holmes' sudden movement almost made the women lose their hold on him.

"Thank you, Hannah. Mr. Holmes, please keep still!"

Holmes felt the slight jolt as the nurse shrugged. "He was going to find out anyway, Mary. Better now than later."

"I could not agree more! Would you care to explain why you have taken to injuring yourself, madam?"

"I needed some blood for a diversion, and I was the only available donor. It was a simple enough ruse: I sliced my arm with the bodkin from my sewing kit and let it drip on the floor for a minute. All I had to do then was add a few theatrics when the doctor came back." Holmes could feel Mary's laugh ripple through her arms. "Honestly, that must be one of the oldest tricks ever invented – I'm amazed the man was even taken in by it!"

"Joubert thought that you... that you had..."

"The word you're tiptoeing around, Mr. Holmes, is 'miscarried', and yes, thankfully he did. It was easy enough to... shall we say, catch him off guard. We had quite an interesting conversation after that, once he was able to speak again."

Holmes winced in sympathy. "I see... How did you come to be involved, Fräulein?"

"Mary stayed in hiding for the next few hours until I came on duty, she told me everything." The nurse sighed. "Sad to say, my father's actions do not greatly surprise me – he has always been overprotective, even before my mother died. If he had simply told me of the threat, perhaps we could have done more to shield the three of you until you had recovered, mein Herr. As it is, he and I will also have to flee, once the sedative Mary gave him wears off. Do you have any place to go?"

Holmes nodded. "I sent the Inspector back to the Schultz' residence, although I have no idea whether he managed to reach them, or contact my brother. We shall simply have to feel our way forward, as carefully as possible."

"Speaking of which," Mary interrupted, "I do believe... Do you feel that, Mr. Holmes?" Indeed, the cool breath of a draught on his face, carrying the scent of pine; they were almost out. Holmes reached up and lifted the scarf from his eyes, uncaring of his surroundings now, eager for his first taste of the outside world without the barrier of walls or windows. "Set him down, Hannah; I'll douse the lantern." The darkness pressed back around, but to the detective's relief, there was a weak silver light filtering through the brush at the tunnel's entrance.

"A quarter moon... We couldn't have chosen a much better night for flight," he murmured with a faint smile.

"Quietly, now – I think..." The three stiffened as a twig snapped out in the forest to their right. Mary swiftly produced a revolver from somewhere, muttering something decidedly ungenteel in French – where had she learned such language? Then a curious sound reached their ears, a kind of screeching yelp, repeated several times. Mary suddenly chuckled. "If that's an actual fox, the poor creature must be deathly ill!" She returned the sounds, markedly different to the first.

121

"He really needs to brush up on his calls, he's had more than enough chances to practice."

"Mary?" The bushes parted to reveal two figures silhouetted in the faint moonlight, one extremely familiar. "Thank God, you're all right! Mr. Holmes, is that you?"

"As you can see, Lestrade. It would seem it is my turn to surprise you."

Lestrade's relieved grin matched Holmes'. "You're telling me, sir! Honestly, I wasn't sure we'd be able to get you out this way... no offence."

"None taken, Inspector – this is all Mary's doing." The truth might have been embarrassing, but credit should go where it was due. The second man released Mary from the bear hug he had been crushing her in, turning to Holmes and Fräulein Bessner with a broad smile. It was simple enough to deduce the man's identity: *"Herr Schultz?"*

"Yes, Herr Holmes." The man leaned down and carefully engulfed Holmes' extended hand in his own. *"It's an honour."*

"Thank you, mein Herr... but the honour... is mine," the detective murmured, colouring. His lack of competence in German was not helping his discomfort in the slightest.

"I hate to interrupt you two," Lestrade cut in, "But we'd best be going. Herr Schultz, would you...?"

"Pardon me, mein Herr." The burly foreman wrapped the blanket more securely around Holmes and lifted him effortlessly. *"Are you also coming with us, Fräulein?"*

"Sadly, no." Fräulein Bessner smiled regretfully. *"I must return.* Goodbye, Herr Holmes, Mary. May God be with all of you."

"And with you, Hannah." The two women embraced. "Travel safely, and give your father my deepest regards." The nurse laughed, a wicked glint in her eye, then relit the lantern and vanished back down the narrow tunnel to the hospital. Mary tore her gaze away with difficulty and turned to Lestrade. "Inspector, how did you know we would be here?"

"Actually, I didn't... but we can fill in all the gaps later. We need to leave, Roland's waiting for us at the river."

"The river?"

"Did you honestly think we'd be remaining in Zurich, Mary, after all this? Herr Schultz, lead the way."

Holmes tried to remain awake for the journey – the forest was eerie yet beautiful in the moonlight, and this was the first time he had knowingly been outside in weeks – but the stress of the last several hours was inevitably beginning to take its toll. Finally, he conceded defeat, leaning his head on Herr Schultz' broad shoulder and closing his eyes... not for long, just a few minutes...

* * *

The next time the detective opened his eyes, the scene had changed. He was lying on a couch in the main living area of a well-kept chalet, covered by a patchwork blanket, sunlight streaming through the windows. Before he could take in more of his surroundings, Lestrade's footsteps sounded on the outside veranda and the man himself appeared in the open doorway, heavy-eyed but smiling.

"Good morning, Herr Holmes! How are you?"

"Good morning, Lestrade... Enlighten me, are you attempting to speak the language or murder it?"

"I know, I know. It was Mary's idea, though, and even I'm not stupid enough to argue with her. But you still haven't answered the question: how are you feeling?"

"Marginally improved." Actually, now that Holmes considered it, decidedly so. The coiled-spring tension that had gripped him yesterday seemed to have dissipated, and a fair amount of the pain along with it. His body no longer felt weighted down with lead, and although his wounds still irritated him, they had ceased to burn. "Where are we, exactly? I gather from our direction in the forest last night that we are somewhere to the north of Zurich."

"Northwest. We're about three miles east of Baden, it's a spa town – very popular with the tourists, I understand. Herr Schultz recommended we bring you here to speed your recovery. Apparently, the region's thermal springs are second to none."

"A few Turkish baths are hardly going to miraculously restore me back to full health, Inspector." Not to mention the risk involved – visiting the baths in Holmes' current state was certain to attract attention. Even if he disguised his features, the gruesome marks on the rest of him would be more than sufficient to give him away.

"Which is why we're staying for a month."

Holmes' jaw dropped. "Surely you jest, Lestrade! Moran..."

"...doesn't want you dead, or Mary, not yet..." Lestrade sighed and pulled up a chair next to the couch. "Look at it like this, Mr. Holmes. At the moment, we've got three choices: run, fight or hide. I'll admit, none of those are ideal options, but right now you're in no condition to travel far, or to face the Colonel. Besides, given what you two know of each other, what's Moran least likely to expect you to do?"

"Assuming you are correct..." The detective did not appreciate Lestrade's less-than-subtle aspersion on his judgement. "Why here?"

"Because I'd say that Moran is far less likely to search for you this close to Zurich." Hiding in plain sight... Was this mad enough to actually work? "Schultz said we can stay in his family chalet until you're back on your feet. He's planning to come up here again in about four weeks, though, so I'd suggest you use the time wisely."

"Why is that?"

"Because, according to your brother, he'll be bringing someone else with him. And no, I've not the least idea who – though I rather doubt it'll be Mycroft."

"Then you were able to contact him yesterday?"

"Got his answering telegram here, if you want to read it." Stifling a yawn, Lestrade pulled a yellow slip of paper out of his pocket and unfolded it. Since his fingers were still out of commission, Holmes reached out and took the paper with both hands, ignoring his complaining shoulders.

HASTEN SWAN TO GOTTFRIED STOP HERALD NEAR WITH PAGES STOP ELSA BEWARE TELRAMUND STOP HEINRICH FINAL STOP

It only took Holmes a few moments to grasp the meaning. Wagner's 'Lohengrin' comprised some of his preferred composer's best work, although definitely lacking in terms of plot. 'Hasten swan to Gottfried' – he would heal as swiftly as he was able, thank you; his brother's concern for his welfare was truly touching. 'Herald near with pages' – so Mycroft *was* sending another agent, the four pages were the number of weeks until his arrival. 'Elsa beware Telramund' – Holmes already knew Moran was after Mary, did his brother think him a fool? As for the man signing himself as the king... Holmes had to suppress a snort – and Mycroft called *him* vain...

125

He gave Lestrade a sideways look. "And you were able to decipher this, Lestrade?"

The Inspector grinned unashamedly. "Actually, Mary did, on the boat last night. I suspect that's why Mycroft used the opera reference – he probably knew she'd understand better than me, or anyone else who might intercept it."

"Speaking of Mary, where is she?" The chalet and the surrounding clearing suddenly seemed ominously quiet.

"Gone into town with Roland; somebody had to get supplies. Relax, Mr. Holmes, it's market day. She and the lad will have no trouble blending in, which is more than can be said for the two of us! Hence the German – Mary thinks it'll be good for us both to learn the language, so we can maintain a lower profile and, frankly, help to keep you from getting bored. I have to admit, it would be nice to understand what the people around me are saying, especially Roland. I'm getting tired of gesturing or asking Mary to translate all the time."

Roland... Holmes and young Brenner had not come face to face since Reichenbach, a state of affairs the detective was not anxious to remedy. In spite of Lestrade's account of the boy's later efforts on their behalf, Holmes was by no means convinced that it had not been Roland who let slip Mary's condition to their enemies. Living under the same roof as a former pawn of Moriarty for the next four weeks – one who would doubtless be following Mary around like a love-sick puppy – promised to be an *interesting* experience. Groaning, Holmes crumpled Mycroft's missive and rolled gingerly onto his right side, his back to Lestrade, pulling the blanket over his head. Somebody wake him in a month...

Chapter 13

Turning the Tide

"Do not test me, Mr. Holmes! The three of us have been accommodating as possible, but enough is enough!" Thirty-six hours later, and Holmes still had not moved or spoken, except to rebuff any and all approaches from his fellow houseguests – and now it seemed that Mary's patience had finally been exhausted. "I am not your thrice-sainted landlady, sir, and you would do well to remember that!" Too true, Mrs. Hudson had never interfered regarding his personal hygiene... Why was Mary suddenly so concerned about him bathing now, anyhow? "Let me put it to you another way: it is summer, you needn't sleep inside. I have no qualms whatsoever about making you share quarters with the donkey, if you insist on smelling like her!"

That threat got Holmes' full attention, and he lifted his head from under the blanket to glare at the woman blearily – he had not managed to get much sleep, either. "Absolutely not!"

Mary smiled grimly. "Very well then... Inspector, Mr. Holmes wishes to bathe. If you would be so kind?" She nodded her head towards the couch and its mutinous occupant.

"Right you are." Lestrade rose from the kitchen table, where he had been conversing with Roland in halting German, grinning.

"Lestrade..." Holmes hissed, glaring venomously.

"Sorry, Mr. Holmes, you heard the lady!" Without further ado, Lestrade whisked the blanket away and gathered the detective roughly into his arms. For several moments, Holmes' sheer outrage at the man's audacity held him immobile, until he realised Lestrade was carrying him outside. Deducing where they must be going freed Holmes from his paralysis, but he still did not dare to struggle in case the Inspector lost his grip on him.

"Take me back, Lestrade, at once! This is most undignified!" As if this were not mortifying enough, Roland was following them with a cake of soap and a wool robe, trying in vain to smother a smile.

"Hard not to be, with you shouting like that." As Holmes had suspected, they rounded the corner and approached a deep wooden trough with a pump at one end lying under the eaves, which currently held at least three feet of water.

"For God's sake, Lestrade, animals have been drinking from there! How is that sanitary?"

"I'd say they were a lot cleaner than you right now." The Inspector was entirely unmoved, continuing on inexorably.

Holmes made one last attempt. "This will not be forgiven, Inspector..."

"Oh, well, in that case..." Lestrade dropped Holmes straight into the trough. Flailing for the side, the detective rose spluttering to the surface, having neglected to close his mouth when Lestrade let go. Through the water in his ears, Holmes heard the Inspector say cheerfully, but with a band of iron in his voice, "Something you clearly haven't deduced yet, sir: I'd far rather have *you* angry at me than Mary, any day of the year. The water's clean, here's the soap..." The fist-sized bar landed in front of Holmes, splashing more water into his face. "And you won't be needing this." His sodden hospital gown was stripped off, leaving him with only his bandages and the water for cover.

Holmes' face was scarlet with anger and embarrassment, but the Inspector paid no attention, dropping the robe on the grass next to the trough and turning away. "Don't worry about your dressings, there'll be fresh bandages and clothes waiting inside when you're done. *Come on, Roland, we're leaving.*" Lestrade began walking off with Roland in tow, the lad's shoulders visibly quivering with suppressed mirth.

"And how exactly am I meant to get back inside?"

"You're the genius, Mr. Holmes, not me," came the cavalier response, delivered without even a backward glance. "But given the way you were thrashing a minute ago, I'd say that won't be a problem, anyhow. Enjoy your bath."

Left alone, Holmes spent an uncomfortable quarter of an hour just sitting and shivering, seething with indignation. In the end, however, common sense conquered pride, and he reached for the soap. He might as well, since he was here... His hand bandages made surprisingly decent sponges, although washing his hair was a little more difficult, and finally getting clean did make a considerable difference to his frame of mind. Next time, he would ask for hot water.

Lestrade was right, damn him. After several attempts, Holmes succeeded in levering himself over the side and dropped to the grass, legs folding under him like a new-born colt, shaking with cold and fatigue. Once he was out, though, the afternoon sun was a blessing, quickly drying him where he sat slumped, gathering strength for the journey back.

For a brief moment, he was tempted to return to the house just as he was, but that might be a pyrrhic victory at best – or at worst, seriously offend Mary's sensibilities, again. He wasn't that suicidal. The detective reached for the robe, eased his aching arms carefully into the sleeves and secured the folds around his waist with the cord as best he could. His legs still couldn't hold him up yet, therefore his best option was to crawl. At least he did not have an audience, this time... He thrust the lurking memories back into the dark and concentrated on making his reluctant limbs work in unison.

Mary emerged from the house just as Holmes reached the top of the veranda steps. Kneeling, she put her arms around him and helped him to stand, supporting him enough that he could limp indoors. Clearly, his days of being carried everywhere were done. The woman sat him back down on the couch and eased the robe off his shoulders, leaving it tied around his waist for the sake of modesty. The other two were nowhere in sight, thankfully – this was awkward enough.

His old bandages were unwound and put aside. Mary cleaned each wound in turn with spirits, salving them afterwards with gentle hands and applying fresh dressings where necessary, although the injuries that needed rebinding were considerably fewer now. Some kind of ointment was rubbed into his shoulder muscles; Mary handed Holmes a cloth pad daubed with the same substance and instructed him to massage it into his right knee.

"What is this?" The ointment smelled pleasantly like peppermint.

"Wintergreen. It will reduce the swelling – Klara Schultz swears by it." A large nightshirt, no doubt one of Herr Schultz', was airing by the fire. Holmes managed to pull it on with minimal assistance, savouring the feeling of the warm, crisp linen.

Lastly, Mary turned her attention to his hands, removing the stained wrappings and splints. Most of the bruising had healed, but the new scars would be a long time in fading, and his nails were still very much a mess. Grimacing, the detective tried to hide his hands inside his sleeves, until Mary prevented him. "Your hands need air, let them breathe."

She replaced the splint on his left palm, then turned her attention to his right hand – the index and middle fingers were still mildly swollen. "Be patient, Mr. Holmes; another week or so and you can take the splints off entirely. Until then, I think we need only splint these two fingers, and let you exercise the rest." She finished working, then packed the leftover materials away into a large basket, which held enough medical supplies for a small country practice. "If you're wondering where all this came from, Hannah raided the supply cupboard at the hospital before we left."

130

"I surmised as much." Mary rose and placed the basket on the sideboard, her expression troubled. It wasn't hard to fathom the reason. "Mary, Fräulein Bessner will be all right. She is a brave, capable woman..." Much like Mary herself. "I have little doubt that she and her father were able to get away safely, as we did."

The worry in her eyes had receded a little as she returned with a cup of water and a comb. Holmes could deal with the first, at least, managing to drink on his own without spilling, but the comb was too thin for his awkward grasp. Mary took it from him with an understanding nod, knelt on the couch next to him and began to untangle his overgrown mane. Although it was frustrating not being able to perform so simple a task, the sheer ordinariness of the activity was soothing, and the tension gradually began to ebb from him. Heavens, he was exhausted – he had not properly slept since their escape, two nights ago. Wait, that... reminded him of something...

"Mary, there is one thing I am curious about. How did Lestrade and Herr Schultz know about the tunnel out of the hospital? Did Fräulein Bessner send a message?"

"No, she didn't need to. Werner's known about that particular exit for years."

"How would he – ow – know something like that? Gently, Mary, please."

"I'm sorry, Mr. Holmes, this knot is being stubborn... but have you forgotten what the man does for a living? He's a builder, he has been in the trade for close on thirty years, and the hospital wing was only built back in '78." So Herr Schultz had been one of the workers – he might even have helped to dig the tunnel. "As for how we all managed to arrive in the same place at the right time..." Mary smiled sagely. "I haven't the slightest idea. Perhaps there were more mysterious forces at work that night than just us." It would certainly be a relief to know that somebody up there was on their side. "I have never doubted that, Mr. Holmes – not for a moment."

Good Lord, had Holmes said that out loud? He must be more tired than he thought. Perhaps he should get some sleep before the other two returned. "Where are Lestrade and Roland? They have been gone for some time."

"Werner told us of a thermal spring up the hill, about half a mile from here; they went in search of it. Assuming they find it, they can take you there tomorrow, if the weather permits."

"And leave you here by yourself?" Out of the question – either Mary accompanied them, or Roland would have to remain behind with her. It was simply not safe for any of them to be alone, although how he was going to convince the woman of that without divulging the reason...

"I am occasionally able to look after myself, Mr. Holmes. I'm not made of porcelain, and from what the Inspector has told me of Colonel Moran..."

"He *told* you?" Wonderful, another reason to doubt the man's sanity. If Moran wanted to kill Lestrade as well, he'd have to get in line.

Mary's stern voice cut through Holmes' fuming. "I had the right to know, sir: something the Inspector understands, even if you don't." Wait a moment, why was *he* the one getting lectured? "You have an alarming tendency to try to protect those you care about by keeping them in the dark. How does not telling people of the dangers that lie ahead shield them in any way?" In Watson's case, a little more ignorance would have saved his life. "Forewarned is forearmed, is it not?"

"Not always," Holmes muttered. "Sometimes ignorance truly is bliss..."

Mary's eyes widened in sudden understanding. "You were worried about how the stress of that knowledge might affect the baby, weren't you?" Holmes nodded miserably, and she touched his shoulder, voice softening. "Oh, Sherlock..." He stiffened in surprise, both from the contact and her use of his given name, for the first time ever. Mary let her hand fall away, seeing his discomfort, and continued work with the comb.

"Bearing a child... poses enough dangers in itself..." Holmes stared at his hands, face red with embarrassment at having to discuss such matters.

"And learning that someone wants to kill me was hardly going to change that side of things, Sherlock. I knew the risks when John and I began trying for a family – one of the hazards of being a doctor's wife, I'm afraid."

"When did you know...?"

"I suspected I might be while away in the country, but I wasn't certain until the gendarmerie in Geneva."

"Ah... So, the police report..." The detective still couldn't believe Lestrade had allowed her to read that file.

"...was certainly upsetting, but I had already been feeling ill beforehand. You might say it was the final straw on the camel's back." Mary laid the comb aside and sat back down next to Holmes, brow furrowed. "I still don't think the Inspector has completely forgiven me for not telling him at the outset. I've never seen him so angry before, although he didn't do much actual shouting, to his credit. At the time, I was afraid that he would send me back if he knew, regardless of what we had already agreed. I simply couldn't bear the thought of having to

133

sit uselessly at home and wait... and I wanted John to be the first to know..."

The quiet pain in her voice made Holmes wince. "Forgive me for asking, Mary..." This was probably not the best timing, but he needed to know. "What made you change your mind?"

"I don't understand."

"Roland; he knew you were with child at Meiringen."

"Ah, yes... The Inspector told me of your suspicions." No doubt Holmes was about to receive another tirade. "I'm afraid you're mistaken, Sherlock. Yes, Roland knew about my condition, and I imagine Erik did inform Moran... but it would have been Klaus who told Erik, not Roland."

That took him by surprise. "Erik's henchman?"

"At the theatre, when Klaus was holding the knife to my throat, he had his other arm around my waist... I hadn't worn a corset since leaving home..." Mary shivered. "He tensed and asked, 'Expecting?' I denied it, of course, but he simply grinned and said, 'Congratulations!' before bringing me in." Her expression was grave. "I assume the Inspector has informed you of what occurred afterwards – or rather, what didn't occur – thanks solely to Roland, I might add. You owe him an apology."

Far more than that... Holmes had to agree with Lestrade: Klaus and Harrison had not received one tenth of what they'd deserved. "Indeed – I will speak with him when he returns." But Roland was not the only one to whom the detective needed to apologise, and there would be no better time than this. He paused uncomfortably, gathering the courage to say what was long overdue. "Mary, I... I am aware..." Painfully so... "...that I have not yet thanked you for all you have done – not only at the hospital, but at every step of the way thus far."

"It doesn't matter, Sherlock." Mary smiled at him reassuringly, but there was a flicker of astonishment in her face, verifying exactly how childish his conduct had been these last two days. He stared at the floor, his next words an abashed murmur.

"On the contrary, madam. You have been unfailingly kind, in spite of everything..." Holmes forced himself to meet her gaze; he would not shrink from the truth again. "And I have mostly repaid you for your trouble with ingratitude and curses."

"Sherlock, please – you need not reproach yourself so." The sympathy in Mary's eyes stabbed him to the heart. "I do understand, believe me. You have suffered greatly... far more than I could ever imagine."

"Nevertheless, my behaviour of late has been atrocious." And Holmes was horrified at what she had just said – did Mary truly believe her own sorrow insignificant compared to his? "To my shame, I had forgotten that... I am not the only one affected by all of this. Lestrade has described in detail your efforts to... to find Watson and I, a journey that has been nothing short of heroic. I know... all too well... that you did not do it for me..." Holmes' insides twisted at the involuntary movement Mary's hands made, unconsciously coming to rest on her abdomen.

"And... I wish... oh, God...!" The last words emerged as a strangled whisper, and Holmes bowed his head, covering his face with his hands, eyes stinging. Mary didn't need him breaking apart like this right now, she had enough pain of her own to deal with. To have come so far, holding so tightly to hope... only to discover at the last that just one of them was left... *the wrong one...*

"Oh, Sherlock..." Mary put her arms around Holmes' shoulders and held him close. Little by little, he relaxed into her embrace, letting his hands come to rest in his lap at first, uncertain whether or not to return the hug. In the end, it dawned on him that she had need of this as well, and tentatively put his arms around her. The moment he did so, however, his tears began to well up; he tried desperately to hold them back.

He scrubbed his eyes with his sleeve, muttering wretchedly, "I never should have... allowed him to follow me... *Why* did I?" A question he had asked himself a thousand times, and he was still no closer to an answer. "There must have been... *something* I could have said!"

Mary shook her head, her own eyes glistening. "No, Sherlock. There was nothing you could have said to make him turn back, nothing in the world! John loved you as a brother; he never would have abandoned you in such a way, you know that." She rocked him gently, murmuring, "You need not be ashamed to weep, Sherlock; John's death was not your fault... You have as much right as anyone to mourn for him." Her words unravelled something inside of him, he could feel his control dissolving... "It's all right, Sherlock..."

That last compassionate whisper opened the floodgates, and he started to weep uncontrollably, his whole body shaking with grief. Gasping for breath, he managed to choke out the words between sobs: "Mary... I am... *so* sorry...!"

Mary's arms tightened around Holmes; he hung limply in their circle, carried helplessly by the torrent. Even after the flood finally subsided, she did not relax her hold until he stirred himself, passing him her own handkerchief as he fumbled unthinkingly for one in a garment with no pockets. His head felt stuffed with cotton, his eyes and face burning hot. Mary brought him more water, then made him lie back down on the couch and washed his face with a cool cloth that smelled faintly of lavender... She really should... be letting him do that... nice, though... so tired... warm... his blanket was back...

"...Mary...?"

"Shhh... I'm here, Sherlock. Go to sleep... You're going to be all right..." The last thing Holmes was aware of before slipping away was Mary's hand smoothing his hair.

Chapter 14

Present Mercies

The voices drifted through Holmes' dreams, a murmuring undercurrent to the roaring water that tugged at his legs, threatening to dislodge him from his crumbling perch above the abyss...

"How is he?"

"Shh... He's sleeping."

"Thank Heaven. Has he eaten at all?"

"No, it... didn't seem the right time, somehow. He has had some water, at least."

"Dear God – his face... Has he been...?"

"Yes... I hate to see him like this, Geoffrey! He's in so much pain..."

"So are you, Mary... Remember, you can't always hide your own sorrow away to deal with his – and if he can't understand that..."

"No, Geoffrey, it wasn't like that. He actually did apologise when he came back."

"Seriously? Blimey, I should have doused him a lot sooner..."

"Geoffrey!"

"Ow! What was that for?"

"Just... try to have a little compassion, will you? You weren't here – you didn't see the look in his eyes while we were talking."

"Oh, hell... He's still blaming himself, isn't he? What am I saying – of course he is! Of all the bloody stubborn, mule-headed idiots..."

"If only he'd eat something. He's going to make himself ill, Geoffrey; another fever like the last one could set him back for months, if he even survived! What are we going to do?"

"I don't know. There's only so much we can do, Mary. At the end of the day, Mr. Holmes has to decide whether it's worth staying alive. We can't make the choice for him."

"No... you're absolutely right."

"Mary? What is it? You've got that look in your eye again."

"Because you've given me an idea. Where's Roland?"

"Grooming Brigitta. I swear, those two are starting to look like each other... All right, Mary, I'm sorry! You want me to tell him supper's ready?"

"Yes, thank you – and you'll be lucky to get any at the rate you're going."

"What about Mr. Holmes?"

"No, let him sleep. He needs that most at present..."

* * *

Footsteps on the path, muffled by the falls... Holmes glances up from his contemplation of the cascading torrent, nodding pleasantly at the new arrival, a single eyebrow raised in apparent surprise. "Ah, good morning, my dear Moriarty! How fortuitous to encounter you here."

Moriarty's eyes narrow slightly above an icy smile. "Oh, indeed. 'Journeys end in lovers' meetings?'"

Holmes' lips twitch. "You continue to astound me, sir – I had no idea you were an admirer of the Bard."

The Professor's head moves smoothly from its habitual sway into a sardonic tilt. "William Shakespeare is an essential part of any well-rounded education." Holmes' eyes glint briefly at the poorly disguised insult as Moriarty's voice tightens. "But I did not come here to speak of my knowledge of literature." The older man turns to Roland, smiling suddenly in a revoltingly paternal fashion. "*You may go now, young man, thank you.*"

Roland uncurls himself from where he has been leaning against the cliff face, studiously avoiding the gaze of both men, although his troubled eyes flicker briefly towards Holmes. Despite any misgivings he might have, however, the young man wastes no time in absenting himself from the scene, combined fear and relief written plainly across his back and shoulders.

Holmes nods casually after the vanishing boy. "An intriguing choice of minion, Professor. Would I be correct in assuming that there is a distinct shortage of your preferred breed of henchman in the world these days?" He cannot quite conceal the derisive smile which tugs at the corners of his mouth. "At liberty, at any rate..."

Moriarty's smile is as tight as his voice. "I should say that there are few who could pass themselves off as innocent Swiss youths, my dear Holmes. I have never been one to waste a valuable resource, however inconsequential it may appear to others." The malevolent gleam in the man's eye speaks volumes, and Holmes has an increased idea of how Moriarty has been keeping himself apprised of his and Watson's movements since their disappearing act from the Continental express.

Holmes casts a practised glance over his opponent. "And may I say, my dear Moriarty, how extraordinarily well you are looking – the mountain air clearly agrees with you. How fortunate that you should yet be in a position to enjoy its benefits."

"You have your own *professional* colleagues to thank for that, Holmes." The Professor inclines his head mockingly. "It is truly heartening to find that even blundering, incompetent fools have their uses on occasion."

The subtly exultant tone sends a chill down the detective's spine as he realises Moriarty is not merely referring to his apparently miraculous escape. As far as Holmes knew at the time, the cordon surrounding the Professor had been secure, leaving the man no option but to surrender. Now, it seems that there was at least one informant at the heart of Scotland Yard itself, undermining the operation the entire time from within. It is pointless to repine on the subject at this late stage, however. The most he can hope for is that Lestrade has learnt enough from his colleague that he will not consider anyone above suspicion while investigating the leak, should it even occur to him to do so.

He shrugs casually, loathe to pander further to the Professor's already inflated sense of self-importance. "Quite the masterpiece, that letter, my dear sir. It might even have deceived me, had I not been expecting some such artifice from you." Holmes can only be thankful that Watson suspected nothing – although admittedly, the Doctor never had a chance to observe the landlord's actual handwriting, Holmes having signed the guest register for both of them on arrival at the hotel. The detective draws his cigarette case from his breast pocket, courteously offering its contents first to Moriarty. "Will you, Professor? No sense in letting them go to waste, after all."

Moriarty's eyes widen in true surprise for a moment, before taking the proffered cigarette, nodding his thanks with an infinitesimal smirk. "Perhaps you could leave the case for Dr. Watson..."

Holmes barely manages to keep from dropping the match as he lights Moriarty's cigarette. Stilling his quivering fingers enough to light his own, he flicks the burning splinter over the edge and takes a deep drag, allowing the smoke filling his lungs to calm him, before turning back to the Professor as nonchalantly as he is able, eyebrow arched in unspoken inquiry.

Moriarty blows smoke from his nose for several seconds, clearly enjoying prolonging the suspense, before finally continuing. "You need not fear for the good Doctor's safety, Holmes – I've no further interest in him. He may return home freely and unmolested."

Doing his best to keep the relief flooding through him from showing in his eyes, Holmes nods in quiet acknowledgement of the favour. "If you have a few minutes at your disposal, Professor, I would consider myself in your debt if you will allow me to leave Dr. Watson one last message. I should not like him to wonder over my fate indefinitely."

Moriarty inclines his head graciously. "As you wish, my dear Holmes."

"You are too kind, sir," Holmes replies lightly, but with his gratitude audible. This truly is the greatest mercy he can show his friend now, however poor it might seem – the detective well knows that Watson will never be able to move on with his life with the dread spectre of hope haunting his every waking moment. Holmes closes his eyes briefly as he gathers his thoughts, before beginning to write: '*My dear Watson, I write these few lines through the courtesy of Mr. Moriarty...*'

His regrettably brief note complete, Holmes tears the pages from his notepad and lays them reverently upon the rock behind him, weighing them down with his cigarette case, bereft now of all but one. *Smoke it at my grave, my dear fellow – if Mycroft can be persuaded to inter an empty casket...* The detective leans back against the boulder, a curious serenity stealing over him as he turns his head to regard his long-standing opponent thoughtfully.

"It seems almost a pity – does it not, Professor – for our... singular acquaintance to conclude in such a manner." He smiles wryly at the older man's bemused expression. "You paid me a great compliment upon our first encounter; and, I must confess, it has been as great a pleasure for me to match wits with a man of your superb intellect." His profound bow is executed without the least trace of irony. "You truly have been a most worthy adversary."

The corners of Moriarty's mouth lift into something closer to a genuine smile than any of his previous ones. "As have you, my dear Holmes." The Professor gazes at Holmes with an almost hungry gleam in his eye, continuing softly, "Indeed, it is a pity that we should find ourselves on opposite sides of the law, as they say."

Holmes nods, sighing regretfully. "To be sure, sir; but as you have stated previously, with matters as they are, there can be but one conclusion..." He leaves his alpenstock propped against the rock and straightens, squaring his shoulders, allowing the steel to return to his features – he dare not allow any respect for his nemesis to jeopardise the only acceptable outcome to this whole affair.

"Quite so." Moriarty's eyes narrow, his own expression becoming implacable once more. "Very well then, Mr. Holmes." The Professor nods along the path in the direction of the falls. "Shall we settle our accounts now?"

Taking one last pull on his cigarette, Holmes tosses the remainder over the edge, copied by Moriarty as he finishes his own. The detective inclines his head politely to his adversary, pulse quickening, eyes gleaming in anticipation of their impending last battle. "By all means, my dear sir. Let us proceed." Coolly, he turns his back on the Professor and walks towards the end of the path, the pounding of his heart even louder in his ears than the roar of the water...

* * *

143

Holmes woke with a gasp, limbs tangled in his sweat-soaked nightshirt and blanket, the thunder of the falls still echoing in his ears and on the chalet roof... Dear God, was he still dreaming? No, wait, it was... *rain...* He was awake, thank Heaven... and judging from the grey light filtering through the closed shutters, it was a little after dawn. Breathing easier, he untangled himself from his covers and sat up stiffly, noticing as he did that he was still holding Mary's handkerchief from yesterday. He wiped the sweat from his face with his sleeve, cheeks burning at the memory of his unrestrained breakdown, although the mortifying recollection was not as bitter as he would have imagined.

He remembered Mary's unfaltering arms around him, her gentle words, soothing him, picking up the fragments as he fell apart. He shook his head in wonder; what could he possibly have done to deserve such compassion? She could hardly be sincere in saying that she did not blame him for her husband's death – could she? His head was beginning to swim... He abandoned the question, yet another mystery well beyond his comprehension, at least for the moment.

As he contemplated the challenges of getting up, he heard light footsteps behind him and turned his head to see Mary enter the room, dressed in a simple blouse and skirt – borrowed from Frau Schultz, no doubt. *"Good morning..."* The German phrase escaped him unthinkingly. Good Lord, Lestrade must be rubbing off on Holmes, a terrible thought... although if Mary was determined to have them both fluent in the language, there was probably no escape.

The detective was suddenly glad he'd made the effort as she smiled with pleasure. *"Good morning, Sherlock.* This is a surprise; I didn't expect you to be awake so early."

"I could say the same for you."

"Well, unfortunately, breakfast won't make itself." Oh, God... Did she have to remind him? Mary saw Holmes' pained expression and sat down beside him, eyes full of concern. "Sherlock, I know this is difficult, but you haven't eaten in over two days. I didn't wake you for supper last night because you needed to sleep; however, we do have to start addressing your issues with food at some point, and now seems an ideal time." That was *her* opinion... "Are you hungry at the moment?"

Holmes blinked in surprise – he hadn't expected her to actually ask. "I... don't know." The thought of food still made his stomach lurch, although whether it was from hunger, nausea or both, he couldn't even tell anymore. "I am thirsty, though."

"Well, that's a step in the right direction." Mary looked thoughtful. "I'd like to try something with you this morning, Sherlock: a long-term experiment, of sorts. Are you interested?"

"I must confess, you have me intrigued..." And also decidedly nervous.

"Good – because I want to begin teaching you to cook." Mary hurried on as he blanched, opening his mouth to protest. "Hear me out, Sherlock, please. Honestly, I think the best way for you to grow comfortable with food again is by learning to work with it, a little bit each day. We'll move ahead slowly – there's plenty of time – and you'll be serving yourself at every meal." She smiled reassuringly. "No feeding tubes, I promise." No, never again... "Now, this morning, you don't have to eat breakfast, or even help at all... but I would like you to sit in the kitchen and watch me work. Do you think you can do that?"

"I suppose..." In the cellar, Holmes had been forced to eat what refuse was thrown to him or starve – and the hospital really hadn't been much different, in terms of choice or quality. Knowing that no-one here was about to shove swill down his throat did help to fractionally loosen the knot in his gut. It could be worth a try, at least.

"Bravo, Sherlock. Come with me." Mary helped Holmes to his feet and they slowly shuffled into the kitchen. Seated at the well-scrubbed table, he felt decidedly ill at ease, despite not having to do anything but look on, as Mary fed the fire and coaxed the hulking kitchen range into life. Being a bachelor meant he'd had to be able to turn basic ingredients into a meal on occasion, but his limited skills had grown rather rusty, thanks to his worthy landlady's untiring efforts. Come to think of it, he had seldom ever ventured into her domain, not even after Watson moved out...

Holmes hoped fervently that Mrs. Hudson was all right. He had been in no position to ascertain her well-being after Moriarty's men had set fire to the flat, but surely Mycroft would have made certain she was taken care of; not that the fierce old mother hen would ever have admitted to needing it. What he wouldn't give to have her affectionate scolding aimed at him this minute... No, on second thought, the last thing he wanted was for her to see him in this state. Most likely, she'd never let him step out the front door of 221B on his own ever again... not that he had a choice any longer...

The detective blinked hard, swallowing the lump in his throat, and tried to focus on the present. While his thoughts were spiralling downwards, Mary had been hard at work. Breakfast for everyone else this morning seemed to be mainly porridge – he shuddered, better them than him – along with toast, apples and... He stiffened, nostrils flaring at the aroma that suddenly wafted across the kitchen and greeted him cheerfully. His mouth began to water treacherously, with complete disregard for the warring opinions from the rest of him, as Mary set a steaming cup of black coffee on the table a mere arm's length away.

"Leave that alone, it's for the Inspector. I'm sure you know what a bear he can be first thing in the morning." All too well, in fact, but the growing temptation was making Holmes' fingers itch. When Mary turned away to stir the porridge, he reached out and captured the handle, drawing the heavy mug carefully over the tabletop towards him. Cupping his hands gingerly around his prize, he lowered his face over the rising steam, breathing deeply. "Ahem..."

146

He gave Mary's raised eyebrow an innocent look. "What? I am merely warming my hands."

"Well, don't let the Inspector see you with that; he might think you've done something to it."

"I cannot imagine why..." She really shouldn't have given Holmes ideas, especially after yesterday's incident.

Mary chuckled, took the cup away and stirred in generous amounts of cream and sugar, before handing it back. "Very well, you may continue to guard it for him until he emerges."

The smell was even more tantalising now, the sharpness of the coffee turned softer, sweeter... After a few more moments' hesitation, Holmes dipped his finger into the white-gold foam, unable to resist, tentatively putting it in his mouth... and had to stifle a gasp as the flavour flooded over his tongue. To a man accustomed to insipid hospital fare for more than a week, the taste of rich, creamy froth was almost overwhelming.

Trembling hands grasped the cup without waiting for orders from the detective's brain and lifted it to his lips – just a sip, Mary wasn't looking – but when he regained his senses, he found the cup was inexplicably half-empty. How in the world had that happened? He glanced guiltily across the kitchen, where Mary's twinkling eyes told him she'd been watching the whole time. Grinning sheepishly, he wiped the evidence from his upper lip, licking his fingers clean. "Please don't tell Lestrade."

To Holmes' relief, she laughed. "All right, Sherlock, don't worry! I'll pour him a fresh cup when he wakes up." Relaxing, he took another mouthful, then suddenly realised: Lestrade drank his coffee black...and it would have grown cold long before the Inspector made an appearance. Mary smiled mischievously as his eyes widened in understanding, but she said nothing. Shaking his head at the woman's utter deviousness, Holmes continued to sip his coffee slowly, savouring the taste and the welcome feeling of a warm, full stomach for the first time in weeks. Mary seemed to understand him far too well for comfort, but perhaps working in the kitchen wasn't such a bad idea.

When Lestrade and Roland finally wandered in, the detective casually greeted them both in German, enjoying their twin looks of surprise. Switching to French, in which he was much more fluent, Holmes addressed Roland and meekly requested a few moments of his time after breakfast. Roland blinked, then nodded slowly. Holmes felt his ears growing warm; the lad's latest impressions of him had obviously not been agreeable. He wondered whether Roland had read 'A Study in Scarlet' yet, and if so, how much of Holmes' recent demeanour had been a match for his callous, self-centred literary counterpart.

While the other three were eating, Holmes used the time to wash and change into actual clothes. Mary had purchased some second-hand peasant's clothing on market day for him and the other two... well, men, for lack of a better collective word: plain trousers, homespun shirts and coloured waistcoats. Not having a draught around his legs felt decidedly strange, and the buttons on his shirt were the work of several frustrating minutes; however, the rush of pride when he finally completed the task was well worth the effort. He was still without shoes, but he wouldn't be needing them for a while longer, in any case – learning to walk again would be easier while barefoot.

Holmes rubbed the growing stubble on his chin, debating whether or not to shave. In the end, he decided not. A beard was a halfway decent disguise in itself and would help to hide any remaining scars. Besides, he wasn't about to have another blade near his face yet, if ever... His hair was a little wild, but he still couldn't quite manage a comb or hairbrush – he tidied it as best he could with his unsplinted fingers.

148

Hobbling back into the living area after breakfast, Lestrade's arms holding him steady, the detective was floored by the unexpected sight which greeted him. Roland stood by the fireplace, smiling bashfully, holding a pair of slender wooden crutches almost as tall as the lad himself, and exactly the right height for Holmes. *"They're for you, monsieur. You don't have to crawl anymore."*

Holmes stared, speechless for several moments, before finally managing to stammer out, *"Roland... I don't know... what to say. Did you make these?"*

"With a little help from Monsieur l'Inspecteur." Roland handed him the crutches one at a time, he and Lestrade helping Holmes to get comfortable and find his balance. *"Do you like them?"*

"Yes, Roland... very much. Thank you..." Roland had even padded the underarm supports with sheepskin; but the most humbling part was the knowledge that he had to have been working on them while Holmes was still in the midst of his black mood.

Roland shrugged, modestly. *"You're welcome, Monsieur Holmes. It was nothing."*

"No... no, Roland, on the contrary. This was... very kind of you." Begging the young man's pardon had suddenly become ten times more difficult, but Holmes would not put it off a moment longer, coals on his forehead notwithstanding. *"And... I believe that we have... much to talk about."*

Roland nodded. *"Of course, monsieur, if you wish. Shall we?"* Wait, why was Roland gesturing at the front door? It was still pouring down outside, and Holmes was only in shirt sleeves – but then, so were the other two. Oh, well...

"Lestrade, would you mind assisting me? I'm not certain I can manage these on the veranda steps just yet."

"Actually, sir, I wouldn't worry about those for the moment. If I know Roland at all, they'll only get in the way where you're going." With those enigmatic words, Lestrade lent Holmes his shoulder again, leaning the crutches against the wall, and they slowly followed Roland out into the teeming rain. Holmes would be fortunate to avoid getting a chill at this rate, and Mary was no doubt going to have all three of their hides for this... but in spite of the impending repercussions, the detective still couldn't quite manage to keep from smiling.

Chapter 15

A Time to Heal

The three men were already half-soaked by the time they negotiated the veranda steps and rounded the corner of the chalet, retracing their route from the day before. Lestrade grinned at Holmes' chagrined expression as they passed by the water trough, now drained of its old soapy water and gradually refilling from the rain; but that was clearly not their destination this morning.

Roland led them on towards the outbuilding behind the house, which Holmes had barely noticed yesterday while he was sulking in his makeshift bath. Although mainly given to storage, the barn was large enough to double as a stable. Its single occupant poked a hairy, silver-grey head out of the stall as they entered, ears and nose twitching. This, then, must be Brigitta.

"Good morning, Brigitta! I hope you slept well?" Roland confirmed Holmes' surmise with his affectionate greeting in German, scratching the donkey behind the ears, laughing as she butted him in the chest. *"Yes, I missed you, too. You're a good girl, aren't you?"*

"Sickening, isn't it? Honestly, those two'll be publishing the banns any day now," Lestrade murmured in amused tones to Holmes as the lad fussed over the elderly animal, who was blissfully absorbing the attention. Roland gave the Inspector a half-hearted glower, stroking Brigitta's nose, and his next comment forced Holmes to turn a snort into a cough. It didn't work – Lestrade's eyes narrowed suspiciously. "Do I want to know what he just said?"

"Probably not..." Least said was soonest mended; although Holmes would have given a lot to see the Inspector's face on hearing his comprehension of German compared unfavourably with the donkey's. Lestrade raised an eyebrow, but wisely decided not to pursue the question further.

The Inspector set Holmes down on a straw bale next to Brigitta's stall and headed back to the house, leaving Holmes and Roland alone to talk. The detective could understand now why the lad had brought him out here. Any awkward silence that threatened to gather was gently diffused by the animal's placid shifting and Roland quietly getting on with mucking out the stall, while he waited for Holmes to begin speaking. Even so, he was having trouble ordering his thoughts... which were broken up again a moment later by Brigitta lipping at his hair, making him start.

"Here, monsieur, she's looking for this." Roland handed Holmes an apple from his pocket, left over from breakfast; the lad had mercifully switched back to French. "Feed her an apple and you'll have a friend for life; she's completely shameless."

"To whom does Brigitta belong? She can hardly live here all year round." The apple vanished with impressive speed, Brigitta nosing at Holmes' neck in thanks, her warm, fruit-scented breath tickling his face. He was surprised to find the scent vaguely pleasant, patting her absently as Roland filled the wall-mounted manger with hay from the loft.

"She does belong to Herr and Frau Schultz, but they stable her with a family in the next valley when they don't need her." The lad saw Holmes' frown and smiled reassuringly. "Don't worry, monsieur, Herr Schultz didn't tell them anything. As far as they're concerned, you three are just another group of tourists. Chalets often get rented out in these parts during the summer because of the springs, although most of the water has been piped into the centre of town. There are still a few untapped ones on the outskirts, though."

"Mary said you were out looking for one yesterday."

"Yes, and we did manage to find it, eventually... but you'll have to wait for the weather to clear again before going up there. Brigitta hates the rain – don't you, girl?"

"Something she and I have in common." Talking of things shared... "Roland... I gather that you know why I asked to speak with you this morning?"

"Yes, monsieur..." To Holmes' dismay, Roland's smile was rapidly fading; the lad's eyes were downcast and filled with... shame? "I've been expecting you to call me to account. When do you wish me to leave?"

"What?" The lad's air of calm resignation was chilling.

"It's all right, Monsieur Holmes; I honestly didn't think you'd allow me to stay. You've been incredibly patient in tolerating me for this long." Roland's voice, so sincere and earnest in its self-reproach, sent a wave of horror washing over Holmes.

"No, Roland – that isn't what I wanted to say, not at all!" Had the young man genuinely believed... after all this time? "Have I truly seemed so heartless, so unrelenting... that you thought I would simply send you away, without a word of kindness, without making any sort of gesture to..." But Holmes' conscience was jabbing at him, telling him in no uncertain terms to replace 'seemed' with 'been'. His attitude over the last two days, combined with the memory of his cold, contemptuous scrutiny at the falls as he idly picked the boy apart with his oh-so-insightful deductions... Why would Roland not have assumed the worst? "Dear God... What you must think of me..."

"But monsieur... after what I did... to you and the Doctor... to Maria... what must you think of *me*? How can you even bear to look at me?" Roland turned his face away, eyes glistening with tears... and Holmes began to understand, a little, how Mary had been able to comfort him yesterday, in spite of her own deep pain. Roland's words were a near-perfect match for the questions Holmes had thus far lacked the courage to ask her, but which echoed at the back of his mind every moment.

"Roland, please... You need not..." His voice trailed off, he didn't have the words for this, what he wouldn't give for Watson's talents right now – but perhaps that was part of the problem. "Roland... the book Frau Schultz gave you, 'A Study in Scarlet' – you've read it?" The young man nodded, jerkily. "I am so sorry." That made Roland's head come back around, staring at Holmes in surprise. "I fear that Watson's account, although well-intentioned, has had quite an adverse effect in this instance. However, the fault does not lie with the Doctor; rather, with myself."

Holmes sighed deeply at the boy's bewildered expression. "Roland, I wish with all my heart that I could erase every word of that story from your mind – for the impressions it gives of Watson and I, not to mention the Inspector, are highly inaccurate. The Holmes you have been reading of: he may be dedicated, determined, even brilliant... but he is by no means the great man you believe him to be, far from it. That honour belongs to the friend at his side, John Watson: the kindest, wisest, most courageous man I have ever known..." The detective smiled sadly. "And modest to the point of self-effacement."

"I don't understand, monsieur..." Roland's anguished whisper wrung Holmes' heart.

"What I am trying to say – and rather poorly, it seems – is that appearances can be incredibly deceiving, particularly first impressions. I am not the Sherlock Holmes in those pages, although I can fully comprehend why you would think so." Holmes gestured at the space on the bale next to him until Roland reluctantly took the hint and seated himself, tense as a wound spring. "And the same principle applies to you, Roland. From what I have seen of your actions lately, and from Lestrade's and Mary's accounts of your part in their journey, it has become clear to me that there is far more to you than the little I observed at Meiringen. I misjudged you greatly... and for that, I ask your pardon."

"Monsieur!" Roland's face was a study in stunned disbelief.

"Mary spoke the truth, Roland, that day at the hospital: you had no idea of what the Professor intended for me. You meant no harm." Holmes smiled sheepishly at the boy's quizzical look. "Yes, I must confess I was listening; please forgive that, also."

"That still doesn't excuse my actions, Monsieur Holmes. If I hadn't been so blind about Erik..." Roland's fists clenched. "*Why* did it take me so long to see his true character? At the very least, you must think me incredibly naïve!"

"No... Believe me, Roland, I do understand; I too have a brother." Although, mercifully, there was a world of difference between Mycroft and Erik. Holmes was suddenly filled with longing for his pompous, irritating, yet kindly elder sibling, whose excessive concern had, this time, been well-warranted. What Mycroft must have had to endure, while waiting for news of him all these weeks... Yet the ache in Holmes' chest was tempered by sympathy for the despondent youth sitting beside him. Thanks to Erik's treachery, Roland now had to re-examine every good memory he had thought he possessed of his brother, and decide if any of them were worth keeping. "Family is important – something we forget all too often – and you did everything you could to hold your family together, in spite of Erik's choices... and your father's disapproval. Regardless of any errors in judgement, your courage, at least, has been of the first order."

Holmes placed his hand gently on Roland's hunched shoulder, turning him so that he could look the young man in the face. Roland was blushing crimson at the praise, but still looked unconvinced. "And that was the other reason I wanted to speak with you, Roland: to thank you for all that you have done. The three of us could not have asked for a better friend in time of need, especially Mary. Had it not been for your intervention at the theatre..."

The detective faltered, unwilling to finish the thought, moving swiftly on to the next, one just as uncomfortable. "Even if I wished you to leave – and I promise you, I do not – I would have no right to demand it of you, especially not after the mistakes I have made... which, unlike you, I have not yet begun to atone for." If that was even possible... and now he was the one who had to look away, staring bleakly out through the doorway at the falling rain.

Holmes felt rather than heard Roland's quiet chuckle, and turned to see the boy shaking his head with a rueful smile. "Oh, monsieur... We make quite the foolish pair, don't we? Both of us willing for each other to go free, yet we have great difficulty unlocking our own chains." A mental image Holmes could have done without at the moment. "Surely Maria has told you by now that she doesn't blame you for what happened?"

"Yes, but... Roland, after you left us at the hospital..." Holmes shivered as he remembered his baptism of fire and ice from Mary's scornful gaze. "I don't know if Mary told you what we talked about..."

"You mean when she scolded you like a fishwife for planning to run off and let your best friend think you were dead?"

Holmes winced at the forthright question – the young man had as much diplomacy as the Inspector. "If you're trying to make me feel better, Roland, it's not working."

"Well, I don't know how you could possibly feel any worse at the moment." True; up seemed to be the only way Holmes could go from here. The thought was not nearly as comforting as he would have hoped. "If it helps, monsieur: Maria was only angry with you for what you *meant* to do, not for what you did do."

"Yes, she did say as much yesterday; I just wish I understood why."

"That makes two of us, Monsieur Holmes – but then, who says we have to?" Roland nudged Holmes' shoulder with his own, reclining back against the wall. "Would it kill us to simply know that we *are* forgiven, without understanding why?"

"Maybe not you."

"Or you, monsieur, believe it or not." The young man grinned encouragingly as Holmes leaned back as well, finally letting himself relax. "It's an idea worth considering, at least – although I don't imagine it'll be easy, for either of us."

"Hm, Lestrade's been giving you lessons in understatement."

Roland snickered. "Speaking of lessons..." Oh, God – seriously, did they have to do this right now? "I'm sorry, monsieur, but Maria wants you and the Inspector fluent in German by the time Herr Schultz returns. Sadly, that also means I'm not supposed to talk to you in French any more, unless absolutely necessary." Blast, there went Holmes' greatest advantage. "*Don't worry, mein Herr, you're a lot better than the Inspektor.*" Well, that wasn't saying much... "*Shall we begin?*"

They remained in the barn for the next hour, painstakingly correcting Holmes' grasp of the language, mostly grammar. Holmes was amused to note that Brigitta was paying attention as well, pricking up her ears at odd words– the animal's understanding really did seem to rival Lestrade's. By midmorning, the rain had stopped; the Inspector returned with a request for Holmes to join Mary in the kitchen at his earliest convenience. Suppressing a groan, the detective levered himself from his comfortable seat and all three slowly headed back to the house.

Surprisingly, Holmes' excursion in the rain merely earned him a mild scolding from Mary for not wearing a coat, before being persuaded to help her make shortbread. His efforts only reached as far as sifting the dry ingredients, but it was a start, and the smell that presently filled the house was heavenly. He didn't need any convincing to try a biscuit; after the first bite, he had trouble keeping himself from inhaling the whole tray. Mary let him have a small plateful and another cup of coffee, promising him more after lunch if he helped with the washing up.

"I thought you said there wasn't going to be any coercion involved?" he sniffed. "This is blackmail, madam, of the worst kind!"

"So I should hope," Mary smiled impishly, carrying the dirty dishes to the stone sink. "Having been a governess does come in useful occasionally." She flapped a clean dishtowel in Holmes' direction with a meaningful look. Sighing, he followed her into the scullery.

Worn out from the morning's activities, he missed lunch in favour of a rest, waking rather later than he'd intended. After collecting his back-dated payment of coffee and biscuits, the detective spent the remainder of the afternoon practicing on his crutches, moving carefully around the chalet, negotiating the various rooms and furniture. Eventually, he swung out onto the veranda to watch Lestrade chop firewood in the cool of the early evening, enjoying the sight of the Inspector breaking a sweat, for a change.

"Don't look so smug, Mr. Holmes; it'll be your turn, one of these days," Lestrade warned with a grin. "In the meantime, get down here and lose those crutches. You can help Roland with the stacking." By suppertime, Holmes was fast asleep on the couch again, covered in dirt and splinters, too bone-weary even to dream.

The next several days followed much the same pattern, with the addition of visits to the outlying mineral spring. It was too soon to tell what effect the water was having – Holmes wasn't expecting miracles, anyhow. As far as he could determine, the most beneficial part of the journey was riding the donkey. His arms and legs received a thorough workout just trying to stay on Brigitta's back, since Roland wouldn't let him use a saddle.

Helping Lestrade keep the woodpile replenished became a regular activity, the loads Holmes was able to manage slowly getting heavier as his limbs and back strengthened. He still couldn't even lift the axe, though; he wasn't sorry about that, not in the least. He wouldn't admit it to anyone else, but the sound of every stroke set his teeth on edge.

In the kitchen, Mary gradually introduced Holmes to different foods, talking with him about their effects on his senses and the memories they invoked; the tasks he was given steadily increased in difficulty as his grip improved. Two days after his palm and finger splints finally came off, Mary gave him his first knife – up until then, she had been doing all the blade work – and sat beside him as he gingerly began to cut into an apple. To the detective's profound chagrin, he was shaking so badly that she had to steady his hands with hers. "It's all right, Sherlock; we don't have to do this today."

Holmes shook his head firmly, biting his lip; he had to deal with this. Knives were a fact of life – he couldn't avoid using them indefinitely. He closed his eyes and inhaled the scent of the apple. The smell reminded him of the first morning in the barn, making friends with Brigitta... He braced himself, right hand tightening on the handle... and pushed down firmly, slicing the apple cleanly in half. Such a simple thing... but a huge step forward for a man who had been on the receiving end of far too many blades. Letting out the breath he hadn't even known he was holding, he replaced the knife hurriedly on the table, resisting the urge to scrub his hands on his shirt.

Now for the second step: cautiously, Holmes picked up one half of the fruit and slowly bit into it. He had eaten apple on a previous occasion, but Mary had cut and peeled that one for him. He was relieved to find that this tasted much the same; if anything, it tasted better... cool, sweet flesh, the skin firm and tart... he was beginning to understand Brigitta's weakness for them...

"...Sherlock...?"

What on earth... she was crying! "Mary... My dear, whatever is the matter?"

"Nothing, Sherlock! You were smiling..." And so was she, through her tears. "You've never done that in here before, not even with coffee!"

"...good heavens..." Holmes' own eyes were beginning to water... Mary threw her arms around him and hugged him tightly, taking him by surprise; but he was very glad to follow her example, whispering, "Thank you, Mary... Thank you for this!" He still had a long way to go, but for the first time since he'd woken up in hospital, he could feel something that vaguely resembled hope.

Mary's tears continued to flow, now that she had finally let them begin, her relief swiftly being overtaken by all the pent-up sorrow and fear from the last week, well overdue for release. The detective let his memory guide him where his instincts failed, rocking her gently, as she had done for him. She'd been trying so hard to be strong for everyone else for far too long – when was the last time *she* had been able to let her guard down?

Holmes smoothed her hair, murmuring, "It's all right, Mary... I'm here, dear heart, I've got you... Just hold tight... I'm right here... I won't let you go..." The sound of her wrenching, shuddering sobs tore his own heart to shreds, but there was little he could do to help her, except to simply hold on... and vow from the depths of whatever soul he had left to never cause her another moment's pain... never again...

Chapter 16

Means to an End

"Come on, Herr Holmes, hurry up! What's the problem?"

"Patience is a virtue, Lestrade!" Holmes called through the front door, to where the others were waiting with the donkey. Another fortnight had passed, and all four of them were making the trip to Baden that morning for market day.

"What?" Lestrade was still a long way behind the detective in his German lessons.

"I said, 'Patience is a virtue!'"

"Yes, and with you, it's a... bloody requirement! Move your arse, or we'll leave you behind – sorry, Mary..." Lestrade ducked as Mary moved to slap the back of his head.

"Yes, I'm coming – one minute! Mary, have you seen my stick?" Although no longer using crutches, Holmes still needed a little extra support occasionally. He had made numerous journeys on foot into the forest with Roland and Brigitta, but this would be the detective's first trip into town, and it was a three-mile walk.

Mary sighed. *"Beside the fireplace, where you left it."* Ah, of course. Holmes grabbed the stick and joined the others outside, shutting the door behind him. "Honestly, Sherlock, you don't need to bring that. *If you get tired, ride Brigitta."*

"Brigitta can't carry Herr Holmes for much longer, Maria," Roland grinned, adjusting the donkey's panniers. *"He's getting too heavy!"*

"I heard that, Roland," Holmes glowered, unamused. "This is your fault, Mary, I hope you realise?" Thanks to the ongoing kitchen work and Mary's cooking, he was well on the way to regaining his lost

weight, but he was still rather sensitive regarding his appearance. One of his latest recurring nightmares was of standing in front of a mirror and finding his reflection looked exactly like Mycroft.

"Nonsense, Sherlock, it's all a question of self-control: you haven't any," Mary teased, then suddenly looked thoughtful. "Perhaps I should simply stop baking for a few days..."

Holmes eyed her uncertainly. "You wouldn't..."

"Try me," she smiled pleasantly, raising an eyebrow. He hastily abandoned the subject.

Finally ready, the four set off down the path through the forest to the main road – Roland leading Brigitta at an easy pace, with Mary and Holmes flanking her, and Lestrade bringing up the rear. The day was bright and warm, but with a fresh breeze promising rain for the afternoon. For the most part, they walked in comfortable silence, something which had taken surprisingly little time to achieve.

After continuous days and nights spent in each other's company – working, talking, arguing and just generally learning how to live under the same roof – the four of them had become a mostly functional... team? No, Holmes supposed that 'family' really was the only term for it. It could never take the place of what he had known with Watson... but the detective had been relieved beyond measure to find that the other three had instinctively understood that. What was growing here didn't feel like a replacement, as such – merely... an extra, something that could even have been present back home, had he had the mind to acknowledge it...

"*Sherlock – what is it?*" Mary's concerned voice broke Holmes' reverie. "*Are you all right?*"

"*Yes... yes, of course,*" he lied, unwilling to disclose his thoughts on this occasion. "Although I still cannot conceive how you managed to talk me into this," he sighed, attempting a subtle turn of the conversation.

"For the last time, Sherlock: you need shoes, and we can't exactly ask the town cobbler to come out here for a fitting." The look in Mary's eye told the detective she was in no way deceived by the evasion. "Besides, you're all but turning into a hermit with just the three of us for company. *This will be good for you.*"

"Famous last words..." Holmes muttered. He didn't even want to think about all the different ways this expedition could go wrong – the variables were too many to count.

"You're ready, Sherlock, don't worry." Mary smiled encouragingly at him across Brigitta's back. "Your German's good enough, and your French was flawless to begin with. And given the way you look now, I don't think even your brother would recognise you!"

Doubtful... and hardly comforting, considering that Mycroft was not the one they needed to worry about. However, Holmes' still-sparse beard did mostly hide the fading scars on his face. His hair now reached down to his shoulders, the regrowth from the torn-out patches blending in almost seamlessly, and most of his other souvenirs were well covered by his peasant clothes. His hands were the one exception – there was nothing he could do about them. Wearing gloves in summer would only attract attention, and the detective was entirely without any sort of makeup to camouflage their latest marks or the damaged nails. He would simply have to try and act naturally, and hope that was enough of a disguise for him to pass unremarked.

At least he had mostly regained his old dexterity, Holmes mused gratefully, the result of many days' dogged effort. After his first success in the kitchen with the apple, Roland had approached him the next morning and presented him with a large block of wood and a clasp knife, insisting that he begin carving during their German lessons. It had taken him several sessions to grow accustomed to the touch of cold steel, his memories having a field day in his head.

Fortunately, being given a benevolent activity to use the tool for had helped, as had Roland sitting beside Holmes, calmly guiding him through a maze of nouns and verbs, giving his thoughts a different focus point. By the end of the first session, Holmes had been the not-so-proud owner of several new blisters, which had since hardened to calluses, but the endeavour had done much to strengthen his grasp and loosen his stiff fingers. Besides, the lad's avid curiosity as to what object his student was carving had been mildly amusing... and when the detective worked it out himself, Roland would be the first to know.

Mary had started Holmes on another new therapy for his hands the previous week, to his great disgust: sewing. He had mended his own clothes in the past, but only under duress. He'd never realised before how many rips, frays and lost buttons three men could accumulate, until it became his job to see to them. Just the simple act of threading a needle was enough to try the patience of a saint – something Holmes most certainly wasn't, even at the best of times. His face reddened as he remembered how matters came to a head the very evening he began...

* * *

...after losing the needle for what feels like the hundredth time. In a surge of bitter frustration, Holmes throws the shirt he is meant to be patching aside, then stands and walks stiffly out of the chalet into the gathering dusk, not wishing Mary to see the angry tears that stupidly threaten to well up. Knowing deep down exactly how childish he is being over such a trivial matter merely serves to strengthen Holmes' burning irritation – not only at his own persistent awkwardness, but at everything and everyone that has played a part in his getting to this moment, including himself and even... God forgive him, even *Watson*... The creeping guilt he feels at the unworthy thought pales in comparison to the gnawing pain in his chest, a pain that has not faded in the least since its conception two months ago.

Dear God... two months... How is it possible? Two months since the world should, by rights, have ended... and yet Holmes is still here, still functioning, just barely... and for what? So that Moran can have a more challenging pursuit, right before he finally slaughters Mary and everyone else the detective cares about? The Colonel will not be so merciful as to kill Holmes himself, oh no... not when leaving him alive – shattered, heartbroken and completely, utterly *alone* – is a far sweeter vengeance... He stumbles, and his knee twinges warningly. He is forced to pause in his blind wandering for a moment to lean against the nearest tree, cursing himself for leaving his stick behind.

Suddenly, he stiffens, heart racing as fast as his thoughts. Why should any of them have to go through all of that? Why wait to be hunted down... when in one bold move, Holmes can simply overturn the Colonel's plans, here and now? With his opponent removed from the game, Moran will have no reason to harm Mary, or the baby. Lestrade can take her and Roland away from here without any more fear for their lives – they can go home... All that's needed is a little resolve. Holmes is a dead man walking, anyhow, regardless of the outcome; at least this way, the bloodshed will be minimal. Squaring his shoulders, he pushes himself upright again and limps back to the house. He'll swallow his pride one last time and apologise for losing his temper... and pray that the others, especially Mary, will one day understand what he has to do, even if they cannot forgive.

Steal... *Acquiring* the Inspector's revolver from the master bedroom, which Lestrade and Roland have been companionably sharing, is far easier than Holmes imagined; the back of the bureau drawer has to be the world's worst hiding place. The only thing left to do after that is wait. There's no point in leaving a note – what can he possibly write that will make this the slightest bit easier on anyone? An hour after everyone else has gone to bed, he quietly rises from the couch, dresses and slips out into the moonlit night, this time remembering his alpenstock. At least Brigitta won't be surprised to see Holmes; this isn't the first time he's come out here at night, whenever he was in need of company or simply unable to sleep. Only one difference this time around – and thankfully, the capricious animal does not detest the dark as she does the rain.

As the detective hoped, Brigitta is her usual baffled but pleased self to see him at such an unreasonable hour, lumbering to her feet and nosing hopefully at his pockets. *"I'm sorry, old girl,"* he murmurs, stroking her neck. *"I know it's late, but I need your help. We're going on one last journey, you and I..."* Working by touch, he manages to get the halter over her head, but when he tries to lead the donkey out of the stall, she simply plants her hooves and refuses to budge. *"Come on, Brigitta; move, please!"* he sighs impatiently – the animal couldn't have chosen a worse time to be stubborn. *"An apple later, yes? Good girl..."* Holmes tugs on her halter rope encouragingly, then harder in rising frustration... but there is no force on earth that can move a donkey who doesn't want to be moved, and Brigitta is no exception to the rule.

"Forget it, Mr. Holmes!" a harsh, familiar voice rings out behind Holmes, making his heart miss a beat in fright. "That beast is a damn sight smarter than you!" Lestrade stands in the barn doorway, also fully dressed, face hidden by the shadows; even so, Holmes can see that the man's eyes are literally blazing with fury. "What the *hell* d'you think you're doing?" Fists clenched, the Inspector advances on the detective, who barely manages to resist the urge to take a step back, although Brigitta snorts in alarm and edges away from the brewing storm. "As if I couldn't guess, the moment I saw you'd stolen my firearm... Oh, you *can* still blush? There was me thinking you'd lost all sense of shame, along with your mind!"

166

"I know what I'm doing, Inspector," Holmes glares, trying to pretend his burning cheeks are merely the result of his anger at being spied on. "This does not concern you!"

"Oh no, of course not! You're just taking Brigitta out for a pleasant moonlit walk; what could I possibly have to worry about?" The Inspector jabs Holmes hard in the chest with his forefinger. "Look me in the eye, sir, if you can, and tell me that you're not planning to take any kind of *shortcut!*" Holmes suddenly cannot meet Lestrade's piercing gaze, and the man nods grimly, "Like I thought..."

The next moment, the detective is reeling backwards from the crashing blow he didn't even see coming. Lestrade's punishing right hook is notorious at the Yard, among criminals and colleagues alike, and now Holmes knows exactly why. He could have done without the firsthand experience, he thinks blearily, as the world tilts and spins, then fades to black...

When Holmes regains consciousness, head pounding, he is surprised to find himself unrestrained and propped up against the wall of the now lantern-lit stall... with Lestrade's pistol retrieved from his coat pocket and resting in his lap. The Inspector stands opposite, leaning against the closed gate. Holmes' alpenstock is hanging on the manger, and Brigitta is nowhere in sight. "She's tied up outside, Mr. Holmes. Guns make her nervous for some reason – can't say I blame her, really... which is probably why she didn't want to know about your little midnight stroll."

"What the devil are you playing at, Lestrade?" the detective groans, fingers gingerly exploring his throbbing jaw.

"I'm going to ignore the incredible irony of what you just said for the moment, sir... and ask you the same question."

"Why bother, Inspector, when you've obviously already drawn the correct conclusion?" Holmes hisses, as caustically as he is able through the pain. One of his lower incisors feels loose.

"I'll grant you, it didn't take a detective to realise you meant to kill yourself – I'm merely a little hazy on the details." To Holmes' disbelief, the man actually produces his notebook and pencil and prepares to write. "In your own time, sir."

"I'm not one of your damned interrogations, Lestrade!" Furious at what appears to be blatant mockery, Holmes staggers to his feet, swaying, and gestures with the pistol in the Inspector's direction. "Move out of the way!"

"Gladly..." Lestrade puts the notebook away and folds his arms, chin jutting. "Just as soon as you pull the trigger."

"What?"

"That *is* how you were planning to do the deed, isn't it?" Without waiting for a response, Lestrade nods calmly. "Fine, go ahead, I won't stop you! You've got six bullets in that gun – try not to miss with all of them."

"No!" Holmes' voice is sharp with horror at the idea. "You don't understand, Lestrade..." The Inspector can't actually want his colleague to go through with it – can he? "Not here... not like this!"

"Oh? And what did *your* brilliant plan consist of: getting far enough away to not wake anyone with the gunshot? Softening the blow by letting complete strangers find your body first?" Lestrade's eyes narrow. "Or were you simply going to make it look like Moran had finished the job he started at Reichenbach?"

"...not exactly..." Although Lestrade's surmise isn't far off.

168

"Then what? Believe me, Mr. Holmes, you have my full attention right now!" Sarcasm does not become the Inspector in the slightest.

"I was going to take Brigitta into town, wait until dawn..." One final moment in the light... "...then send Moran the message: that I forfeit his game." A message in the form of a bullet to Holmes' own heart. Failure would never have tasted so sweet as in those last few seconds, or victory so bitter for his nemesis when the Colonel's men brought him the news.

"What?"

"Moran would never have bothered with any of you, if you hadn't come after me!" The pressure building inside of Holmes demands release, and he begins to pace the stall like a restless horse. "If I'm dead, there's no reason for him to harm Mary, or the child – they can go home... And you, Lestrade, and Roland... All of you can go home!"

"And what about you, you bloody idiot?" Lestrade abandons his post and grabs the detective by the shoulders, shoving him back up against the wall, voice thick with angry concern. "D'you honestly think...?"

"This isn't about me!" Holmes snarls, face twisting in rage and anguish. "I don't matter, Lestrade, I haven't since Moriarty died! It should have been the end for both of us that day – it was supposed to be! But I was a blind, stubborn fool, arrogant enough to try to cheat death, and now... *Watson* is dead... Mary a widow... and I..." He wrenches free of the Inspector's grasp and holds his ragged hands up in front of the man's face, choking on the words, "Just... *look* at me!" Lestrade coolly follows the instruction, gaze unflinching. The total lack of reaction suddenly takes the wind from Holmes' sails, and the fury begins to drain out of him, leaving him weak and trembling in the aftermath.

169

"There's nothing left of me, Lestrade – the man you knew is gone..." he whispers wretchedly. "Sherlock Holmes perished at Reichenbach Falls, the same moment as John Watson!" Holmes slides down the wall to sit on the floor again, knees drawn up, and buries his face in his arms, his next words full of bleak despair: "You came all this way, only to find *two* dead men..." One of them simply happens to be still breathing, for now...

"*Bull!*" The strident oath rings in the detective's ears like a hammer on an anvil; he cannot help jerking his head back up to stare speechlessly at the bristling Inspector. "You heard what I said, Mr. Holmes! That's the biggest load of horse shit I ever heard – even Gregson couldn't match that!" Holmes' lips twitch in spite of his inner turmoil; some things never change, it seems. "I've got some news for you, sir: you're still *very* much alive – thank God! Although if we're being brutally honest..." Lestrade's expression is grim as ever, yet there is something else behind it... "I'll admit there are times when I'd far rather be playing nursemaid to a corpse; for one thing, it would probably listen better than you!"

Now there is no mistaking the gleam in the Inspector's eyes: amusement, combined with a large amount of exasperated affection. Lestrade's mouth is also starting to twitch uncontrollably at the ludicrous thought, and the sight makes Holmes turn his head in a desperate bid not to catch the smile... which fails completely when he hears the Inspector snort. The next moment, the tension in the air is shattered as both of them begin to laugh helplessly, gasping for air, and the fist clenched around Holmes' insides slowly relaxes its hold. He can't even remember the last time he laughed – a lifetime ago, whatever the occasion – although there can be little doubt as to who he was with at the time...

Lestrade leans weakly against the wall, wiping his eyes, then sits down beside Holmes, sighing as he collects his thoughts. "Seriously, sir... I'm well aware that at least one man too many died at the falls.

170

And maybe you're right – maybe the Sherlock Holmes I knew back then was one of them! But even if that's true, we've clearly got some edition of the man still hanging around, whining and wallowing in self-pity..." Lestrade digs his elbow into Holmes' ribs in a friendly fashion, ignoring the detective's annoyed frown. "When he isn't busy saving his colleague from being hauled away in a straitjacket; or keeping his best friend's widow from fretting herself *and* her unborn child into an early grave... Yes, that's all *your* doing! You're not useless, sir, not by a long way – that's just what Moran wants you to think."

Lestrade gives him a pointed look. "And since when should anyone take the word of an enemy at face value? We need you, Mr. Holmes." Holmes doesn't have to ask why, his dejected shrug is eloquent enough for the Inspector. "Because there's one more job left to do, sir, whether or not you choose to kill yourself afterwards. Even if Moran wasn't targeting the people you care about, the man's still a damned menace... and if we don't stop him, who will?"

"And what exactly did you have in mind?" Holmes is too weary to even bother putting any irony into the question. "You're not in England now, Inspector – this is Moran's territory. He's not going to stand still and wait for you to slap on the handcuffs."

"I'm not planning to arrest him, Mr. Holmes." The evenness of Lestrade's tone sends a chill down Holmes' spine. "As far as I'm concerned, sir, the Colonel's just a less civilized version of Moriarty; and I'm sure you remember what I said about *him*..."

The Inspector's words from their first conversation at the hospital hang solemnly between them in the grave silence."And if it makes you feel any better: there's a good chance that you're not going to survive this, in any case." Lestrade claps Holmes on the shoulder, then climbs stiffly to his feet and offers the detective a hand up. "This way, at least, you might be able to look the Doctor in the eye the next time you see him."

"That isn't funny, Lestrade," Holmes whispers, throat tightening.

"I'm not laughing, sir..."

After a long moment, Holmes takes Lestrade's hand and lets the Inspector pull him upright, regarding the man curiously. "You really aren't going to try and stop me, are you?"

Lestrade shrugs. "How could I? You'd find an opportunity in the end, anyway – although if I were you, I wouldn't rely on somebody else's weapon next time." Lestrade holds out a hand for the revolver that Holmes has somehow managed to keep hold of all this time. He passes the firearm back, colouring, and the Inspector breaks it open. At first glance, the contents seem unchanged from when Holmes first checked it earlier this evening. Then Lestrade draws one of the bullets from its chamber... which turns out to be an empty casing.

"You must have a very poor opinion of my intelligence, sir, if you thought I'd be foolish enough to leave a loaded revolver lying around, with you in the state you're in." Yawning, the Inspector turns away and opens the stall gate. "I'm going to bed, don't forget to put Brigitta away. Oh, and just so you know: you can tell the other two whatever story you want about the bruise on your face."

Holmes shakes his head in grudging respect for his colleague's ingenuity, wincing as his jaw gives another twinge. "Not to worry, Lestrade – I will simply blame it on the ass..."

* * *

"...Mr. Holmes? Sir!"

"Hm?" Holmes came back to himself with a start, to find the four of them standing still on the road; house rooftops and the battlements of the town's ancient ruined fortress were now in sight above the treeline.

"We're almost at Baden, sir; it's time to split up."

"Ah, of course – my apologies. I was... lost in thought." The detective realised he was absently rubbing his chin, and hastily pulled himself together.

"Well, that's encouraging!" Mary smiled, looking relieved.

"How so?"

"I think the lady means you weren't as pale as a ghost, for a change." Lestrade surreptitiously tapped his own chin, smirking as Holmes gave him a warning glare.

"Thank you, Inspektor..."

"You're welcome!" Lestrade shook hands with Holmes as Mary took Brigitta's halter rope from Roland. *"Good luck, mein Herr."*

"And you, Lestrade, Mary. Be careful." Lestrade and Mary began walking at a slower pace with the donkey, giving Holmes and Roland a chance to put some distance between the two parties before they reached the town.

"Of course, Sherlock," Mary smiled. *"Remember, Roland, we'll meet you at the bridge when you're finished – and no sightseeing!"*

"Don't worry, Maria!" Roland gave Holmes a mischievous grin, switching to French for the first time in a fortnight. "Come on, monsieur, the cobbler lives on the other side of the church square. What Maria doesn't know won't hurt her..."

Chapter 17

Crossfire

One of these days, Holmes reflected grimly, as he stalked up the sloping street, he might actually learn to trust his own instincts, instead of relying on the assurances of well-meaning but idiotic companions. At least he'd had enough foresight to bring his alpenstock, which was currently being far more of a help than Roland in getting him where he needed to go – namely, away from the river.

"Monsieur, wait! Do you even know where you're going?"

"Obviously..." the detective grated, jaw still clenched with leftover tension. Towards the church, of course, although the town streets were something of a maze and required a slightly oblique approach to navigating. As long as he kept zigzagging uphill, using the spire as a fixed point, he should eventually get to the Kirchplatz, without the need for assistance from his irksome hanger-on.

"I'm sorry, monsieur, I didn't know Maria hadn't told you!"

"Yes, one would think someone could at least have taken a moment to mention it!" Finding out at the last minute that the only way of crossing the Limmat was more of a tunnel than a bridge had made Holmes extremely anxious to have a pointed word with Mary at the first available opportunity. Unfortunately, that would have to wait until he was finished at the cobbler's; and if Mary believed Holmes was going to wait for her and Lestrade anywhere near that hellmouth afterwards, the woman was mad.

"Well, would you have agreed to this trip in the first place if you'd known it was a covered bridge?"

"That is not the point." And Mary had scolded *Holmes* for withholding crucial information. "I do not appreciate being treated like a child." And if Roland dared to voice that next thought...

"Monsieur..."

"What?"

To Holmes' surprise, Roland merely pointed up a narrow side street, which had appeared to be a dead end. "You're going the long way round; there's a shortcut to the square through here."

Relieved, yet oddly annoyed at the boy's unexpected diplomacy, Holmes nodded as carelessly as he could manage. "Very well, if you're that anxious to be rid of me..."

"Not at all, monsieur, you're being charming company this morning!" Roland gave him a forced smile. "I honestly can't think why Maria decided not to tell you about the bridge in advance."

"Sarcasm becomes you as well as Lestrade, Roland," the detective sniffed.

"And if the teacher's pet doesn't stop sulking, he won't get a sweet." Roland's patronising tone set Holmes' teeth on edge.

"Teacher's pet?"

"Oh, as if you're not secretly glad the Inspector's not as good as you at German!"

Holmes snorted in derision. "My dear Roland, Brigitta is better at German than Lestrade."

"At least he practices more than you – hm, that's a good point," Roland grinned. "*I bet you can't complain nearly as well in German.*"

"Well, if you're going to be petty about this..." Holmes shrugged, not deigning to give Roland satisfaction by responding in kind.

"*Excuse me, mein Herr? I didn't understand that,*" Roland purred, putting a hand theatrically to his ear.

"Fine; I won't bother trying to talk to you, then!" Holmes snapped, his simmering temper once again coming to the boil.

"Wonderful!" Roland retorted sharply, sounding delighted at the prospect.

"Oh? I thought you said you couldn't understand me."

"Who's being petty now?" Roland shook his head in disgust. "I hope you're not going to act like this at the cobbler's?"

Holmes raised both eyebrows, offended by the half-serious question. "You really think I would do that, don't you?"

"Well, I'm not the one who seems to have forgotten we're supposed to be keeping a low profile!" Roland glowered, as they reached the top of the street and approached a flight of steps built into the stone wall. "After you, monsieur."

"No, please, I insist!" Holmes stood back and bowed mockingly. "If you think I can survive without a nursemaid for the next minute?"

"Would you prefer me to go around the other way and leave you to it, then?" Roland's voice dripped with condescension. "Let the little boy feel like one of the adults for a change?"

"Look who's talking!" the detective sneered. "I'm not the one who has been gandering at Mary for the last month – you ought to be ashamed of yourself!" Even before he'd finished speaking, he knew the words had struck true. Roland's face paled, then darkened with embarrassment. The young man's eyes were downcast, and the expression in them left Holmes with a sudden, uneasy feeling that he couldn't quite put a name to.

"You're right, monsieur," Roland murmured, almost too low for Holmes to hear. "I do look at her. You think of me as nothing more than a moonstruck youth, Monsieur Holmes... and I don't blame you.

176

When have I given you a reason to think otherwise? I'd rather be silent and seem a fool, than open my mouth and prove it..."

It was Holmes' turn to flush scarlet, as the import of the lad's words sank in. Now that the heat of his anger had cooled, he couldn't even remember half of the things he'd just said, or why they had seemed so clever at the time. The only thing he was absolutely certain of was that he must be the greatest fool on earth for not fully understanding before now, in spite of what Lestrade had already let slip at the hospital.

"You love her." A statement, not a question, and one Roland didn't need to answer in words. The look in the young man's eyes as he met Holmes' gaze was enough. "God... Roland – I am so sorry." A truly pathetic thing to say, but what else was there? Roland must know as well as Holmes did that his case was a hopeless one.

"Why, monsieur? None of this is your doing... or Maria's..." Roland sat down heavily on the steps, head bowed, hands clasped. "I can't change how I feel about her – God help me, I wish I could! All I can do is hold my tongue, if only for her sake." The lad hunched his shoulders as Holmes sat down beside him. "Do you think she knows?"

"No." One thing Holmes and Lestrade could agree on, at least: sometimes the lie was kinder. "No, Roland; I'm sure she doesn't." Holmes could only imagine how hard it must have been for the young man these last few weeks, living in such close quarters with Mary, unable to speak or make any kind of gesture that might be thought inappropriate. The detective couldn't even be certain whether his not noticing the lad's distress was due to Roland's self-control, or Holmes being too absorbed with his own problems. He fervently hoped it was the former. "It probably helps that you still call her 'little mother'. You have been like a son to her, Roland – that's something you should be proud of."

"Not only me, monsieur; you've done your share as well." Roland finally looked up and gave Holmes a weak smile. "I'm sorry for what I said earlier. I have to admit, when you made that comment about not being treated like a child..."

"Don't say it, please," Holmes grinned ruefully. "I'm well aware of the irony, believe me." He sighed deeply; he hated having to do this, but he had no-one to blame but himself. "I'm sorry as well, Roland. What I said before was thoughtless and cruel, you didn't deserve that." The fault was his, for lashing out blindly in the first place, without a second thought as to where the blow might fall. He was amazed that Roland had managed to keep his own temper for as long as he had.

"Well, you did speak the truth, monsieur, even if you didn't know the reason." Roland's forbearance never failed to surprise Holmes, or to put him to shame.

"But I didn't say it because it was true, lad – I said it because I knew it would hurt you." The uncomfortable truth struck a chill through the detective for what else it implied. "Dear God... what's happening to me?" He had never thought he would be thankful that Watson wasn't here... If the Doctor could have seen Holmes now, would his friend even have recognised him?

"Nothing, monsieur!" Roland leant his head against Holmes' shoulder. "Nothing that should not be, at least. After all that you've endured, the only wonder is that you haven't gone completely mad!" Hadn't he? Roland raised his head again, smiling gently. "I promise you, monsieur, you *are* a man, not a monster... You couldn't mourn for the Doctor, or for Maria, if you were."

"I miss him, Roland," Holmes whispered, throat tight with misery. "I miss him so much I can scarcely breathe..." His eyes were stinging, but this was not the time or the place for tears. "He was my friend... and I never once told him how much he meant to me! He didn't even get to read the letter..."

"Do you really think he needed to, monsieur?"

178

"How else would he know?" And even if Watson had read it, would his ingenuous friend have been able to read between the lines?

"Oh, monsieur... You have to ask?" Roland's voice was a mixture of compassion and amusement. "I didn't see much of you and the Doctor together at the hotel, but from the little I did... When you looked at him, monsieur, it reminded me of how Papa... how Papa would look at Mama, before she died." The lad's smile turned sad. "My father was a hard man, monsieur; life cast him that way, and he would have broken before he bent. Even so... he still found ways to show my mother what was in his heart: little things, so small that on their own one might overlook them, but when put together..." Roland looked Holmes in the face steadily. "The Doctor knew, monsieur – I'm certain of that."

"I wish I shared your confidence, Roland," the detective sighed, bowing his head and running his hands through his hair.

"Well, if you can't take my word for it, monsieur, go and ask Maria; she'll tell you much the same thing, I'll wager." Roland nudged Holmes' shoulder with his. "First things first, though: I believe we're supposed to be somewhere else." Good Lord, the cobbler's – they ought to have been there by now. Roland stood and carefully pulled Holmes to his feet. "I wouldn't worry too much, monsieur. Maria and the Inspector will be some time at the market, but we should be going, all the same. Fortunately, the church is on the way."

"Now might not be the best time for sightseeing, lad." They climbed the steps slowly, Holmes managing to swallow his pride enough to take Roland's arm. After all this, it really wouldn't do to miss his footing and break an ankle – Lestrade would never let him hear the end of it.

"It'll only take a minute, monsieur. Trust me, it's worth it." They reached the top of the wall, and found themselves standing on the southern edge of the church square.

"Not very impressive at first glance, is it?" The building was some kind of brown stone, plain and unadorned, at least on this side. The only notable detail about the exterior was the bright chevron stripes on the roof of the spire.

Roland snorted. "And you're supposed to be the one who isn't fooled by appearances, Monsieur Holmes! Just wait until you see the inside..."

They crossed the small square and entered through a low-roofed porch... and the moment they stepped inside, Holmes was rendered speechless. Quite apart from the fact that his last few weeks had been spent mainly in small spaces – the cellar, his room at the hospital, the chalet – the interior of the Stadtkirche was a far cry from anything he had ever seen in England. There were few vaulted Gothic arches or heavy timbers here, hardly even any stained glass. If asked for an overall impression of the place, Holmes might have said it was like being surrounded by a wedding cake; the ceiling and upper walls were covered in delicate mouldings of leaves, vines and cherubim, all in white.

At ground level, the altar was an edifice of black and grey-green marble, picked out with gold, framing an exquisitely painted panel, although he couldn't make out the scene from here. More paintings adorned the walls on either side, framed in the same fashion. Delicate glass chandeliers hung from the ceiling above the simple wooden pews, their candles unlit at present. The late morning sun streamed in through the mostly plain windows, filling the airy space with a cool, pearly light.

The detective stood immobile, lost in rapt contemplation... until the sound of voices brought him back. He turned to his right to see Roland talking with a black-robed priest – short and thin, clean-shaven, tonsured brown hair threaded with silver. The ease of their conversation indicated that Roland had been in here before with Mary,

180

which was confirmed when Holmes heard the priest say the name 'Marta', the alias that Mary used in town.

"*Uncle,*" Roland called softly, his voice carrying in the echoing quiet. "*Come and meet Father Leopold. Father, this is my uncle Stefan.*"

"*Welcome, my son. It is a pleasure to meet you.*" Father Leopold extended a hand in greeting. Not wishing to draw attention to his own hands, Holmes elected to give a polite nod in response, which the priest returned without a blink. "*I hope you are well?*"

A weighted question, and one Holmes had no intention of answering honestly. "*Never better, Father, thank you. Excuse us, please.*" The priest's calm, steady regard was making the detective nervous, and he was anxious to be gone. "*Raül, we should leave now, or we'll be late.*"

"*Yes, Uncle.*" Roland nodded reluctantly and turned back to the priest. "*Goodbye, Father. I'll tell Marta you asked after her.*"

"*God be with you, my sons. Go carefully...*" Holmes could feel the priest's curious gaze on his back as they departed.

"What was that about, monsieur?" Roland demanded as soon as they were outside. "Father Leopold's been a good friend to Maria and I ever since we got here – you didn't have to be so abrupt!"

"Really? And how many times have you and Mary been to confession?" They left the church square and joined the main throng of people flocking towards the arch at the base of a tall, white clock tower. Holmes could see the market square on the other side of the arch, already packed.

"How stupid do you think I am, monsieur? Seal of the confessional aside, I'm not about to start putting us or innocent bystanders at risk like that, and neither is Maria!" Roland's annoyed frown suddenly lightened. "Besides, Maria isn't Catholic, she's Protestant..."

"One more reason why you won't press your suit, I suppose?" Holmes asked lightly, responding to the jest, grateful for the truce it represented.

"Nothing gets past you, does it?" Roland grinned. "Mama always told me never to mix religion or politics in matters of the heart." They stopped short of the tower and turned right into another side street, Rathausgasse, where the shop front at No. 7 bore the modest sign: 'Girard Lefevre, Cordonnier,' above a large window display of leather shoes. "There's the cobbler, monsieur – shall we? This shouldn't take long."

Chapter 18

Trading Blows

The bell above the cobbler's door tinkled with sickening cheerfulness as they entered. Holmes suppressed a wince as the noise brought a stout, balding, middle-aged man bustling out from the back of the shop to greet them, beaming in genuine pleasure.

"Welcome, messieurs! Please be seated." The man ushered them both to comfortable chairs, calling over his shoulder, "Viktor! We have guests – stir yourself! Allow me to introduce myself: Girard Lefevre, at your service. Whom do I have the honour of addressing?"

"Stefan Austerlitz, monsieur, and my nephew, Raül. I trust we find you well?"

Their host bowed deeply. "Indeed, Herr Austerlitz, and all the better for making your acquaintance! How may I serve you?"

"As you can see, Monsieur Lefevre," Holmes nodded downwards at his unshod feet, "I am in rather urgent need of shoes – today, if possible."

"My good man, you need look no further! All shall be done in a trice." A dark youth a little older than Roland emerged from the back passage, looking decidedly resentful at being disturbed. "Ah, Viktor, how kind of you to grace us with your presence! Coffee for these gentlemen." The young man's expression darkened as he surveyed the new arrivals, but gave a grudging nod and disappeared again in slightly more haste. "And what about you, young sir?"

"Nothing, monsieur, thank you. We're only here for my uncle today." Roland shook his head regretfully, tearing his attention away from the sturdy pair of boots he had been eyeing.

Monsieur Lefevre tutted, eyes twinkling. "Nonsense, young man, your boots say otherwise! I insist you allow my apprentice to replace those frayed laces and missing nails, at least – free of charge!"

"Uncle?" Roland perked up and smiled hopefully at Holmes.

"If it is not too much trouble, monsieur..." Although the gesture was a welcome one, as their funds were low these days, despite Mary's careful economy.

"No trouble, Herr Austerlitz, I assure you. I should be ashamed if your nephew were to walk out of my establishment with his heels in that sorry state! Viktor will welcome the company, I am sure."

"Thank you, monsieur." The eagerness in Roland's voice gave Holmes a guilty twinge. The poor lad had been all but starved of association with his peers for the last two months. No doubt it would be good for him to spend time with someone his own age, for a change.

Monsieur Lefevre waved Roland towards the back with a fatherly smile. "Off with you, then; the kitchen is at the end of the passage. And tell the lazy boy to remember the biscuits this time!" As soon as Roland had left the room, the man knelt at Holmes' feet and pulled a tape measure from his apron pocket. "And now... Monsieur Sherlock Holmes..." Holmes' heart missed a beat, hands tightening on the handle of his alpenstock... "I must ask you what in God's name you are doing here – in broad daylight, no less?"

The demand was anxious, not hostile, as was the man's face; Holmes relaxed his grip on the stick. "You know me?" The cobbler was clearly no enemy, or he would never have put himself in such a vulnerable position.

Monsieur Lefevre continued to measure as if nothing were amiss, etching figures on a wax tablet, his voice still a worried murmur. "Your description, at least, monsieur – the marks on your hands are unmistakeable. Did you think that those villains would not be looking for you here?" In town, perhaps, but why at the cobbler's in particular? "They ordered me to send word if I saw you."

"So why did you warn me?" Not that Holmes wasn't grateful, but trusting a total stranger went completely against his instincts after everything that had happened so far.

The man's eyes flashed scornfully. "I am not such a coward, monsieur. Animals like them are beneath contempt... and I bow to no-one under my own roof, save God and my customers. You trust the boy Raül, if that is his name?"

"Indeed." The detective saw no reason to divulge Roland's true identity just yet.

"Then you both may take shelter here for as long as you wish. I can give Viktor a day off, the lad knows nothing."

"You are most kind, monsieur," and it was only the need to maintain the role of ordinary customer that kept Holmes from shaking the man's hand. "But there are..."

All at once, a shivering crash sounded from down the passage, followed swiftly by a muffled thud. The sinister noise turned Holmes' blood to ice, but he recovered enough the next moment to follow Monsieur Lefevre's example, who jumped to his feet with a curse and stormed down the back passage towards the kitchen with Holmes a few steps behind. "Viktor, you clumsy young oaf! If you have broken my grandmother's sugar bowl again..." Then... "Oh, dear God – Raül!"

The sharp urgency in the cobbler's voice twisted Holmes' insides as the shorter man rushed into the room, revealing a sight that almost made the detective's heart stop entirely. Roland lay crumpled in the middle of the kitchen flagstones, unmoving. Shattered crockery and puddles of steaming coffee covered half the floor, and Viktor was nowhere to be seen.

"Roland!" Without a thought for the hazards to his bare feet, Holmes plunged forward and dropped to his knees beside the boy's limp form, gathering him into his arms. "Roland... for the love of Heaven, wake up – please!" The young man moaned faintly, face creasing; he was alive at least, thank God... Weak with relief, Holmes clutched Roland to him, heedless of the coffee staining his clothes.

A firm hand clasped the detective's shoulder, startling him. "Calm yourself, monsieur, the boy will be all right. Help me put him on the couch." Flushing crimson at his sudden panic, but still more shaken than he would ever care to admit, Holmes assisted the cobbler in lifting Roland to the nearby settle and making him comfortable. After an interminable minute, the young man revived enough to open his eyes, wincing as he tried to lift his head.

"Uhh... monsieur...?"

"Easy, Roland, lie still for now. You've taken a blow to the head." The lump on Roland's crown was rapidly swelling in spite of the cold compress; Holmes would have given much to have Mary's wintergreen to hand.

Roland's eyes suddenly widened in alarm. "Viktor...?"

"Viktor's gone, lad. What happened?" Holmes ignored the cobbler's disapproving look, enough time had already been lost.

"I'm so sorry, monsieur... he caught me off guard." Roland looked mortified. "He must know who you are. I found him opening that hatch when I came in..." The lad weakly pointed towards a closed trapdoor in the corner.

"Oh, that foolish boy!" Monsieur Lefevre's hand flew to his mouth, colour draining from his face. "He must have gone out through the Black Falcon."

"The tavern in the church square?" Holmes shot a piercing glare at the thunderstruck cobbler as he helped Roland to sit up slowly.

"It backs onto this building; I forgot the two cellars are connected, there was never a need..." Frowning deeply, Monsieur Lefevre brought Roland a cup of water, which the lad gulped thirstily. "Forgive me, messieurs, I truly believed Viktor knew nothing of this."

"Where would the boy go to make his report? Did you have any kind of written directions he could have found?" How long did they have left until their enemies closed in, and could Roland be moved before then?

"No, monsieur, nothing! They merely told me to rearrange my window display, put a certain pair of shoes on the far right."

"Then they must have approached him separately for added insurance. What family does Viktor have?" Although there was little need to ask, given what Holmes knew of Moran's methods of ensuring loyalty.

"His mother lives in Regensdorf. The poor lad! I should have known..."

"You are not to blame, monsieur; however, we don't have much time. I'm sorry to ask this of you, Roland, but we need to leave as soon as possible. Can you walk?" Holmes gave Roland his alpenstock and eased the young man to his feet, steadying him as he swayed.

"Don't worry about me, Monsieur Holmes, I'll be all right..." Roland gave Holmes a shaky grin. "And Maria would kill me if I let you go off alone, anyhow. What do we do?"

"We need to find Mary and Lestrade at the market, then get out of town." Whether they could get back to the chalet remained to be seen, but they certainly couldn't live there any longer. Monsieur Lefevre lent his support to Roland's other side, and the three men made their way back down the passage to the front of the shop. Holmes was profoundly thankful that neither of the other two had suggested taking the same escape route as Viktor.

"But monsieur, you still have no shoes!"

"I've survived this long without them, lad..." Holmes was interrupted by the cobbler reaching behind the counter as they passed and pulling a pair of plain, stout brogues from a pigeonhole.

"Here, monsieur, take these. They will be comfortable, I assure you." The man chuckled at Holmes' sceptical expression, supporting Roland as the detective swiftly put on the shoes and laced them. "I would be a poor example of my profession, Monsieur Holmes, if I could not fit any foot with ease."

"There's a number chalked inside, Monsieur Lefevre. For whom were they really intended?" The man was as good as his word: the shoes fit Holmes as if they'd been made for him, although it would take some time to get used to wearing such things again.

"The farrier – and believe me, the shape of your feet is all you have in common." Monsieur Lefevre peered through the front window at the street, apparently seeing nothing as yet to cause alarm.

"What we owe you, monsieur..." Although this really wasn't the time to be haggling, as the cobbler held the door open for the pair to pass through.

"Stay alive, my friends, that will be payment enough."

"You're not coming with us?" Roland's voice was far too strained for Holmes' liking – he'd have to keep a close watch on the boy for signs of concussion. The sooner they found Mary, the better.

"No, lad, I can do more here by sending those scoundrels in the wrong direction when they arrive."

"Then put the signal in the window, monsieur; it will make no difference now. They mustn't know you assisted us."

"Very well – now, go! I will tell them you were heading for the castle." Girard Lefevre's normally genial face was set hard, and Holmes was suddenly struck by the fierce gleam in the man's eye, painfully familiar... On impulse, he extended his scarred hand to the cobbler, who grasped it firmly without hesitation.

"Thank you, monsieur; we are indebted to you."

"Not at all, Monsieur Holmes. God be with you both." The man closed the door behind them and began moving the shoes around in the window, as they headed towards the clock tower. Holmes silently prayed that their enemies weren't coming from that direction, and that Mary and Lestrade hadn't left the market yet. The square on the other side of the arch was still thronged with people, booths and barrows. Locating the other two in this multitude would be a mission in itself. Hopefully, that would also make the search just as difficult for their pursuers, on the off chance they didn't follow the cobbler's misdirection. The castle ruin atop the hill towered above the town to the west, but anyone trying to spot them from that vantage point would have their work cut out for them.

"How are we going to find them, monsieur?" Roland had to raise his voice to make himself heard above the din.

Only one viable option: "We have to separate. I'll cut through the middle, you circle around; we'll meet on the far side." There was no way the detective was going to let Roland get mixed up in that crowd after what the boy had just been through. "How's your head?"

"I'll live, monsieur." Roland's brave smile suddenly faded. "Wait, what about Brigitta?"

"What about her?" Holmes had to admit, he hadn't given the animal a second's thought; but now that Roland mentioned it...

"She's coming with us?"

"She'll have to, lad. If we leave her here, the gang might be able to trace us back to the Schultz' chalet." Or worse, to her other home in the next valley. "Go on, now."

Making his way through the crush was as much of a penance for Holmes as it would have been for his injured companion. He had to silently bless Monsieur Lefevre for the wise selection of footwear, as his feet were trodden on several times. However, most of his attention was necessarily taken up with scanning the faces in the crowd, doing his best to block out all the other demands on his senses, the press of people around him, the sounds, the scents, the bewildering variety of wares on display. He reached out blindly for the nearest solid object, it was all too much, too soon, he wasn't ready for this yet, his head was beginning to spin, why had he given Roland his stick... Then mercifully, he caught sight of Mary, and the shifting world steadied a little.

Holmes took a deep breath and covered the last few yards to where she'd just finished buying apples at the fruit vendor's cart. Mary's eyes widened in surprise the instant she saw him, and he had to take a moment to realise what this must look like to her: he was without Roland or his alpenstock, wearing shoes and coffee-stained clothing. *"What's happened, Stefan? Where's Raül?"*

190

He took her elbow, muttering urgently, "There's no time, Mary, we have to find Lestrade..." And suddenly she stiffened, arching forwards slightly, face pale. There was no need to ask why, Holmes had become aware of the reason almost the same moment she did. The man who had just come up behind them had something digging into Mary's back... a man Holmes remembered passing a minute earlier but hadn't seen the face of, and whom he wished fervently he didn't recognise now. The detective had to forcibly restrain himself from making any sudden movements, no easy task with fury flowing through his veins at the sight of Mary being held at gunpoint by such vermin.

"Now, now, Mister 'Olmes, jus' calm yerself..." The crawling voice was every bit as repellent as Holmes remembered. "Step away and keep yer 'ands where I can see 'em... Fold yer arms."

"Simmonds..." There seemed little option at this moment but to obey instructions. The detective's mind raced – how had Ned Simmonds gotten out of prison? He and Watson had 'assisted' Lestrade in breaking up that smuggling operation less than a year ago.

"Flattered you remember me, Mister 'Olmes... You and the lady can jus' sit tight till the others get 'ere."

"Sherlock?" Mary's voice was tense but controlled, hands tight on the handle of her basket, her eyes locked on Holmes'. She was afraid, but not panicking, thank Heaven – she'd follow his lead.

"Stay calm, Mary. You're a long way from Dartmoor, Simmonds; Lestrade's not going to be pleased." And where the devil was the Inspector? Typical that the man only turned up when he *wasn't* welcome.

"Lot o' that goin' around at the moment, Mr. 'Olmes." Simmonds' eyes narrowed suspiciously as Holmes leaned casually against the nearest stall, arms still crossed. "Led us a right merry dance, you 'ave!"

"Well, I would hate Moran to underestimate my ability to be a thorn in his side..." Holmes barely managed to keep from flinching when he felt a stealthy pressure on his newly-shod foot, then the familiar touch of a stick on his ankle. Relief washed over him as he realised Roland was under the stall; the odds had just increased in their favour. The detective blinked and lifted one hand to rub his eye, masking any telltale reaction and keeping Simmonds' attention focused on himself... and the next few seconds became fraught with activity.

From under the stall, the crook of an alpenstock reached out and hooked over Simmonds' wrist, yanking his arm sideways and down, making the thug's finger instinctively tighten on the trigger. Mercifully, the bullet only struck the ground, but the thunder of the gunshot unsurprisingly caused chaos to break out around them. As Simmonds cursed and tried to regain his balance amid the crowd of people shouting and ducking for cover, Mary turned and swung the basket of apples straight into the man's stomach; the thug doubled over, breathless. Holmes snatched the alpenstock from Roland as the lad scrambled out from under the stall and viciously clubbed Simmonds over the head, who dropped to the cobbles like a sack of coal.

Rage and adrenaline still coursing through him, Holmes was about to deliver another blow to the man's unprotected head, when a strong hand grasped the detective's arm, making him lower the stick. Lestrade's authoritative bellow cut through the shocked cries of the crowd: "*He had a gun! Take him to the police!* All right, Mr. Holmes?"

The Inspector's cool inquiry amidst the uproar enabled Holmes to calm down enough to respond appropriately. "It's about time, Lestrade – did you lose your invitation?" And when had the Inspector gotten that fluent in German?

Undisturbed by the sarcasm, Lestrade raised both eyebrows at Holmes' odd appearance, trying hard not to smile as Mary and Roland came up beside them. "Lord's sakes, sir – can't take you anywhere, can we?" The four companions retreated through the crowd as the shaken townsfolk began to pick themselves up and converge on the luckless Simmonds, just beginning to come to.

"Where's Brigitta?" Holmes plucked one of the remaining apples from Mary's basket.

"I hitched her by the fountain." Lestrade pointed, frowning. "Time to run, is it?"

"Brilliant deduction, Inspector. Mary, I hope you were finished shopping, because we won't be coming back here."

"Sherlock, what on earth...?" The woman seemed a little stunned, and no wonder, but this really wasn't the time for explanations.

"Just trust me, Mary, please. The important thing right now is getting back over that bridge." Holmes waited until the struggling Simmonds had been hauled away through the arch, before striding over to the donkey. Brigitta was still distraught from the gunshot, but Roland managed to soothe her, and the apple proved a sufficient bribe to make the reluctant animal move in the right direction: down one of the side streets off the market square, towards the river. "But remind me to discuss the subject of bridges with you again in the near future."

Holmes smiled grimly as Mary coloured, then returned his thoughts to the problem at hand. Considering that the covered bridge was the only way they could all get across the Limmat, short of swimming, it seemed certain that at least one of Moran's men would be waiting for them there. "Lestrade, I hope you reloaded that revolver."

Chapter 19

Best Laid Plans

Holmes slipped quietly back down the steps leading up to the street and around the corner. Mary was waiting for him on the narrow footpath on the west riverbank, where the last row of houses met the water. One look at his face told her it wasn't good news. She nodded calmly and handed him back his alpenstock, whispering, "How many?"

"Two." Parker, the sentinel who had unintentionally saved Holmes from being choked by Moran, ironically proficient with a garrotting wire himself... and a second man Holmes had never seen before: swarthy, red-haired, with a scar on his chin and a large knife concealed inside his jacket. Both men stood at the crossroads of the next street called Kronengasse, which ran parallel to this path, and the street that faced the bridge. The thugs' vantage point was perfect in that they could get a good look at anyone trying to cross the river. Roland was going to have one long, nerve-wracking walk; Holmes prayed the young man's acting skills were equal to his courage. "Signal Lestrade."

Mary turned and waved her headscarf twice in the Inspector's direction. Lestrade was concealed at the other end of the river path, and should now be giving Roland his cue to begin leading Brigitta along the Kronengasse, straight towards the two watchers. "You do realise the Inspector is going to kill you if anything happens to Roland?" Mary's grim undertone stated clearly that there would be a queue for the privilege.

"I didn't hear either of you arguing when he volunteered," Holmes muttered. Now was hardly the moment to admit that he wasn't nearly as confident about this as he pretended to be. If Roland did come to harm, neither of the other two could possibly berate Holmes as much as he would himself. All the same, someone had to take Brigitta across, and a lone peasant boy leading a donkey away from the market ought not to arouse undue suspicion from either sentinel.

It was the second part of the plan which concerned Holmes the most. If Lestrade's diversion failed to draw both thugs away from their station, Holmes and Mary would have to incapacitate whoever was left, with the aid of either speed or stealth – the situation simply wouldn't allow for the use of both. If only Lestrade could fire his revolver sooner... but Roland must get Brigitta off the bridge and out of sight first. The fewer people involved in this next stage, the greater their chance of escaping unscathed.

The clip-clop of Brigitta's hooves on the cobblestones intruded on his thoughts and grew steadily louder. Unable to resist, Holmes stole back up the steps, only lifting his head above street level as Roland and Brigitta emerged from the Kronengasse and turned left towards the bridge. To Holmes' profound relief, the two thugs merely continued to lounge against the nearest wall, Roland's appearance clearly not exciting any kind of interest. Incredibly, the young man looked entirely unruffled, even smiling and calling a greeting to the pair, who shifted uneasily and nodded back, faces grim. Don't overdo it, lad, Holmes silently urged; don't attract attention, just keep moving!

Boy and donkey gained the bridge and began to cross, Brigitta's pace slowing slightly and Roland cheerfully coaxing her along in German. Learning that the animal was equally unimpressed with the enclosed space did nothing to make Holmes feel better about his impending turn. At least he'd have Mary at his side; and no panic attacks this time, he told himself sternly, deep breaths, focus on the daylight at the other end...

The detective jumped slightly as Mary took his free hand firmly in hers, he'd never even heard her climbing the steps. What he had heard was a change in the sound of hooves clattering on the wooden boards: Roland and Brigitta had left the bridge. Holmes turned and breathed to

Mary, "Be ready!" Another ten seconds, nine, eight, seven... and the two of them suddenly stiffened in alarm at the sound of gunshots: too early, too many, and from more than one gun!

"Geoffrey!" The name escaped Mary's lips in a smothered gasp of horror, her hand tightening convulsively on Holmes'... but in the next instant, they saw both Parker and his colleague abandoning their post with strident oaths and rushing down the street towards the commotion.

"Now!" Holmes hissed, and the two of them surged up the last few steps and sprinted back towards the bridge, as yet more shots rang out from downriver. The darkness of the tunnel still pressed in on him, but claustrophobia was currently the least of his worries. He and Mary skidded to a halt by the bridge's north-facing window at the halfway point and peered out through the slats, to see the Inspector running full-tilt towards the river instead of along it, pistol still in hand, with three ruffians shooting at him.

"Run, Lestrade!" The words burst from Holmes before he could stop them, despite the fact there was no possible way the Inspector could actually hear him. An instant later, Lestrade reached the brink and dived in without slowing down, his pursuers blazing away at the spot where he'd vanished. After a few more seconds, and no sign of the Inspector, dead or alive, they ceased firing, scowling and cursing at each other. The third man retreated towards the bridge, while the original two swiftly made their way downriver along the path, scanning the surface of the water.

"Let's go!" Holmes whispered sharply to Mary, his heart still in his mouth from watching Lestrade's dramatic exit. They weren't out of danger yet – if they stayed where they were, they'd be seen the next minute. The two emerged at a swift, silent lope from the bridge onto the eastern bank, the vacant guard house towering above them, and ducked through the archway, hidden from view now by the trees that thickly lined this side of the river. Roland and Brigitta were nowhere to be seen on the road, but Holmes could easily tell where they'd gone. Fresh hoofmarks led north along the river path – the lad must have been alerted by the extra gunshots and ridden off after Lestrade. It shouldn't take too long to catch them up... but then Holmes glanced over at Mary, who was leaning against a tree, panting, one hand flat on her abdomen... "Mary! Are you...?"

Mary raised her head and gave him a strained smile. "I'm fine, Sherlock, honestly, just tired... but I don't think I can keep up, you'll have to go on without me." She straightened, wincing, and waved Holmes away, cutting off his protests with her best governess' glare. "Don't argue, Sherlock; Roland might need help to get the Inspector out of the water! All I need to do is stay inside the treeline and follow the road back to the chalet. I'll meet you at the spring, as we agreed." The detective hesitated a moment longer, torn between conflicting duties, instincts screaming that this was a huge mistake, he shouldn't leave her alone like this, Heaven only knew what else could go wrong at this point... "*Go*, Sherlock, you're wasting time! Geoffrey's a good swimmer, but that current is probably a lot stronger than it looks!"

Still very much in two minds about the issue, Holmes thrust his alpenstock back into Mary's hands and set off along the road, calling back over his shoulder, "Stay hidden in the forest, Mary, do you understand? You're not to set foot inside that chalet!" Most of their belongings were still there, including all the medical supplies, but it was simply not worth the risk of Mary trapping herself alone in a building with only one exit. However, it wasn't until he lost sight of her in the trees on the other side of the road that he realised she'd never actually answered him... Damn the woman!

Holmes' hands clenched and he increased his speed, ears and eyes straining for any odd sounds or signs of movement. Please God, let Lestrade still be alive, don't let him be drowned or shot, not Lestrade, God, not him too... The detective stopped to rest for a few seconds, chest burning, right knee beginning to twinge. Then, to his immense relief, he could hear the faint sound of splashing from farther down the river, and he put on another burst of speed, fear and adrenaline giving him a strength he could never have mustered on his own.

He spied Brigitta first, and scrambled down the bank to where she was standing untethered next to the water's edge, nervously watching the two figures struggling in the river. Roland had one arm around Lestrade, making a valiant effort to get the Inspector back to shore; Lestrade looked in much worse condition than he should have been for a relatively short swim. They were only three yards away from dry land, but the bank was too high for them to climb out here without aid.

Knowing better than to dive in as well – he still wasn't strong enough to be of any help in the water – Holmes unclipped the leading rope from Brigitta's halter and hurried along the bank. "Roland!" The boy's head whipped around, eyes shining in relief. Holmes wrapped one end of the rope around his hand and wrist, and threw out the rest for Roland to catch, digging his heels into the earth.

The young man clamped his free hand onto the rope, with the same grim determination of a hawk pouncing on a mouse, shouting in Lestrade's ear, "*Please, Inspektor, stay awake!*" Holmes saw with growing alarm that his colleague was ghostly pale. It took at least another minute to haul him out of the water, even with Roland assisting from below.

Lestrade did his best to help Holmes with getting Roland up the steep bank next, then collapsed the instant the young man was safely out, shivering with cold and what Holmes strongly suspected was shock. He opened Lestrade's shirt and confirmed his suspicions – there was an angry-looking groove scored along the Inspector's left side, seeping blood, a souvenir from his narrow escape, which no doubt the careless idiot hadn't even noticed at the time. Fortunately, the bullet had missed his ribs, but they needed to get the wound seen to as soon as possible, and the river water wouldn't have helped at all, in terms of cleanliness or temperature.

"Roland, fetch Brigitta." Holmes stripped off Lestrade's waistcoat and shirt, then his own, draping the somewhat-drier shirt around the Inspector's shoulders. Silently apologising to Mary for giving her yet more work next washing day, Holmes folded his coffee-stained waistcoat to a clean place and pressed the cloth to the wound, wincing sympathetically as the Inspector hissed in pain. "Sorry, Lestrade; you don't get to die, that's too easy..."

Lestrade grinned weakly at the quote. "Th-thought we ag-greed... y-you wouldn't come b-back for me, s-sir."

"And when have I ever actually listened to you, Lestrade?"

Lestrade tried to look stern and failed completely. "Hmph, th-that w-would be 'n-never.'"

"Besides, Roland was the one who dived in after you." Once again, the young man had put his life on the line to save one of theirs – it seemed to be turning into a tradition.

"D-don't I know it! Only p-problem is, I c-can't s-scold him properly in G-German yet..."

"You might just have to settle for thanking him, then." And Holmes would be next in line after Lestrade.

Roland returned with Brigitta, carefully easing her saddle blanket out from beneath the loaded panniers. The two wrapped the blanket around Lestrade and hoisted the Inspector onto the animal's back. Holmes was about to boost the young man up behind Lestrade, when Roland stopped him. *"No, Herr Holmes, I'll walk – I need to stay warm!"* The young man reattached the rope to Brigitta's halter as Holmes gathered Lestrade's soaked garments, wringing them out. *"You should ride, mein Herr, your knee's hurting you again. Are we going to the spring?"*

"Yes, Mary will meet us there." Holmes clambered up behind the Inspector and wrapped an arm around the man's upper torso to hold him steady. *"Let's go."*

"Forward, Brigitta." Roland clicked his tongue encouragingly at the donkey and began leading her off the road, eastwards into the forest.

"So t-tell me, Mr. Holmes, w-what on earth p-possessed you to let M-Mary go off al-lone?" Impressive: even through chattering teeth, the Inspector still managed to sound completely humourless.

"Since when does one 'let' Mary Watson do anything, Inspector? She insisted we separate to make better time." Holmes decided not to burden the Inspector with more worry at present – if the stubborn woman had decided to take a detour, there wasn't a damn thing any of them could do about it. He changed the subject abruptly: "So what happened at your end, Lestrade? You seemed to have attracted some trouble back there." Trust the Inspector to turn a simple diversion into an all out battle.

"You could s-say that," Lestrade nodded grimly. "I w-was all set to sh-shoot and run, w-when t-two more thugs came r-round the other c-corner. I c-couldn't exactly delay the s-signal, so I decided to make g-good use of the b-bullets. C-clipped one of them in the sh-shoulder, put him on the g-ground, b-but by then, the other t-two were p-pounding up the street... I h-had to head for the r-river, it w-was the easiest w-way out."

"You didn't tell me you could swim, Inspector." And he really could have done with someone informing him of the fact *before* Lestrade's spur-of-the-moment plunge.

"You n-never asked, s-sir. Would have th-thought you'd d-deduced that ab-bout me by n-now, anyhow." A very good point, considering how much water Lestrade had had to cross since he and Mary left England. Now that Holmes considered it, Lestrade had never once indicated a fear of water, sea-sickness being an entirely different issue.

"It would seem you have severely overestimated my abilities again, Lestrade," the detective sighed. Suitably ironic, considering that Holmes had been *under*estimating Lestrade from the very outset, despite being given constant proof of the Inspector's hidden depths.

"Hardly, s-sir," Lestrade shook his head emphatically. "If y-you're b-blaming yourself for th-this, d-don't bother. It w-was a good p-plan, j-just bad t-timing, is all; th-there was no w-way you could have kn-known about the other t-two gang m-members. And w-we did all m-manage to get out in one p-piece."

This from the man with the newly-acquired flesh wound? "Barely, Inspector..."

"W-well, I can r-recall a few c-closer shaves th-than that one, M-Mr. Holmes." Lestrade gingerly dug an elbow backwards into Holmes' ribs, wincing at the movement. "Ch-cheer up – we're all s-still alive, aren't we?" That remained to be seen... because if Mary wasn't at the spring when the three of them arrived, Holmes would wring her neck when he saw her again – and she had better still be alive for him to do so!

Chapter 20

Loose Threads

Getting to the rendezvous was more difficult than any of them suspected, thanks largely to the unfamiliar terrain – none of the three men had approached the spring from this direction before. They were forced to adopt Mary's method of following the treeline, while maintaining a safe distance from the main road. What disturbed Holmes the most was that Lestrade showed no signs of improvement, rather the opposite.

The saddle blanket was now wrapped around them both so that Holmes could use his own body heat to keep Lestrade warm, but the Inspector was still shivering half an hour on. He was also having increasing difficulty staying awake, despite their best efforts to keep him talking. At least his wound had stopped bleeding for now, but infection was another serious worry; although the Limmat was a good deal cleaner than the Thames, one would still be foolish to drink straight from it.

After what felt like hours, the chalet finally came into view through the trees. "Not long now, Lestrade, hold on..." Holmes murmured. *"Roland, stop here a moment."* The young man halted Brigitta, peering ahead the last few dozen yards. *"Is anyone out there?"*

"I don't think so, mein Herr, everything seems quiet. Should we...?"

"No, we should keep going." Even if Mary had been here before them, she'd have left by now, and Lestrade was rapidly getting worse – they couldn't stop here. Giving the clearing a wide berth, they continued on up the hill to the northeast, Roland daring to lead Brigitta at a faster pace now that they were on familiar ground.

Ten minutes brisk trot brought them to the spring, Holmes' heart leaping as Mary emerged from hiding, apparently unhurt. The relief in the woman's face at seeing all three of them alive was rapidly replaced by grave concern as she took a closer look at Lestrade. "Oh, dear God – Geoffrey..." Holmes slid to the ground, ignoring his protesting knee; he and Roland eased the barely conscious Inspector down off Brigitta's back and carried him over to the gently steaming spring. "What happened, Sherlock?"

"One of his pursuers shot him before he got to the river, the bullet grazed his side. We couldn't get him warm..." The detective hoped he didn't sound as anxious as he felt.

"Well, let's get him into the spring, that should help." Mary's demeanour had swiftly changed from worried to decisive. "You'll need to hold him so he doesn't slip under. *Roland, you're soaked as well – change your clothes.*"

A shivering Roland gratefully retreated into the trees a short distance with a bundle of dry clothes that Mary handed him from a large burlap bag – clearly salvaged from the chalet, Holmes noted grimly. Putting the thought aside for later, he kicked off his shoes and stepped into the waist-deep pool, still half dressed. Mary applied a temporary dressing to Lestrade's bullet wound, then helped Holmes to gather the Inspector into his arms. The detective lowered Lestrade in carefully until he was submerged up to his neck; fortunately for Holmes, the water supported most of the man's weight.

Mary kept a close watch on her patient, constantly checking Lestrade's heartbeat. There was no obvious change for the first few minutes, but eventually the colour began to return to the Inspector's face, and his breathing became less shallow. Mary let out a long breath of her own. "He's going to be all right, Sherlock; he's warming up."

"How long should he stay in here?"

"I'm not certain – until he can speak coherently, at least."

"That could take a few weeks." If anything was going to bring the Inspector round...

"...heard that... sir..."

...it'd be a joke at his expense. "Good of you to join us, Lestrade. How are you feeling?"

"Less like... an icicle... thank God..."

Holmes couldn't agree more with that last sentiment. "How's your side?"

"...smarts a bit..." Lestrade shifted in Holmes' arms, jaw tense, clearly in much more discomfort than he was prepared to admit.

"Well, you did practically shake hands with a bullet."

"Hm, remind me... not to... do that again..." Lestrade's eyes closed and the lines of pain on his face began to smooth out.

"Lestrade? Lestrade!"

"It's all right, Sherlock," Mary laid a reassuring hand on Holmes' arm. "Let him rest, he's out of danger now. I'll get you both some fresh clothes." She crossed the clearing and began searching in the bag. Roland returned from changing, beaming at the Inspector's improved appearance, then started to unload the weary Brigitta and rub her down. "We'll have to dry all these wet things the hard way; we can't build a fire in case anyone sees the smoke."

Unfortunately, the weather had other ideas. The sky clouded over around midday, and the heralded rain presented itself in a steady drizzle soon after. By that time, they'd managed to build an adequate shelter for Lestrade, who returned to sleep after changing bandages and clothes, but the rest of them had to simply take cover under the trees and wait it out.

The most perturbed by this turn of events was, of course, Brigitta. The disgusted donkey knew perfectly well that they were only half a mile from home, and kept attempting to escape her tether so that she could return to her warm, dry stall. After half an hour of trying to keep her calm, Holmes was more than a little tempted to let the fractious animal do exactly that, despite the risks. That reminded him... He asked Roland to take over from him, and joined Mary in watching over the Inspector in his rough lean-to.

"Mary..." The detective hesitated, trying to choose his words with care. As he had said to Lestrade, she was certainly not the sort of woman to meekly accept a scolding, and Holmes' fears for her safety didn't automatically grant him any kind of authority over her – far from it. He sighed; how on earth would Watson have handled this situation? After living first with Holmes, then Mary, his friend could probably have rivalled the skills of the entire diplomatic corps...

"Sherlock?"

He returned to the present with a start, shaking his head. "Forgive me, I was..."

"Lost in thought again? Perhaps we ought to keep a search party on standby," she teased, then sobered at the sight of Holmes' concerned frown, correctly guessing his thoughts. "I'm sorry, Sherlock – I know you were worried about me. Believe me, I wouldn't have gone back inside the chalet if I didn't think it was necessary. It only took a minute, I already had most of it packed."

"But that isn't really the issue here, is it?" Holmes asked, as calmly as he could manage. "Mary, you knew I was trusting you to take the wisest course of action – and instead, you went into a building with a single exit, alone, without anyone to stand guard. Just because you didn't actually promise to stay out of trouble..." Mary's eyes narrowed, a familiar danger signal, but he wasn't going to back down now. "I'll admit, this is one serious predicament we're in – but if the four of us can't rely on each other completely, how are we ever going to survive?"

Her brow furrowed, plainly indicating the internal war between dignity and honesty. "You're still angry with me about the bridge, aren't you?"

"Well, now that you mention it..." Although Holmes hadn't planned on compounding the lecture. "Mary, I can understand why you didn't want to tell me; but considering what you said earlier, about forewarned being forearmed..."

Mary looked sheepishly at the ground. "I did say that, didn't I? I'll have to be much more careful in future, you have far too good a memory!" She looked back up at Holmes, eyes troubled. "But you're right, Sherlock. It was foolish of me not to warn you – will you forgive me?"

He was completely taken aback by the serious question. "Mary... You need to ask me that?"

"Well, considering the distress it obviously caused you...!" How had she known about that? "Sherlock, your hands were shaking when we were on the steps by the bridge. They only stopped when we heard the gunshots, because then you had the Inspector to worry about." Which would never have been necessary if Holmes had thought of a better escape plan. "And Geoffrey's going to be just fine, thanks to you and Roland. You two saved his life."

"Only after I put him in danger to begin with!"

"To use your words, Sherlock: you didn't hear either of us arguing at the time. There was always a chance someone would get hurt, no matter what plan we decided on. Geoffrey and I were well aware of the risks involved in this journey, even before we left home." It took Holmes a second to realise that Mary meant London, rather than the chalet. "Sherlock, you know I didn't come here only for John's sake – or our child's – any more than the Inspector came looking for you because of Mycroft." Wait... Mycroft didn't send Lestrade? "Geoffrey offered to go, the moment your brother told him you were missing... but I can see from your expression that that isn't what he told you."

"No..." Holmes stared at her in confusion, before turning his bewildered gaze to the sleeping Lestrade. "I don't understand – why didn't he tell me?"

"I've no idea, Sherlock; you'd have to ask him." Which meant that Holmes would never know – he'd rather cut his own tongue out than ask the Inspector that question; and the detective knew enough about his colleague to be certain that Lestrade would never volunteer the answer.

The drizzling rain eventually petered out in the late afternoon, although the clouds refused to disperse. They appeared to be in for a long, cold night, as a campfire was still out of the question. The good news was that Lestrade was awake again and much more alert. His bullet wound also looked decidedly healthier, thanks to his immersion in the spring water. They'd be able to move on in the morning, but that was the question up for debate at the moment: where were they going to go next?

Mycroft's agent might be on his way, but they didn't dare stop and wait for him now, and any messages sent to Herr Schultz in Zurich could be intercepted far too easily. Their best option seemed to be to head north again. According to the maps in the chalet, the Rhine river that served as the Swiss-German border was only a few miles north from here through the forest. Hopefully, that should negate the need for travel papers, until they could get back in contact with Mycroft. Beyond that, the future was far too uncertain to make any definite plans, which was probably for the best.

Despite Mary's patent disapproval, Lestrade insisted on getting up soon after he woke, so that Roland could take his place in the shelter. The exhausted youth was asleep in moments – not terribly surprising, after the morning he'd had. The older three considerately retreated a short distance, quietly filling in the gaps in the day's events, Mary and Lestrade still being unaware of what had happened to Holmes and Roland during their absence. Deciding that least said was soonest mended, Holmes cut straight to their adventure at the cobbler's, also skimming over Viktor's betrayal as much as possible.

Having spent so much time in Roland's company, Holmes couldn't find it in his heart now to blame the cobbler's apprentice for his actions. Given the choice between his mother's life and that of a stranger, Holmes could understand how Viktor, much like Dr. Joubert, had simply taken what must have seemed to him the least unforgiveable road. The detective even found himself hoping that the young man had not come to harm for his subsequent failure. There was also the question of his valiant employer. What if Monsieur Lefevre had not managed to convince Moran's men of his co-operation in their search? Sadly, there was no way of knowing what had happened after Holmes and Roland left the shop. All Holmes could do was pray, something he'd been doing almost constantly at the back of his mind over the last few hours. He only wished he shared Mary's confidence that anyone was listening.

As there was barely enough room in the shelter for one, and everywhere else was still wet from the rain, the four of them had to take turns sleeping in three-hour shifts, which became increasingly frustrating as the night progressed. Holmes tried to convince Lestrade to take his sleeping shift as well, but the Inspector flatly refused, pointing out that the detective was no good to the rest of them if *he* was half-dead with fatigue, either; and if he tried being so stupidly noble again, he'd get a thick ear – sir.

Shaking his head in exasperation at the man's stubbornness, Holmes reluctantly bedded down in the distressingly narrow space, which Roland had just vacated. All the same, it didn't take him long to fall into a sound sleep. When he was re-awoken by Mary at the end of his three hours, he had difficulty believing it hadn't been just a few minutes. Rubbing his eyes, the detective crawled slowly out into the chill night air, mind and body filled with lead. What he wouldn't give for a cup of coffee right now, or better yet, a syringe – although Watson would probably have disputed the beneficial effects of coffee injected directly into the bloodstream...

Mary gratefully took Holmes' place in the shelter – he had tried persuading her to exchange shifts earlier, out of Lestrade's hearing, but she'd insisted on going last. The detective had noticed her sleep patterns were a little unusual of late. The baby was doubtless making its presence felt, in ways Holmes could only guess at, Mary being extremely reserved on the subject. Her reticence worried him, mainly due to the grim knowledge that he was no doctor... If anything were to go wrong, what could he possibly do about it? Come to that, how would any of them know if something was wrong until too late, even Mary?

Joubert must have given her some counsel at the hospital when he first examined her, since he was not then in fear for his stepdaughter's life, but that had been a month ago. Was there anything important the man had neglected to tell her back then, believing that there would be time enough later? The sooner the four of them left Switzerland, the happier Holmes would be; but the undisputable fact remained that Mary could not go on like this indefinitely, as evidenced by her discomfort during their earlier flight. Sooner or later, the woman would have to come to a complete halt, if only for the sake of the child, a state of affairs that the Colonel would do his utmost to exploit.

Holmes was under no illusions on that issue – their period of grace had clearly come to an end. Whether the detective was prepared or not,

Moran was now coming for Mary, intent on burning what remained of his opponent's heart to ash... Curious, Holmes could almost smell the smoke, his imagination seemed to be working overtime... Wait, that was *real* smoke, what the devil...?

He scanned the area frantically. Was Roland lighting a fire? No – the boy was on the other side of the clearing, trying to calm Brigitta. The animal pranced from foot to foot, tossing her head; Holmes had never seen her so distressed... and he could see them both much more clearly than he should have been able to in the light of a single lantern. The detective's gaze darted to the sky above the trees, where a lurid orange glow was growing rapidly in the southwest, obscured every few moments by thick billows of black smoke. "Lestrade!"

The Inspector made no attempt to restrain the colourful oath that escaped his lips as he came up beside Holmes, eyes wide with horror at the spectacle. "Bloody Christ, sir... Is that what I think it is?"

Regrettably, yes... the Schultz' chalet was on fire. "It would appear that the gang have traced us, Lestrade – you need to wake Mary!" Holmes hastened to assist Roland, still doing his best to soothe Brigitta. "*Roland, can we keep her under control?*"

"*I don't know, Herr Holmes, she's terrified!*" The young man looked almost as agitated himself. "*I certainly wouldn't try to ride her...*"

"*Just the panniers, then; the four of us will walk.*" Mary brushed past Holmes, her face lined with exhaustion and concern, and put a gentle hand on the anxious boy's arm. "*Roland, are you all right?*"

Roland hunched his shoulders, staring at the ground in embarrassment. "*Yes, Maria, it's just...*"

"*I know,*" Mary smiled kindly. "*Come with me. Geoffrey, you and Sherlock load Brigitta.*" She and Roland began gathering up stray items of equipment and still-wet clothing, leaving the two older men to their task of persuading the unenthusiastic donkey to carry her heavy baskets again.

"Any idea what that was about?" Lestrade murmured to Holmes as they worked.

Holmes looked at the Inspector gravely, as the answer suddenly occurred to him. "You told me at the hospital, Lestrade, remember: how his father died..."

"Oh, hell, I'd forgotten!" Lestrade looked guilt-stricken. "Thank God Mary remembered... Poor lad – d'you think he was there when it happened?"

"You can ask him later on, Inspector; we have more pressing concerns at present."

"True. On to Germany, then?"

"Indeed." Their fluency in the language was about to be put to the test, it seemed, particularly Lestrade's. "What time is it?"

"Well, my watch didn't take kindly to going for a swim – but I'd say it was somewhere around eleven." Lestrade grinned at Holmes' sceptical expression. "You can't do night patrols in London fog without developing a halfway decent sense of time, sir."

Seven hours until dawn... Traversing the forest in the dark without a guide might be risky at best, foolhardy at worst – but what choice did they have? Their enemies were all but breathing down their necks, and they couldn't take the risk that Moran's men didn't know about the spring. Assuming there was meant to be a moon tonight, it was well and truly hidden from view; they'd simply have to do the best they could with the lantern and the flames from the chalet reflecting off the clouds...

Holmes was abruptly brought back to the present by Lestrade snapping his fingers in front of his face. "I hate to interrupt, sir, but it looks like we've got another problem." The Inspector nodded to where Mary and Roland appeared to be arguing, and from their postures, it was currently a draw. "Not keeping you two waiting, are we?"

Mary looked around at Lestrade's pointed question, frowning deeply. "Sherlock, talk to him, will you? He's being unbelievably stubborn!"

Said the pot to the kettle... "Perhaps if I knew what you were referring to," Holmes sighed. *"Roland, what is it?"* Now really wasn't the time for this, but something in both their faces made him uneasy.

Roland's voice was worried but determined. "I'm not coming with you to Germany, mein Herr – I need to go back."

For a moment, Holmes thought he might have misheard, but Mary's upset expression told the detective there was no mistake, and his apprehension increased tenfold. "Roland, if this is about what we were discussing in town..." which should be vague enough to avoid discomfiting the lad in front of Mary.

Roland looked grateful for the discretion, but shook his head emphatically. "It isn't that, Herr Holmes! I have to return to Zurich to warn Herr and Frau Schultz about what's happened, and there's also your brother's agent to think of."

To be fair, the boy's argument was logically sound, but Holmes could well understand Mary's reluctance to even consider the notion. After recent events, the idea of leaving Roland behind in enemy territory, alone and unprotected, was just as objectionable to him. "Roland, are you certain about this? If Moran's men find you..." However, it was plain from the tilt of the lad's chin that Holmes was wasting his breath. Roland had chosen his course, had certainly more than earned the right to do so, and Heaven help anyone who tried to stop him.

"You don't have to worry, mein Herr; I'd rather die than tell them anything!" Roland's face was a picture of defiant courage, although why the boy believed such assurances were necessary now...

"You know that's not what I meant, lad." Holmes placed his hands on the young man's shoulders, his anxious eyes meeting Roland's clear ones. "Roland... when we found you on the floor... I..." God forgive him, he still didn't have the words...

"I know, Herr Holmes – I'm so sorry." Holmes was appalled at Roland's look of remorse. "I should have been more careful."

"That wasn't your fault, Roland, don't you dare apologise!" It should have been Holmes begging the boy's pardon, but he knew that Roland would hear none of it. The detective realised suddenly that he was gripping the lad's shoulders too tight, and relaxed his hold. "You're going back to see Monsieur Lefevre as well, aren't you?" Roland nodded, relieved at Holmes' acceptance of his decision, however unwilling. "Good, tell young Viktor I'll be visiting again soon."

Roland laughed. "I will see you again, mein Herr – all of you. Inspektor..." The young man turned to Lestrade, who had evidently grasped the situation, despite not understanding all of the words.

"Good luck, son..." Lestrade shook Roland's extended hand with both of his, smiling mistily, his expression a mixture of concern and fatherly pride. "Be careful."

"Of course, Inspektor. Maria..."

Mary embraced him, choking, eyes filled with tears. "Goodbye, Roland...!" God only knew how she had managed to hold her tongue against further arguments.

"I'm so sorry, little mother! I'd stay if I could." Roland returned the hug fiercely, letting his arms say all that his mouth might not, before turning back to Holmes. "Herr Holmes?" Unable to speak, the detective simply opened his arms so that Roland could walk into them, wrapping them tightly around the young man's shoulders. Holmes realised with a pang that this was the first hug he'd ever received from Roland... and merciful God, he prayed it would not be the last. He heard the lad whisper softly, "Promise me, Herr Holmes: don't let Maria be alone."

"Of course..." Although the request struck Holmes as rather strange – why hadn't Roland told him to keep Mary safe? Then again, given what he knew of her, perhaps the lad believed that that was too much to ask.

"God be with you, mein Herr."

"And you, little brother." The last words were out of Holmes' mouth before he realised; but once spoken, he wouldn't have taken them back for the world, not with the young man beaming at him like that... He forced himself to let go of Roland, who took the cloth-wrapped bundle Mary handed him, before turning away and walking westwards into the forest without another word, or even looking back.

"Have I missed something? Why's he going back to Baden?"

"Loose threads, Inspector – there's a debt that needs repaying." Holmes didn't expect Lestrade to understand, given that his colleague hadn't been with them at the cobbler's. The detective walked over to Mary, staring after the vanishing boy, tears streaming down her face. Remembering his promise to Roland, which was beginning to make a little more sense, Holmes put his arm around Mary's shoulders... and was completely taken aback when she turned and dealt a furious slap to his left cheek, almost knocking him off balance. Her eyes were ablaze with anger, the firelight reflected in them adding to the effect.

214

Mary swept past Holmes and snatched the halter rope from Lestrade, who was mercifully too dumbfounded to do anything suicidal, such as laugh, although his lips were twitching dangerously. "Let us be off, *gentlemen*..."

Holmes fell into step beside the Inspector as they left the clearing behind, rubbing his smarting cheek. "Don't look so smug, Lestrade; that could just as easily have been you," he muttered.

"With this souvenir, sir? Not likely!" Lestrade nodded down at his wounded side, grinning in sympathy. "If I were you, I'd let Mary do all the negotiating from here on in."

"Be quiet, Lestrade... and find the wintergreen – I don't think I can blame this one on Brigitta."

Chapter 21

Bread and Salt

"...Sway to and fro in the twilight gray, just as the darkness is closing down..." Holmes hovered on the edge of sleep, as the haunting tune gently stole into his ear. "Always it sails at the end of the day, it is the Ferry for Shadowtown..." The singer's voice was sweet yet sad, and entirely familiar... "Rest, little head, on my shoulder so, a sleepy kiss is the only fare..." He struggled upwards out of the shadows, kicked for the surface... "Drifting away from the world we go, Baby and I in the rocking chair..."

The detective opened his eyes a fraction, careful to keep his breathing deep and even; Mary wouldn't thank him for eavesdropping, despite the fact that it was her singing that woke him. He had heard her on occasion at the chalet, but she always kept it for when everyone else was awake – and never anything like this. She must truly believe he and Lestrade were asleep, she would hardly sing a lullaby to her baby if she thought either of them could hear. And why was she still awake – wasn't Lestrade meant to be on watch at the moment? More insomnia, no doubt, courtesy of the child.

"...Sailing away at the close of the day..." Mary's face in the lantern light wrung Holmes' heart. Roland's departure seemed to have driven home exactly how precarious their situation was, especially for her and the infant. All attempts by Holmes and Lestrade to lift her spirits had been unsuccessful at best, and met with outright hostility at worst. Holmes had a greater appreciation now for what the other three had gone through at the chalet with him, before his much-needed dousing.

"...Rock slow, more slow, this is the Ferry for Shadowtown..." At least she had the chance to rest, if not sleep. They'd travelled far enough through the forest that they could no longer navigate by the glow from the burning chalet, although they still hadn't reached the river. That was assuming they were even heading in the right direction;

they could be going in circles for all any of them knew. The clouds were beginning to thin out, but the stars still weren't clear enough to use as a compass. They'd simply have to wait until sunrise for a new bearing. In the meantime, the large pine tree they'd come across had proved an excellent shelter, the thick layer of needles around its roots surprisingly dry. Holmes closed his eyes again, letting Mary's voice carry him away... Thank goodness he was accustomed to Lestrade's snoring...

"...Mr. Holmes? Sir?" Oh God, what now... "It's time to wake up, it'll be sunrise soon." Impossible, he only just got back to sleep...

Holmes groaned, "Remove your hand from my shoulder, Lestrade, before I remove it from your wrist..."

"I'd like to see you try that!" Lestrade sounded criminally cheerful for this hour of the morning. "Come on, get up, or you won't get any coffee."

The detective snorted derisively at the seemingly obvious ploy, but then the scent reached his nostrils, jerking him at least half-awake. Muttering several choice words under his breath, he managed to lever himself vaguely upright and stumble over to the coffeepot, brewing in the embers of a newly-lit campfire. "So tell me, Inspector, which part of 'no fire in case anyone sees the smoke' did you not comprehend?"

"As opposed to starting the day in your charming company *without* coffee? This way, there's slightly less chance of someone getting shot." How very amusing... "Maybe we should keep a canteen full for emergencies."

Not a bad idea, actually, although Holmes wasn't about to admit it at the moment. "And maybe you should be the one to wake Mary," he smirked, cradling his steaming cup. Damned if he was going to get *his* head bitten off by the she-bear this morning. "Or would you prefer to draw lots for the privilege?"

"Oh no, not a chance! I woke her up last night, remember?"

"As if I could forget..." Holmes gestured at the left side of his face, which was still a little tender.

"And is it *my* fault she slapped you? You want someone to blame, she's right over..." Lestrade fell silent as Mary suddenly appeared between them, blanket draped around her shoulders. How was it possible for a pregnant woman to move that quietly?

Mary ignored their twin looks of guilt and sat down by the fire, warming her hands. It must have been a trick of the light, but Holmes could almost see the flames glowing through them. Wordlessly, he handed her his still-untouched coffee and started to rise, when she abruptly placed a hand on his arm, halting him. "Sherlock, wait – please..." Her face was unreadable from this angle, turned towards the fire, but she was biting her lip. Holmes caught Lestrade's eye and the Inspector took the hint, leaving the two of them alone with the transparent excuse of checking on Brigitta.

Another minute passed, both staring awkwardly into the flames. Finally, Holmes cleared his throat, nodding at the cup in Mary's hands when she looked up, startled. "You, er, might want to drink that... It's getting cold..." He felt like kicking himself the next instant – such a blindingly obvious, inane remark – but strangely, that seemed to have been the right thing to say, judging by the relief in Mary's expression.

"Thank you..." The murmured words were almost inaudible, her smile tentative in response to his own.

"For what?" Not that Holmes had to ask, but it was clear that Mary needed to talk, and he'd be the last person to deny her that outlet.

"For letting him go." Good Lord... so much for being able to read her thoughts."You did the right thing, Sherlock; I... I just..." Mary suddenly reached up and touched Holmes' cheek; he barely managed not to flinch. "Sherlock, I'm *so* sorry!" Her eyes were glistening, filled with remorse. "I should never have hit you – that was unforgiveable, especially after..."

"Mary..." Holmes put a finger to her lips, cutting her off in mid-apology. "It's all right." He wrapped his arms around her shoulders and held her close. "I do understand... and Roland will be fine, try not to worry."

Mary rested her head on his shoulder, sighing. "You don't know that."

"No... but I believe it – and Lestrade does, as well." She looked entirely unconvinced. "My dear, do you honestly think either of us could have let him leave if we didn't think he had a chance?"

"Don't lie to me, Sherlock. He would have gone all the same, wouldn't he? I saw it in his face, but... God forgive me, I couldn't..." Mary's voice was a bleak whisper. "...not again..."

"Oh, Mary..." Words failed the detective, he couldn't think what he could possibly say to comfort her right now – or what he'd done with her handkerchief.

To his surprise, instead of weeping, Mary lifted her head and drew a deep breath. "But... I suppose this really isn't the time, is it?" She let Holmes help her up from the ground, giving him a brave smile, one that was far too fragile for his liking. "Roland has work to do... and so do we."

That 'we' occupied most of the detective's thoughts as they continued north through the forest after breaking camp, held steady on their new course by the growing light in the east. The more Holmes considered the issue, the more imperative it seemed to find a place for Mary to hide. Besides the obvious physical toll, her emotional state was rapidly becoming a serious liability, as evidenced by the events of last night. The woman was exhausted, heartbroken, terrified for her baby and now Roland. If any more was asked of her, Moran might cease to be the chief threat to Mary's life, or the child's – there must be somewhere that could give her the sanctuary she so desperately needed...

"Sherlock, stop!" Holmes halted as Mary's sharp warning broke in on his thoughts, realising with a stab of horror that they'd emerged from the forest... and were only a yard or two from the edge of a steep cliff. Where the devil had that come from?

"Honestly, Mr. Holmes, if you're going to get lost in thought while travelling, hold onto Brigitta. At least she looks where she's going!" The detective didn't begrudge Lestrade his sarcasm, his colleague's voice laced with exasperation. The Inspector must be well and truly fed up with Holmes' increasing tendency to lose track of his surroundings – and it was only thanks to his companions that it hadn't had serious, possibly fatal consequences on this occasion.

Holmes nodded at the other two in silent apology, face scarlet, before taking a second look at the landscape before them. The pit he'd narrowly avoided walking into was a large quarry of some kind, which must mean... yes, there was a village, a quarter mile to the northeast on the bank of the Rhine – they'd reached the border.

"Gentlemen, this may sound mad... but I believe I know where we are!" Holmes and Lestrade turned to stare at Mary, who smiled sagely. "Remember the church in Baden, Sherlock? You had to have passed it on the way to the cobbler's." It was a good thing Holmes' blush hadn't faded yet. "The priest there, Father Leopold... he mentioned once that he's from Mellikon, a mining community on the river. That could very well be it."

"Assuming it is, how does that help us, exactly?"

"Because he also said his old mentor still lives there; I just wish I could remember his name!" Mary's brow furrowed. "It was something beginning with 'S'..."

"Well, if his mentor is the local cleric, we shouldn't have great difficulty finding him." A sudden thought struck Holmes. "What's today?"

"Sunday, I reckon... Yes, it must be, market day was yesterday." Lestrade grinned wryly. "Hard to believe, isn't it?"

Indeed – twenty-four hours ago, Holmes had been asleep on the couch in the Schultz' chalet... and how much had happened since then... "Well, wherever we are, we're going to need directions to the nearest bridge. I could be mistaken, but from here it looks as if this town doesn't have one."

They skirted the edge of the quarry and approached the village, the signpost on the main road south confirming Mary's surmise: this was indeed Mellikon. "It appears we'll be attending Mass this morning, gentlemen." Holmes' and Lestrade's pained expressions earned them both a warning glare. "Watch your step, you two – fall asleep in church and we could lose any chance of assistance."

All was strangely quiet as they made their way towards the village green, despite the sun having risen. The sound of Brigitta's hooves on the dirt road caused a few curtains to twitch as they passed the houses, but the arrival of strangers seemed mostly to be of little interest. They found a well at the edge of the green, with a trough built into the wall and a low stone seat alongside. Mary sank gratefully down onto the bench while the two men drew water for Brigitta and refilled the depleted canteens.

"Too bad we've no way of heating the water. What I wouldn't give for a bath right now..."

"Weren't the two you had yesterday enough, Lestrade?"

"*German, gentlemen,*" Mary's low voice cut across Holmes'. "*We have company...*"

A small, elderly woman approached the well, carrying a large enamel jug. Her face was a delicate network of fine wrinkles, but her brown eyes were sharp as a hawk's, no doubt observing as much about the three of them as they were about her. Holmes saw almost instantly that she too was a widow. She wore little black, her wedding ring still on her finger, but her bearing was much the same as Mary's... although her sorrow had clearly been softened by the years. This woman's bereavement was an old, familiar garment, made comfortable by constant wear; it seemed so desperately sad to hope that Mary would one day attain that kind of serenity.

"Good morning, mein Frau!" Holmes suppressed a wince at Lestrade's cheerful greeting. The Inspector's accent was still atrocious, no-one listening could possibly mistake him for anything but English.

The old woman nodded, guardedly. "Good morning, Jungen, Fräulein..." Mary hid a smile on hearing Holmes and Lestrade addressed as 'lads', then politely asked where they might find the village priest. "Father Siegfried?" The widow's eyes narrowed suspiciously. "And what would you three be wanting with him, now?"

"Only to speak with him, good mother," Mary smiled. "We've come from a protégé of his in Baden, a Father Leopold; perhaps you know of him?"

The woman's eyes widened in surprise. "Good heavens – you must mean young Leopold Fischer! Well, well... that's a name I've not heard for some time! And in Baden now, you say?"

"Mein Frau, if we may?" Lestrade gestured politely at the woman's empty jug. She relinquished it with a nod of approval, sitting down on the stone bench beside Mary, as Holmes and the Inspector began winching the bucket back up.

"So how does Leopold fare these days – is he well?"

"He's very well, mother; he will certainly be glad to know you asked after him."

"I'm sure!" the woman sniffed. "You can tell the young rascal the next time you see him that I still haven't forgotten about my chimney – not if I lived to be a hundred, I wouldn't!"

Lestrade raised an eyebrow. "Chimney?"

"You heard me, young man!" wagging a stern finger at the Inspector. "It's a wonder I'm not completely white-haired from all those childish pranks of his!"

"We're sorry to hear it, mein Frau." This really wasn't the time for stories – now that they knew Father Siegfried's name, they could move on to whatever passed for a church in this place. "However..."

"Tell us about it, good mother, please!" Mary swiftly interrupted Holmes' barely begun protest, giving the widow her most winsome smile. "Was Leopold very wild as a boy?"

"Enough to try the patience of a dozen saints!" the woman snorted, shaking her head, but with a faint twinkle in her eye. "Honestly, the scrapes that lad got himself into, even after the good Father took him under his wing..."

Contrary to Holmes' initial misgivings, the time spent listening to stories of the young Leopold's exploits proved extremely fruitful. The widow, known in the village as Mother Weibchen, invited them back to her cottage for breakfast, a welcome supplement to their first meal of black coffee and day-old bread two hours before. Holmes even managed to put away a bowl of porridge without choking, although he

223

firmly declined a second helping. Fortunately, Lestrade and Mary were more than able to do justice to their hostess' standards of hospitality.

Mother Weibchen had noticed Mary's condition at first glance, and spent most of the time fussing over her, which Mary tolerated with surprisingly good grace. Even so, Holmes observed curiously that the widow asked no actual questions about the child, or any of them, come to that. They'd found another well-wisher, one who was wise enough not to pry, thankfully. The less the woman knew, the less danger she'd be in if Moran's men tracked them to Mellikon.

Knowing that the widow would be deeply offended by any offer of payment, Mary insisted that they help with the chores before leaving for church. She and Holmes washed the breakfast dishes, while Lestrade followed Mother Weibchen out the back door, returning with a large armful of logs for the kitchen wood box and a bemused expression.

"All right, Lestrade?"

"Yes, fine; but now I know why the villagers call her 'Mother Hen'... She must have at least a dozen chickens back there! Brigitta seems to be enjoying the company, though."

"You didn't notice the noise they were making before now? For shame, Inspector."

"*You* didn't notice you were walking towards a cliff earlier?" Their hostess' timely return saved Holmes from having to think of an appropriate response.

Mellikon had come to life by the time the bell chimed to signal Mass. The village chapel itself was a tiny affair, which could have fitted easily into the main living area of the Schultz chalet, with barely enough room for the thirty-odd parishioners and their unexpected visitors. Holmes seemed to be the only one bothered by the crush, however. He reserved a bench at the very back for the three of them, ignoring the pointed looks from the family of four who arrived soon after, and who obviously considered this to be their pew. Mary managed to smooth the parents' ruffled feathers, but the look in her eye as she sat down warned Holmes they'd be discussing this later.

Father Siegfried wasn't much taller than their hostess, with a balding head under his biretta, but Holmes could easily believe that Father Leopold had been a protégé of his. The elderly priest had a simple dignity about him which automatically commanded respect. Unfortunately, the detective found himself unable to appreciate that for long. His gaze was constantly being drawn, against his will, to the crucifix above the altar, which was far too graphically depicted for his liking. The blood and scars on the body of Christ kept causing recent memories to resurface...

Just as Holmes was wondering whether he could possibly slip out without causing further offence – no chance of leaving unseen – he felt Mary take his hand and hold it tight. "Put your head down, Sherlock," she whispered softly. "No-one will comment, they'll just think you're praying." He already was... and what infernal muse had made Father Siegfried choose the Scripture reading: 'By His wounds we are healed'? This was the last time the detective would ever put himself through something like this, even Moran could have taken notes. Discarding propriety, he leant forward and put his head between his knees, taking deep, shuddering breaths. He could hear the curious murmurs of the villagers around him, but right now, he didn't give a damn... His ears were ringing... colours dancing in front of his eyes...

When Holmes opened them again, he was lying on his back on the grass outside, looking up at the blurred, anxious face of the Inspector. "Mr. Holmes? Can you hear me?"

The detective groaned, trying to focus. "What happened?"

"You passed out." And Holmes could clearly hear the unspoken: 'You stupid idiot...' "Why didn't you just tell us it was too much, sir? We could have gotten you out of there without causing a scene!"

Because acknowledging his claustrophobia had seemed far more humiliating at the time. "Where's Mary?"

"Inside, doing damage control. Oh, don't look like that, Mr. Holmes. It's not as bad as you might think." Easy for Lestrade to say – Holmes was fairly certain the Inspector had never fainted in church, of all places. "Mary can tell the villagers whatever they need to hear, she's good at that! All we have to do is keep from looking surprised."

Holmes grinned sheepishly as his colleague helped him to sit up. "Are you certain you're equal to the task, Inspector?"

"That's the spirit, sir," Lestrade smiled. "Think you can handle going back in? Although, personally, I've had my fill of religion for one morning – I'd much rather stay out here."

The Inspector's innocent expression didn't deceive Holmes for a moment, but he was grateful for the attempt to spare what little remained of his dignity. "I suppose it would be inconsiderate to interrupt a second time."

"Good point." Lestrade eased Holmes to his feet and they took a seat on the wooden bench by the door. The sound of a hymn being sung unaccompanied came faintly through it, although the detective didn't recognise the tune. "Are you sure you're all right, sir?"

"I believe my pride's the only casualty in this instance," Holmes sighed. "I'll live... but why are only the two of us out here?"

"Oh, believe me, there was no shortage of volunteers to help carry you outside – but somehow I didn't think you'd want an audience when you came round. Which reminds me..." Lestrade pulled a small flask from his pocket, which turned out to contain a fine brandy.

"Compliments of Father Siegfried – easy, Mr. Holmes, no need to inhale it!" as Holmes choked on the sip he'd just taken.

"Brilliant timing, Lestrade," he croaked, wincing as the man thumped his back. If he didn't know better...

"Sorry about that. Seriously, though, I don't think we have to worry about offending the good Father's sensibilities. He does seem the unshockable sort."

"He'd have to be, with Leopold as his protégé." Although Holmes suspected that most of the widow's tales could be taken with a pinch of salt. "How much longer before we can talk with him?"

"Another half hour, I'd say. But if you don't mind my asking, Mr. Holmes: why are you so impatient? You've had a fire lit under you ever since Roland left, and my gut tells me this isn't just about shaking off our enemies. If you've got anything you want to share, now's the time..." Lestrade's gaze nailed Holmes to the bench. "Especially since Mary is out of earshot, finally. Would I be right in thinking this has something to do with her?"

Holmes nodded slowly, frowning. "She's exhausted, Lestrade. You saw what she looked like in camp this morning, and don't tell me that was a healthy pregnant glow! This would be hard enough on her even if we weren't fleeing for our lives, but with everything combined... However strong Mary thinks she is, this can't be good for her, or the child." He bowed his head, hands clenching in agitation. "She can't go on like this, Lestrade; I won't allow it! If anything happens to either of them..."

Holmes didn't dare even finish the thought, but there was no need to do so. Lestrade's grim expression was a match for the detective's own – they both would rather die than allow the unthinkable to occur. "So you're trying to find her a place to hide?"

"If at all possible, which is the chief reason I want to speak with Father Siegfried. If anyone in this region knows of a safe refuge, it'll be him."

Lestrade snorted. "Very likely, but there's a problem you might not have considered: a hiding place only works when the person is willing to stay in it. I gather you haven't actually mentioned any of this to Mary?"

"Not yet."

"Then I suggest you improve your diplomatic skills in short order – because the only way Mary is going to agree to this is if she thinks it's her idea..."

Chapter 22

Sanctuary

"Bless me, Father, for I have sinned." The look on Mary's face when she heard Holmes was going to confession was one memory he would cherish until the end of his days.

"I know," came the unexpected response from the man sitting beside him on the front bench, their backs to the altar and its gruesome effigy. "Although somehow I doubt that is why you are here." Father Siegfried's mouth quirked in mild amusement as Holmes hesitated, uncertain whether to be impressed or worried by the man's insight. "My son, it is an essential part of my profession to see further than most people." Something they had in common, then. "But perhaps you would be more comfortable speaking your native tongue?"

Holmes' eyes widened at the realisation that the priest had been using English for the last half minute and the detective hadn't even noticed. Good Lord, he was actually beginning to *think* in German! He shook his head in disgust at his own ironic lack of awareness, trying to recollect his scattered thoughts. "You're right, Father. I will not insult you by asking for your discretion; but I fear for your safety, should you choose to aid us more than you have already." Speaking of which... Holmes offered the brandy flask back to the cleric, who waved it away with a knowing smile.

"Keep it, lad; I suspect you will be needing a stiff drink more than I in the near future. What did you wish to ask of me – which you did not wish Marta to be privy to?"

The man's perception continued to surprise Holmes. "How much has she told you of our situation?"

"Nothing whatever; although I will admit, the tale she told my flock after your fainting spell was most entertaining." Father Siegfried chuckled lightly at the detective's reddening face. "The woman possesses the gift of storytelling, that much is obvious." As did her husband... "Mother Weibchen took you in without hesitation – the good widow has something of an instinct for the deserving – and that is all I need to know, save for what assistance you require."

"Just one thing, Father: sanctuary for Marta. Her life and her child's are in grave danger; she needs a place where she can rest." Thank God Holmes did not have to explain further.

The priest looked thoughtful. "You do not mean here, I presume?" Holmes shook his head firmly, appalled at the idea.

"Do not look so anxious, my son. I believe I can help you – and you need not journey any great distance, either. Mother Weibchen mentioned that you have encountered my protégé, Leopold, in Baden; are you aware that it has a sister town in Germany, of sorts?"

"Not until this moment – what of it?"

"It also is a spa town; amusingly enough, its name is Baden-Baden. However, it is not merely noted for its thermal springs... On the outskirts of the town stands Lichtenthal Abbey." The priest sighed sadly. "One of the few cloisters still in existence since the recent Kulturkampf." 'Culture conflict'? Something to ask about another time. "I would say that that is Marta's best chance for refuge. The Abbess will be certain to grant sanctuary to her, at least, if not all of you. I can write a letter of introduction, if you wish."

"You are most kind, Father, but the fewer written records of our presence anywhere, the better." Father Siegfried nodded approvingly. "Where is this place?"

"Southwest Germany, just north of the Black Forest. The easiest way to reach it from here is on the Rhine – you merely need to travel downriver until you come abreast of the town."

230

"Do you happen to have a map?" Lichtenthal Abbey was sounding increasingly like the perfect hiding place, and not just for Mary's benefit, either. An idea had begun to take shape at the back of Holmes' mind.

"Of course, in the sacristy."

By the time Holmes and Father Siegfried left the chapel, the sun was high, and Lestrade and Mary were nowhere in sight. "They must have gone back to the widow's house. We will see you tonight, Father."

"Until then, my son. May God smile on your efforts with Marta – you have a difficult task ahead of you." That was putting it mildly.

Heading back to Mother Weibchen's cottage alone meant Holmes had to run a gauntlet of wide-eyed stares from every villager he encountered on the way. He'd forgotten to ask the good Father exactly what tale Mary had fobbed the curious parishioners off with – not that it would have done him much good, anyhow, given a story's propensity to evolve in the retelling. One more thing for him to discuss with Mary later...

He arrived back at the cottage to find Lestrade sitting in the open front doorway with a loaded plate on his lap. "Banished already, Lestrade? That's a new record, even for you." Holmes caught the apple the Inspector lobbed at his head with ease, joining him on the step. "I assume Mary is sleeping?"

"Finally." Lestrade nodded down at the plate of food, indicating that the detective should help himself. "How was 'confession'?"

"Thank you, it was most enlightening."

"Then you found what you were looking for."

Holmes nodded, smiling faintly in anticipation of his colleague's reaction. "Have you ever heard of a spa town in Germany called Baden-Baden?"

Lestrade barely avoided choking on a mouthful of bread and cheese. "You're pulling my leg! Seriously?" The Inspector snickered. "Lord's sakes... Why there, though?"

"Several reasons, the chief one being Mary's prospective new home..." Holmes couldn't resist the slight dramatic pause. "Lichtenthal Abbey."

Lestrade whistled, clearly impressed. "Good God – I'll say this for you, Mr. Holmes, you certainly don't do anything by halves!"

"Well, it was Father Siegfried's suggestion, but I agree with his reasoning. If Mary isn't safe on holy ground, of all places..."

Lestrade snorted, glancing at Holmes dubiously. "Moran's not a ruddy vampire, sir, although that would explain a lot. He's hardly going to burst into flames if he crosses the threshold!"

"I am aware of that, Lestrade!" Holmes glared, offended by his colleague's apparent doubts regarding his grip on reality. "However, the Colonel was *once* a gentleman – and that being the case, there is bound to be some level to which even he wouldn't descend." One had to hope... Holmes' previous encounters with the man had done nothing to fill him with confidence in that respect. "In any event, the abbey is Mary's best option at the moment, even if only for a short while."

"So what will the two of us be doing? You don't mean to wait for Roland to catch up?"

"Of course – but all three of us staying in town would be foolish, in spite of the baths." Holmes believed he had gone as far as he could with that particular treatment, anyhow. "As much as it pains me to admit it, Lestrade," he sighed, "I am still in no condition to hold my own in any kind of a fight, fair or otherwise – something I mean to remedy." Especially with the perilous task ahead of them...

"What did you have in mind?"

"The town lies beside the Black Forest. According to the good Father, a person might wander in there for weeks without meeting another soul." The detective exhaled impatiently as Lestrade looked confused. "I need a place to exercise, Lestrade, and we can hardly use the cloister grounds; the Abbess would show all three of us the door for that kind of disruption!"

The Inspector's eyes narrowed warily as understanding dawned. "So you plan to use the forest as a training ground?"

"Exactly."

Lestrade grimaced. "And you want me to be your trainer, I suppose?"

"If you've no objection. I have seen you drilling the new recruits at the Yard on occasion. You do seem to know how to get the best from your students." A back-handed compliment, perhaps, but a sincere one.

"Lung power and bullying tactics, mostly." The Inspector shook his head, a wolfish grin slowly appearing. "Are you sure you're ready for this, sir?"

"Not at all – but that is hardly the issue."

"True," Lestrade shrugged casually, but with a mischievous glint in his eye. "All right, as you like. When do we leave?"

"Tonight. Father Siegfried is arranging transport downriver for us; but first, you and I have some diplomatic affairs to attend to." Holmes glanced inquiringly at his colleague. "How are your acting skills?"

"I've done my share on the job before now – why?"

"As you pointed out earlier, Inspector, Mary needs to believe this is her idea. A little obstinacy can achieve a great deal, if properly applied."

They discussed strategy while waiting for Mary to wake. Ironically, it was only after they had worked out the details that doubts began to creep in. Holmes' conscience kept jabbing at him, reminding him of the very last time he'd practiced deception in what he thought was a good cause... and for the exact same reason. What if he was mistaken, and taking Mary to the abbey was the worst possible course of action? As he'd promised Roland, she would not be alone, and yet... Not so many days ago, he had vowed never to hurt her again, and now look at him. If he and Lestrade didn't manage to put on a convincing performance, Mary would probably refuse to speak to either of them for at least a year, and Holmes wouldn't blame her in the slightest.

The detective was roused from his brooding by Lestrade nudging him. "It's time, sir, are you ready?"

"As ready as I'll ever be," Holmes muttered, frowning. "Although I must admit to some misgivings... and don't look at me that way, Lestrade, I know it was my idea to begin with!"

"Well, it's not as if Mary doesn't have a choice in the matter, is it? Nobody's forcing her to pick a side – that's up to her. And of all the bloody arrogant fools I've ever had the bad luck to work with, Mr. Holmes, you top the list!" in a slightly louder voice as Mary's footsteps could be heard behind them in the narrow front passage. "It wouldn't kill you to at least think about it!"

No turning back now... "What precisely is there to think about, Inspector? You've certainly done little enough of that while concocting this absurd scheme!"

"What on earth do you two think you're doing?" Mary's voice cut between the two men, sharp with annoyance. "You'll bring the whole village to the door at this rate!"

"Oh, hell." Lestrade gave Holmes his best '*Now* see what you've done' glare, and Mary a sheepish grin. "Sorry if we woke you, Mary. This was *supposed* to be a discussion for all three of us..."

Mary gave Lestrade a reassuring smile, which was only slightly strained. "Well, actually, you didn't – I was already awake. It would be helpful to know what you're talking about, however."

"Lestrade's been contending for village idiot," Holmes glowered, "But he seems to be overqualified."

"Sherlock!" Mary's scandalised face gave him pause; that might have been a step too far. His eyes flickered a fleeting yet heartfelt apology towards the Inspector, who recaptured Mary's attention with the explanation she was still awaiting.

"I had a talk with Father Siegfried earlier while you were sleeping. He suggested where we can go next to let this stubborn... that is, Mr. Holmes, get back to full health – as much as possible, anyhow."

Mary's annoyed expression turned swiftly to curiosity. "Where is this place?"

"A spa town north of the Black Forest; there's some kind of monastery there, he says."

"He said it's a *priory*, Lestrade!" Holmes smirked. "We're all going to blend in perfectly with a cloisterful of nuns!" And he had to fight the urge to snort at the sudden mental image of his colleague in a habit.

"Sanctuary is sanctuary, Mr. Holmes, and beggars can't be choosers! Besides, if anyone can persuade them to take all of us in, it'll be Mary."

Mary flushed pink at the unexpected compliment, smiling shyly. "What did you say the town's name was?"

"Baden-Baden. Apparently, it's something of a sister town to the one we just came from."

Mary looked thoughtful. "And it has mineral baths as well?"

"Well, considering that 'Baden' *means* 'bath' – as if I hadn't had enough of those to last a lifetime..." Holmes muttered peevishly.

Lestrade sighed in apparent frustration. "Admit it, sir: you're still not completely recovered yet, in spite of all the exercise you've been getting."

"Really? So what about the marketplace – that was sheer luck, I suppose?"

"Well, it wasn't just you there, was it? *And* it's only thanks to Roland that Mary didn't get shot! I'd love to see you try to hold your own, one on one."

"Your confidence is truly inspiring, Lestrade," Holmes sniffed. "Besides, if we don't keep moving, Moran's men may catch up before we know it. We've spent far too much time here as it is."

"And exactly how are they going to know where we've gone? The river's the best way we've got to cover our tracks."

"Geoffrey does have a point, Sherlock," Mary interjected calmly. "They'll have no way of knowing where we've put ashore; they could scour both banks in either direction for weeks and never pick up the trail!"

"You forget they have the perfect source of information right here in the village," Holmes growled.

"Assuming they even trace us here, sir," Lestrade retorted sharply, "If you don't think we can trust Father Siegfried to keep silent, why did you even bother going to confession?"

"That is not the point..."

"It's exactly the point!"

"Sherlock," Mary laid a gentle hand on Holmes' arm as he and Lestrade stood glaring at each other, both completely out of arguments. "You're right, we do need to keep moving..." and for one horrified instant, the detective wondered if he'd actually won the fight. That wasn't part of the plan! "But it couldn't hurt to pass through there, at least." Thank God... Holmes caught an echoing glimmer of relief in Lestrade's eyes as Mary turned towards the Inspector, chin tilted at a very familiar angle. "How soon can we leave?"

Careful to maintain his half of the charade, Holmes turned and stalked around the side of the house without another word, although his tension was not merely a façade. They'd succeeded in obtaining, if not exactly what he and Lestrade had hoped for, then a workable compromise, but the detective was still no happier about it. In spite of all their emotional blackmail – there really was no other term for it – Mary had been able to put her personal feelings aside and find the middle road, a truly admirable achievement. Lestrade was not the only one whose limits Holmes might never get; and he suddenly no longer cared whether Mary discovered what they'd done. She could hardly despise him more than he did himself at that very moment.

He found Mother Weibchen in the back garden, feeding her chickens. "*Junge,*" she greeted with an enigmatic smile. Good Lord, Holmes would never grow accustomed to being called 'lad'. The widow nodded her head down at the bucket of feed, inviting him over. He took the pail from her and continued scattering the grain for the jostling hens, while she began searching the nesting boxes for eggs.

Brigitta was contentedly grazing by the hedge. Seeing her reminded Holmes that they hadn't yet discussed what to do with the animal. They certainly couldn't take her with them on the boat. Setting the empty bucket by the back door, he walked over to the donkey, who looked up at his approach briefly before turning her attention back to more important matters. "Hello, old girl, you're looking well," he murmured affectionately, stroking her neck. "Our hostess is spoiling you dreadfully, isn't she?"

"Aye, Brigitta's a sweet thing, she is," came the widow's voice from behind. "But what are you planning to do with her when you leave tonight, I'd like to know?"

"Actually, mein Frau, I wanted to speak with you about that." There was no need to ask how their hostess knew of their plans; no doubt she had been eavesdropping during their dispute, and she'd shown no confusion when Lestrade had occasionally lapsed into English in front of her. "Do you know of anyone in this area in need of a donkey? Brigitta has been a faithful companion, but she can't come with us where we're going."

Mother Weibchen nodded. "I'll see what I can do, lad. She'll have a good home, at least, that much I can promise."

"Thank you, good mother – for everything." Holmes followed her back to the house, cradling the basket of eggs. "We are leaving tonight... but our enemies may follow soon after. Please, do what you must to protect yourself."

"Don't you fret, young one," Mother Weibchen chuckled good-naturedly. "This old bantam knows a thing or two about keeping secrets, believe it or not!"

"Of that, 'Mother Hen', I have no doubt," Holmes replied with mock gravity, earning himself a light swat on the shoulder, the widow's stern reprimand about respecting one's elders tempered by the upturned corners of her mouth.

The other two were talking by the fire in the sitting room when they entered, faces anxious. Holmes nodded stiffly at Mary in grudging apology, but said nothing. Thankfully, she accepted the curt gesture without reserve. Still feeling guilty about the necessary deception, Holmes allowed Mary to coax him out of his 'sulk' with relative ease. The rest of the afternoon passed agreeably, made more so by Holmes relieving his companions' worries about Brigitta's fate. Lestrade also pointed out encouragingly that whereas their pursuers wouldn't know to look for her, the donkey would be a helpful pointer for Roland if he ever came this way.

"Although he'll still have to leave Brigitta wherever she is. I just hope he doesn't get too upset with us for abandoning her here."

"I imagine he'll be far more relieved to know that she's in good health and out of harm's way," Mary smiled reassuringly. Holmes caught Lestrade's eye, their thoughts clearly following the same lines. If only the exasperating woman would show that level of consideration for herself, they'd have much less to worry about! It might be wise to remember that particular quote for another time.

Supper was eaten in comfortable silence, Mother Weibchen chasing them from the kitchen immediately afterwards with a dripping dishcloth. *"Get along, you three. Rest while you can, you'll need it!"* A truer word was never spoken, although sleep proved elusive as they waited for darkness to fall, which seemed to be lagging on purpose.

At last, a few minutes before the kitchen clock was due to cuckoo nine, the three companions gathered up their belongings, bid a grateful farewell to the widow, and slipped out the back door into the moonlit night. Mother Weibchen's cottage stood at the southern end of the village, so the best way to get to the Rhine was by circling the western outskirts, rather than taking the direct route through the streets. The wisdom of that choice became fully apparent as they approached the river.

"Oh, hell..." Lestrade's murmured oath made the hair stand up on the back of Holmes' neck, and all three swiftly melted into the shadow of the nearest hedge. There was indeed a boat of some kind waiting for them, moored to the bank, but to reach it, they'd have to get past the group of half-dozen villagers waiting at the crossroads. What on earth...?Why was there a mob at what was supposed to be their escape route?

"What in blazes is going on?" Lestrade breathed in dismay. "Shouldn't everyone be in bed at this time of night?"

"I think they've come to see us off." Mary's brow was furrowed, torn between gratitude and annoyance. "And we can't get to the boat unseen with all of them standing there!"

"Yes, and how would they know the time and place, unless... you don't think Father Siegfried told them?"

"No, he wouldn't do that – not deliberately, at any rate..." Mary whispered, doubt creeping into her voice.

But as Holmes glanced idly to his left, he noticed a very faint glimmer of light among the trees further down the riverbank, just about where the quarry must be. Relief flooded through him as he realised why this situation felt so familiar, and exactly what the cunning old cleric had been up to. "It's all right, you two," he murmured. "Stay quiet and follow me."

Lestrade and Mary exchanged confused glances, but followed Holmes' lead, saving any questions for a more convenient moment. They crept back the way they'd come, then headed west towards the quarry, circling it anti-clockwise until they came to the Rhine again, far enough downriver that they wouldn't be seen or heard by the gathered townsfolk.

"Now would you mind telling us what's going on?" Lestrade hissed. "Where's Father Siegfried?"

"I am here, my son." The elderly priest stepped out of hiding, still half-lost among the shadows in his black robes, startling even Holmes. "Forgive me if I alarmed you, but a diversion was most necessary, believe me."

"Yes, we saw the farewell party back there. You took a great risk in involving the other villagers, Father."

Father Siegfried chuckled. "One cannot shepherd a community of this size for over fifty years without learning that there is no such thing as a perfectly-kept secret, with eyes in every window and ears in every wall. That being the case, it seemed wise to use the circumstances to their best advantage. I was certain I could trust at least one of you to look beyond the obvious and see the truth, as you did."

"It was mostly luck," the detective shrugged modestly, "Combined with a case of déjà vu. We had to do something similar in Baden."

"A story I would no doubt enjoy hearing... some other time," the cleric smiled in true regret. "But now you must leave, before my poor, unsuspecting flock discover how they have been fleeced. Your vessel awaits."

Their promised transport turned out to be a shabby coal barge, the captain of which was most eager to be gone. No doubt the fear of offending a priest was all that had kept the man from cutting his losses and setting sail long before. It was only once his human cargo was safely aboard that the pilot started making noises about recompense, quelled completely a moment later by Father Siegfried's partially raised eyebrow. Holmes barely refrained from bowing in respect –

he'd previously considered himself something of an authority in intimidating expressions, but the good Father had clearly honed his skills to a fine art over the decades. Suddenly, the detective felt a great deal less anxious about how the people of Mellikon would deal with whoever might come looking for the three of them, be they friend or foe.

The glimmer from Father Siegfried's lantern was soon lost to view, as the river bore the three Londoners away towards their next shelter, and an uncertain future fraught with hazards. On the other hand, Holmes mused grimly, when had his life ever been any different? Nevertheless, the companions at his side knew the risks, they'd made that extremely clear, and for some unfathomable reason had chosen to stand with him in this fight to the very end, whatever that might be. Lestrade – stalwart, tactless, stubborn to a fault; Mary – valiant, resourceful, and unfailingly compassionate, despite her own deep sorrow; and Roland, hopefully absent for only a short while longer – energetic, sanguine, still oddly innocent after all that had occurred, bearing up under his own regrets with a steadfast optimism at which Holmes could only marvel.

Although far from deserving such loyalty, the detective couldn't help but be thankful for it, and pray to any higher power paying attention that he would not fail any of them again. Whatever price was demanded of Holmes, be it the last drop of blood in his veins, he would gladly pay it to see the remaining members of his... of *Watson's* family safely home.

Forgive me, John... forgive me.

End of Part One

To be concluded in 'The Final Solution'.

The Secret Journal of Dr Watson

www.mxpublishing.com

Also from MX Publishing

Winners of the 2011 Howlett Literary Award (Sherlock Holmes book of the year) for '**The Norwood Author**'

From the world's largest Sherlock Holmes publishers dozens of new novels from the top Holmes authors.

www.mxpublishing.com

Including our bestselling short story collections 'Lost Stories of Sherlock Holmes' , 'The Outstanding Mysteries of Sherlock Holmes', 'Untold Adventures of Sherlock Holmes' (and the sequel 'Studies in Legacy) and 'Sherlock Holmes in Pursuit'.

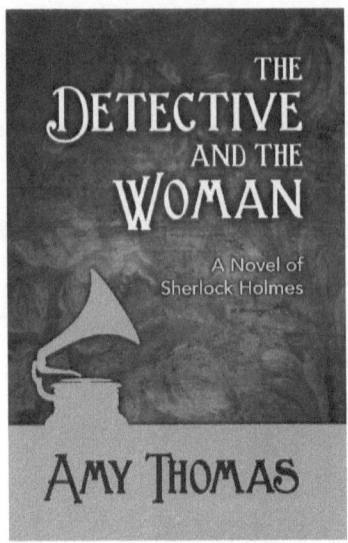 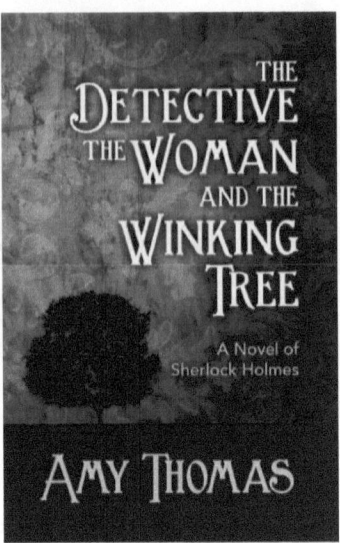

Two acclaimed novels featuring 'The Woman', Irene Adler teaming up with Sherlock Holmes

Links

The Author and the Publishers support the Save Undershaw campaign – the campaign to save and restore Sir Arthur Conan Doyle's former home. Undershaw is where he brought Sherlock Holmes back to life, and should be preserved for future generations of Holmes fans.

Save Undershaw   www.saveundershaw.com

Sherlockology   www.sherlockology.com

MX Publishing   www.mxpublishing.com

You can read more about Sir Arthur Conan Doyle and Undershaw in Alistair Duncan's book (share of royalties to the Undershaw Preservation Trust) – An Entirely New Country and in the amazing compilation Sherlock's Home – The Empty House (all royalties to the Trust).

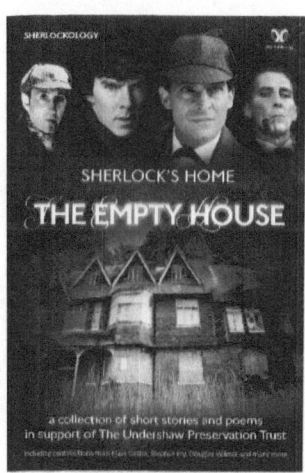

www.ingramcontent.com/pod-product-compliance
Lightning Source LLC
Chambersburg PA
CBHW050414260626
47156CB00003B/1000